HUNTER

AFTER THE FALL

JOHN PHILLIP BACKUS

ILLUSTRATED BY CHAD SCHOENAUER

JONDHI MEDIA GROUP U.S.A.

This novel is a work of fiction—of future events, yet to happen. The characters, incidents, and story are drawn from the author's imagination and should not be construed as real. Any resemblance to actual events or persons, living or dead, is purely coincidental.

 Published by Jondhi Media Group, a division of Jondhi Holdings, LLC., 677 Spartanburg Highway, Suite #172, Hendersonvillle, NC 28792.

Cover art by Duncan Long
Illustrations by Chad Schoenauer

Book One in the AFTER THE FALL™ Series.

FIRST EDITION - June 2010
Library of Congress Control Number: 2010930932
ISBN 978-1-935812-00-5

ACKNOWLEDGEMENTS

The following individuals have graciously contributed their valuable time, talents, and observations directly to this project, and I owe them a tremendous debt of gratitude for their help in bringing this novel to fruition (in alphabetical order):

My tireless reading crew: Chris Backus, Ryan Backus, Troy Backus, Wayne Beardwood, Nancy Guarino, Claire Jones, Stephanie Mason, Jeremiah Miller, Kasia Pimenta, and Koya Pimenta, all of whom read (and re-read) the manuscript, offering insightful comments and invaluable advice and encouragement.

Frances Augusta Hogg, multi-talented writing coach, who offered painfully honest and much needed constructive criticism. *www.FAHOGG.wordpress.com*

Duncan Long, renowned author and illustrator, for his awesome cover art and technical advice on a wide range of subjects. *www.duncanlong.com*

Chad Schoenauer, illustrator-extraordinaire and creative genius, who captured the images from my imagination and brought them to life through his captivating drawings. *Asheville.Illuminator@Gmail.com*

The Saint Petersburg Writer's Group: Colleagues—Liz Burton, Dr. David Mokotoff, and Kathleen Murphy—for encouragement, and perceptive style and editorial suggestions.

Lex Veazey, Esquire, who painstakingly proofread the manuscript for punctuation, paragraphing, and capitalization—offering brilliant recommendations relative to tense and usage.

DEDICATION

To my family's newest generation of reader/writers:

Emily Alaina Backus

Emily Cordelia Alexandria Backus

Christopher Michael James Backus

Gabrielle Christine Pimenta

Alexis Faith Senty

Jeremiah James Senty

and,

To my readers everywhere,

whoever you are,

with deep appreciation...

THIS STORY WAS WRITTEN FOR YOU.

PROLOGUE

SIX MONTHS FROM THE PRESENT

K*EEP MOVING AND don't look back* he told himself, his breath coming in ragged gulps as he sprinted along an empty street in a blacked out city, the hour after midnight. A pale quarter moon hovered timidly in the dark expanse above as the young man scanned the shadows ahead and to the sides, desperate to avoid capture, certain of his fate if caught out after curfew. His mind was reeling with the incredulous events of the past few days, still having a hard time accepting the finality of it all.

Gone... it was all gone! The whole damned system had collapsed—destroyed! The radio said it... before it went dead. Major cities hit by nukes—wiped off the map!

He heard a woman scream from a building off to his right, followed by shouts and gunshots, but he kept on running, heading for the bridge—*Got to get to the river.* Up ahead on the road he saw lights! Ducking into an alley he crouched behind a dumpster and tried to quiet his breathing—*Got to think... Don't panic!*

Men with flashlights passed by speaking in low voices he couldn't decipher. He waited another minute before moving cautiously back to the street and down towards the water. Ahead he could see torches—*watchers on the bridge!* He left the roadway and slipped down the bank, angling towards the abutment. At the water's edge, he took off his shoes and tied the strings together. Wearing them around his neck, he started to step into the river when two figures suddenly rushed out of the shadows, tackling him to the ground. He fought like a cornered animal, but they quickly had him pinned and bound hand and foot with duct tape.

A few minutes later they hoisted him up on the side of the bridge with a noose around his neck and roughly shoved him off. "NOOOOOO!" He screamed, plummeting until the rope snapped his vertebrae, severing his spinal cord. The young man's corpse dangled there alongside dozens of others, young and old, male and female, foolish enough to try to escape. The two hangmen went back to cutting rope and fashioning nooses.

On a hillside overlooking the bridge, Hunter peered through a set of night vision binoculars with thermal capability. He could see the activity on the bridge as clear as day and counted six guards here and another six on the opposite side. Strung out along the riverbank, a dozen two-man teams lay in wait to nab anyone hoping to make it to the river—and freedom. All wore red and black armbands. *Looks like someone's already formed up a militia*, he surmised, stashing the glasses back inside his jacket.

Hunter relaxed and waited. The time to make his move was two hours before dawn when the night was darkest and the sentries most tired. Snapping off a bite of protein bar, he sipped slowly from his canteen, thinking how lucky he was to have been away when it all came down. He glanced over at his newly acquired weapon lying beside him on the ground —a silenced .308 with night vision scope above match grade iron sights. In his backpack were clips filled with ammo—lots of ammo. He sat with his back against a tree and closed his eyes. It was hard to believe it had only been four days.

He received the news while returning from a long weekend solo-backpacking trip in the northern Sierra Nevada Mountains, catching up on some of his favorite outdoor pastimes—hiking, trail running and rock climbing. His wind-up emergency/weather radio came alive on the way back to his truck and at first he thought it must be some kind of a joke. The Emergency Broadcast System warning sounded, and a voice came on saying that major war had erupted, ordering everyone to remain calm and stay inside their homes to await further instructions! It apparently started somewhere in the Middle East—a place he was entirely too familiar with—but this time had spread like wildfire all over the world until all major nations and governments were involved!

When he got to the truck, he tried the radio, but the FM band was silent. He picked up an independent AM station from a small town somewhere in the middle of the Nevada desert that was continuously transmitting the National Anthem followed by short news flashes. Hunter was stunned by the disjointed reports:

> *Washington, D.C. and other major cities had been leveled in midnight nuclear attacks.*
> *The national electrical grid was down.*
> *Military command and control centers had been bombed and were presumed destroyed.*
> *Satellite communications were down.*
> *The president, vice president, full cabinet, and most members of Congress were missing and presumed dead in the attacks on the capitol.*
> *The federal government was virtually non-existent.*
> *With only limited CB radio communications, state and local governments were paralyzed.*
> *Police and military forces were in complete disarray.*
> *Chemical weapons were reportedly used in several cities.*
> *Suspected biological warheads had been deployed.*
> *The financial system was gone.*
> *The transportation/distribution system had halted.*
> *Air transportation had stopped.*

All media, cable TV, Internet, the GPS system, and cell phone service were down.
Social order had devolved into total chaos.
Mass hysteria engulfed the population.
Riots and looting were widespread.
Thousands had died in mob violence.
Plague-infected throngs were fleeing the cities.

Hunter sat motionless a long while as time stood still. He would always remember the date—June 21st—the summer solstice. When the station faded into static, he knew that this was really it, and he was on his own. He quickly compiled a list of essential equipment and supplies he'd need short term. Long term—well that was another prospect altogether. He just wanted to make it through the next forty-eight hours alive and in one piece!

He headed for a local sporting goods store where he sometimes bought ammo for target practice and the little hunting he did. When he got there, it was almost dark. Somebody had backed a delivery truck through the front wall of the place, and there were several bodies on the ground beside it and more in the gravel parking lot outside. Spent shell casings lay all over, and he spotted a handgun partially hidden beneath one of the vehicles.

Grabbing the Glock .40, he cleared the chamber, checking the magazine: *Empty.* He picked up a chunk of the smashed brick façade and threw it into the building: *No response.* Low-crawling to a nearby body, he discovered it was cold and stiff. He squeezed under the truck in the half-light, carefully picking his way along the floor into the store. There were more bodies inside. There must have been quite a fight—blood and spent shells everywhere! He made his way to the counter and sat on the floor with his back against it.

Waiting there in silence for a good ten minutes, he listened, hearing nothing. As darkness fell, he switched on his flashlight and sat it on the counter, dropping his hand away quickly in case someone was hiding there waiting: *Nothing.* Picking it up, he checked around behind the counter. Another body lay sprawled there, a big guy with his hand still wrapped around an empty .50 Desert Eagle; it was the owner. Hunter checked his pockets for keys. He found what he was looking for on a thin chain around his neck. He knew the guy had a safe in a room in the back where he kept the good stuff—*they all did.*

Grabbing a new black range bag off the shelf and a couple of shotgun bandoliers, he checked the paneling along the back wall for smudge prints. Spotting the not-so-hidden latch, he opened the door. The back room was filled with crates and boxes and lined with shelves. Rows of rifles were lined up on racks against the far wall.

In one corner was a gun safe. The key fit the lock, and Hunter tried some numbers on the digital keypad. Street address: *Nothing.* He went back and got the guy's wallet. He tried his birth date: *Nope.* He tried the last 4 of the guy's SS#: *Nada.* He went to the filing cabinet in the opposite corner of the room and looked for a file folder with information on the safe: *Bingo.* He rifled through the file, and the original combination was there in the warranty paperwork. Not obvious, but you had to know where to look. Maybe the guy had been too lazy to customize it, as were many people. He entered the numbers and the thing beeped as the light turned green: *Yes!*

Opening the safe he hit the jackpot—a stack of cash in various denominations, a small pouch of assorted gold sovereigns, a pair each of the latest night vision goggles and binoculars, a concealable twelve gauge shotgun with ten inch barrel and pistol grip, a fully-silenced .308 SR-25 rifle with scope, bipod, sling, and a silenced, laser-sighted .45 Baretta in a custom holster with extra clips! He gathered the weapons and grabbed a bulletproof vest with ceramic plates off a rack before heading back to the front to fill up on ammo. Finally, he loaded a large backpack with the ammo and other useful items from his list and made his way back outside.

It was pitch dark and deathly quiet. A light breeze blew from the east, the air cold and wet, foretelling of rain. He checked the street for movement with the binoculars; nothing was there, but he would have to clear out fast. He was sure others would be showing up anytime, and he wasn't interested in being here when they did.

He spent the rest of that night collecting what he needed from the pharmacy, grocery store, outfitters, hardware store, gas station and military surplus. By daybreak he had everything on his list and drove northeast on the back roads for an hour, towing a loaded utility trailer. Backing up into a secluded draw in the middle of nowhere, he caught a few hours of sorely needed sleep. When dusk settled in again, he headed back out on the road.

Driving at night and sleeping during the day, he crossed the mountains near Lake Tahoe and continued through the Nevada and Utah backcountry, heading to the secluded forty acres and small cabin in western Wyoming he'd purchased, while still in the military, as a place to retire to someday. Looks like someday came sooner than he expected.

Hunter drove with the truck lights out, wearing night vision goggles, and removed the brake and back-up light fuses so he would be nearly impossible to detect in the dark. Along the way, he passed several wrecks and abandoned vehicles, and coming around a curve, he nearly ran over a dead man lying in the middle of the road in the middle of nowhere. On the outskirts of a small town, he heard the report of a rifle and floored it all the way through to the other side. The only people he saw were dead ones from a distance, usually sprawled out in diner parking lots or gas stations along the way. On several occasions, he pulled off the roadway and stopped when he saw headlights approaching in the distance. Those driving the speeding vehicles were definitely not into stopping to check him out.

As the third day dawned, temperatures continued to drop, and a hard rain mixed with sleet started to fall. He pulled down a deserted farm lane and parked. Donning long underwear and cold weather rain gear, he slept in a hammock up a tree fifty yards from the truck cradling his rifle —just in case. In the middle of the fourth night, he reached the Wyoming border.

Approaching the river, he stopped a half-mile back from the bridge adorned in bodies and climbed the hill to check it out. From his vantage point above the bridge, he panned back across the steel span, re-counting the guards and checking their placement. *Getting across that bridge won't be a problem*, he reasoned. *Doing so without bloodshed?* Hunter smiled grimly. *He wouldn't want to bet on it!*

14 YEARS LATER...

CHAPTER ONE

MYSTERIOUS SOJOURNERS

THE CRIMSON DAWN swept silently across the vast North American wilderness, brushing the eastern sky with a hint of pink changing to red and orange until finally giving way to a perfect cobalt blue. The advancing line of sunlight moved steadily west, bathing the sheer granite walls of the Continental Divide in dazzling brilliance and sending long, golden fingers of warmth down into deep forested valleys to chase away the last remaining shadows of the night.

High on a windswept slope, a single shaft of sunlight filtered down through frost-tipped branches, stabbing onto the angular face of the motionless figure below. Seventy feet above the forest floor, Hunter lay motionless in his hammock, cataloging the sights, sounds, and smells of his immediate environment. A cool breeze sifted through the brilliant autumn leaves, as throughout the highlands, active woodland creatures carried out their early morning routines with boundless enthusiasm. On a nearby branch, a western jay hopped nimbly about, plucking crispy black ants from the gray bark with great relish. Sixty feet away through the canopy, an animated red squirrel frantically chased its mate round and round the trunk of a mature lodgepole pine, chattering loudly all the while.

Satisfied that all was well, he eased out onto an adjacent limb and untied the netting that secured his night camp. Balanced there, he stowed his sleeping gear into a sturdy leather backpack, with his senses attuned to his surroundings for any sign of danger or threat. This habit of constant vigilance, second nature to him now, ensured his continued survival against the odds in an unforgiving environment where a moment's carelessness could very well be his last.

Propping his pack against the trunk, he stood and reached inside his vest for the dwindling supply of dried venison. Standing on the wide limb, he bit off a mouthful of the salty meat, replaced the bundle, and climbed into the uppermost branches of the old tree with the fluid grace of a large feline. Soon he was perched atop the ancient oak, halfway up a steep shoulder of land belonging to a series of tall ridges that formed northwestern Wyoming's Wind River Range. From this lofty vantage point, he surveyed the surrounding territory with a pair of well-used field glasses.

Far below, the valley floor lay covered in golden grass sweeping south towards the foothills. A sparkling stream snaked through the bottom like a shiny, silver ribbon pulled along by gravity towards the distant Colorado River. A small herd of deer casually ambled through the vale, nibbling choice shoots and grasses on the way to their favorite morning resting spot half a mile downstream. He watched, amused, as a trio of yearlings chased each other through the early-September grass, their fading white spots of fawnhood barely visible against the reddish-brown umber of their young adult coats.

Standing off from the rest, a battle-scarred buck in full rut and armed with razor-sharp antlers and deadly hooves, remained alert. As a dominant male, he divided his time between mating, marking his territory and sharpening his antler tips in anticipation of crushing the next foolish challenger who would inevitably arrive to test his readiness. He raised his nostrils to sample the wind before lowering his regal head to drink from the rushing brook.

Beyond the stream on the far side of the valley, the land rose steeply, dotted with boulders and clumps of dark green cedar and juniper. The ridgeline was topped with sharp granite outcroppings like shattered shark's teeth stabbing the stark blue sky. High above, a hawk sounded a plaintive cry, and Hunter quickly located her as she wheeled and plummeted earthward, returning to the sky with her struggling prize. As she passed out of sight beyond the far ridge, he turned to put away the binoculars when something unusual caught his eye. Panning back across the horizon, he froze.

The gray-white column of smoke drifted lazily above the skyline. His pulse quickened. After a long, careful look, he replaced the glasses, quickly descending the forty-odd feet to his equipment. Retrieving one piece at a time, he consciously brought his accelerating thoughts under control and pondered the significance of the smoke with mixed emotions.

Hunter had been alone here now for more than seven years. Prior to that, occasional run-ins with 'outsiders' taught him to avoid all contact with what was left of the human race. Call it *antisocial,* but merely surviving the untamed wilderness was a danger-filled activity. Introduce a stranger into the mix, with unknown motives and intentions, and the risk factor multiplied exponentially.

He was alone by choice. Living near others was dangerous, relying on them, suicidal. Sometimes late at night a part of him still longed for human companionship or at least the tender touch of a lover, but the days of friends and lovers had long since passed.

Now he guarded his solitude, secure in his self-imposed exile at a time when even a casual contact with someone unwittingly exposed to one of a host of mutant viruses could prove fatal. Such designer plagues had wiped out entire populations during the waning hours of the End War when automated weapons systems dumped obscene arsenals into Earth's atmosphere in a last ditch effort to annihilate "the enemy."

Today's sign of a foreign human presence was the last thing he had expected, and the abruptness of the intrusion was unsettling. Shouldering his pack, he cinched the hip belt and positioned a quiver stuffed with arrow-like bolts at his side. Stooping down, he picked up one final piece of gear.

The impressive-looking crossbow was powerful enough to drop an adult grizzly bear at fifty yards and accurate well beyond that, thanks to the rifle scope mounted above its polished hardwood stock. For a dozen seasons, it had saved his life more often than he cared to remember. Sliding the formidable weapon into position over his shoulder, he was now ready for whatever might await him beyond the next ridge.

With a final scan of the oak's immediate surroundings, he swung out onto a stout branch and dropped, landing lightly on the balls of his feet. Without hesitation he moved downhill through scattered trees towards the meadow. Sheepskin tunic and leggings made no sound against the twigs and briars that tugged at him. The naturally tanned clothing blended well with the muted colors of the rugged mountain landscape. Tough moose-hide moccasins protected his vulnerable feet and ankles, while flexible leather soles enabled him to sense his way along the ground, avoiding dry sticks or loose stones that might otherwise reveal his position to a potential enemy.

Thirty minutes later he crouched at the edge of the meadow, surveying the valley. The deer had moved on, piles of steaming pellets and bent grass pathways the only visible evidence of their passing. Hunter hesitated. A direct route across the open field would leave him exposed and vulnerable. Under normal circumstances he would keep to the cover of the trees and skirt the meadow to a more concealed crossing point, but today was far from normal. Bending forward at the waist, he moved quickly, stopping just long enough at the stream to fill two canteens before continuing across and up the opposite slope. Climbing rapidly, he melted into his surroundings, taking full advantage of rock outcroppings, clumps of brush and stands of trees. An hour later, he caught his breath in the shadow of a massive boulder overlooking an open plain.

A half-mile below, two figures crouched before their smoldering fire. The smoke drifted lazily into the morning sky, dangerously visible for miles. A makeshift lean-to, barely large enough for one person to lie down in, was their only shelter against the elements.

From the look of the trampled grass, they'd come in from the south arriving at the hills on foot. *But from where?* There were no permanent settlements within hundreds of miles. At this distance, fine details were difficult to make out, but the two appeared to be rather slight of build and poorly equipped for a protracted journey into the wild. With his curiosity piqued, he scoured the terrain below for a route to take him closer to the strangers, while remaining undetected. Selecting an observation point, he headed for a stand of conifers midway to the base of the slope.

He descended the rocky terrain slowly until bisecting a well-traveled game trail, winding around boulders and angling down through dense patches of scrub. On it, he moved smoothly through the rugged landscape as troubling questions bombarded his mind. *Who are these travelers and where are they from? Are they truly alone or just the bait in a cunningly devised trap?* Pondering the possibilities, he circumvented a recent rockslide partially blocking the trail.

Hunter had learned early on not to be too inventive when traversing the backcountry. The deer and elk populations and the predators that shadowed them knew this region far better than any human being ever would. Since the passing of the last Ice Age, their generations had been eking out an existence here, and their trails were the most efficient routes through the otherwise trackless mountain passes. Sticking closely to them generally guaranteed that you wouldn't wind up at the edge of a four-thousand-foot cliff and be forced to retrace your steps, which could add hours or even days to your trek, and might prove fatal should you happen to be injured or pursued by any one of a number of potential enemies.

Dropping through a well-nibbled section bounded by wild grape and raspberry, he moved down across the slope, pausing often to listen and observe. He was puzzled by what he had seen from the crest. The travelers could not have survived long on their own without sufficient gear or an effective means of defense, nor could they have journeyed any great distance on foot. The balance of power among species had shifted dramatically during the fourteen years since the End War, and the fear of man, especially among the larger carnivores, had already diminished.

With the passing of modern civilization, diverse animal populations flourished and expanded into new habitats bringing a new natural order to the Earth. Thundering herds of bison and pronghorn antelope again migrated across North America, west to the Pacific coast. Wild horse and burro bands shared millions of acres of former ranch lands with deer, elk, and moose. At the higher elevations, Rocky Mountain goats and bighorn sheep thrived, no longer challenged by two-legged enemies with large caliber rifles and telescopic sights.

Hunter was content with this new balance in spite of the constant danger it represented. He considered Man's fall from grace fitting retribution for the millennia of havoc his fellow humans wrought upon each other and the natural world. It rather comforted him to know that the heavens were no longer cluttered with satellites and warplanes, and that, across the globe, airliners rusted on the tarmac, overgrown with vines and thorns, inhabited by snakes and birds and other wild things.

Rounding a sharp bend in the trail, he startled a female wild pig grubbing for roots among the berries. Grunting an alarm, she stared back at him with black, beady eyes and trotted warily across his path closely followed by her string of snorting piglets. Briefly tempted to harvest one for later, he changed his mind and let them pass. Moving forward cautiously, he remained constantly on guard for a potential surprise attack by a hungry lion or irate grizzly—or even an agitated bull elk—all life-threatening situations that generally seemed to occur when least expected.

Closing in on the stand of trees, he doubted the two wanderers were actually on their own. More than likely, their companions were off hunting or scouting the foothills. *Probably have a couple of well-placed guards nearby.* The thought suddenly struck him that the two might be on the run, which would explain their meager camp and apparent lack of escorts or provisions.

Switching back across the mountainside in the opposite direction, the trail wound down through scarred granite boulders laced with quartz before opening up again into sagebrush and mesquite. Working his way through a final tangled berry thicket, he arrived suddenly at the edge of the trees.

Crouched in the shadows, he loaded his crossbow, preparing for an ambush that may or may not materialize. Once under the trees, he moved wraith-like from shadow-to-shadow, forefinger playing lightly upon the trigger of the effective weapon cradled comfortably in his callused hands.

A quick reconnoiter of the small wood revealed nothing. Red squirrels chattered. Ever-present jays went about their lives. Nearby, a seeping spring revealed plenty of deer and elk sign among bird and rodent tracks, but nothing distinctly human. Unloading the bow, he scrambled up into a gnarled old cedar to have a better look.

High in his wind-blown lookout, straddling a wide limb with his back against the scaly trunk, Hunter's glasses again swept the plain. At three hundred yards, the camp jumped quickly into focus. From here he could clearly distinguish details and was shocked to discover that both travelers were female, a fair-haired girl in her mid-teens and a dark-haired young woman, probably early to mid-twenties! Both wore travel cloaks and riding boots, but their mounts were nowhere to be seen. Searching for clues, he spied three mugs on a flat rock beside the fire. Concentrating on the lean-to, he surmised the third person's whereabouts and waited.

For the remainder of the morning, he sat in his lofty perch, curiously watching the mystery travelers do nothing unusual—*beyond the fact that they weren't really doing much of anything.* As the column of smoke dissipated, they moved quietly about their camp, tending the small fire, preparing a quick meal and washing their utensils in a nearby stream. Eventually, the fair-haired girl ducked into the shelter for a few moments before rejoining her companion at the fire. Afterwards, they seemed to be willing to make more noise, and Hunter caught faint fragments of conversation on the wind. Every so often, the dark-haired young woman would stand, shade her eyes and stare off towards the south. *Are you waiting for friends,* he wondered, *or perhaps afraid of being followed?*

At regular intervals, he closed his eyes and absorbed the sounds and smells swirling and echoing around him. Against the backdrop of the intermittent s*woosh* of the wind, he identified a dozen bird species as they sang or called out to one another in unique feathered dialects. High in a nearby tree, a western woodpecker hammered away at the tough outer bark, using his specially designed beak and the weight of his skull as a battering ram to get at hidden insects and their larvae. Down below, sparrows, chickadees and jays flitted about from tree to shrub to ground, devouring ripe berries and seeking fat, juicy earthworms and grubs under bits of rotting bark or leaves on the shaded forest floor.

Beyond the small glade, beneath sagebrush and dry grasses, jackrabbits, striped ground squirrels, field mice and many other small earth-bound creatures carried on active lives, nibbling favorite flowers, leaves and shoots, completely undisturbed by Hunter's presence. High above in the cloudless sky, winged predators cried out in eerie solitude, relentlessly stalking their prey with patient, telescopic advantage.

A mile out on the grass-covered plain, a dark, undulating mass slowly edged towards the camp; the outer boundary of a bison herd, numbering in the thousands, grazed contentedly in the cool autumn air. Beyond the shaggy horde, just at the outer limits of his vision, Hunter estimated several hundred pronghorn antelope, probably just the fringe of a larger group, reveling in the afternoon sun.

The relative quiet was punctuated by the nearby trumpeting of a bull elk, declaring his superiority and warning challengers to stay away. Behind him, up the hill, a lion's vicious snarl was followed by the squeal of pigs and silence, as the food chain played out its never-ending drama of survival of the fittest.

Aloft in his tree, Hunter relaxed and drank in his surroundings. Through the years, he'd come to know this place —its rhythms and secrets—and was constantly renewed by its magnificent beauty, nurtured and sustained in body and soul by its bounty, yet honed and toughened by its violence and unforgiving finality. He felt a connection to the nomadic tribesmen formerly inhabiting this land who relied solely on nature to provide for their needs. During his constant scouting of this territory, he often came upon evidence of their passing, in stone implements, arrow and spear points, and bits of broken pottery. Most intriguing of all were the ancient markings and images painted or etched on rocks or hidden cave walls long since abandoned and forgotten.

High in the swaying cedar, the sun hit its zenith and dropped a notch while Hunter remained relaxed, yet focused. A short time later, his patience paid off when a third young woman emerged from the shelter carrying a bundle of furs in her arms! More perplexed than ever, his bewilderment turned to shock as a tiny cry wafted up to him on the afternoon breeze; the bundle she was holding was a baby!

This unexpected development stunned him. Dark memories of an intentionally forgotten past seeped through his carefully constructed emotional defenses, flashing pictures of small children running and playing and laughing—*STOP!* The painful images stirred long-buried sensitivities he chose long ago, never to revisit.

He consciously choked back the unwanted feelings until there was only the Present. Always the Present, *the Now.* He could deal with the present; this he could do something about. The past was gone. *What was done was done.* In the present, he could control his destiny, surviving one day at a time, responsible only for himself. Such was his life now.

However, on this fine autumn afternoon after so many years alone, he was suddenly faced with more than he had bargained for—a child. So many died during the Dark Time, their frail, helpless bodies wasting away as anguished parents tried in vain to comfort and love them better. He let the sad pictures fade to black and looked out again at the flimsy little camp nestled in the ocean of grass.

For the first time in many years, Hunter realized that he was in trouble. To happen upon three travel-worn drifters crossing the mountains was one thing, but three women and an infant alone in the wild after all of these years? This presented a problem. For what could a child represent but the future? Who then was responsible for that future, but those with the skills and determination to fashion one from the post-war rubble?

He focused his thoughts and began a swift descent from the tree. Loud and clear he heard the warning: *Run! Leave! Forget you ever saw them!* Unfortunately, it was too late for that. He had to know whether the unprotected camp was a ploy or if they really were on their own and possibly on the run. If so, he could not just leave them here defenseless, *but neither was he ready to take them all under his wing, or was he?* Long ago he'd written off the human race, yet here were fellow beings in need, and, regardless of his bitterness towards the mistakes of the past, he found himself unable to simply turn his back and walk away.

Besides, it had been more than seven years since he'd spoken with another human being—man or woman—and almost twice that since he'd laid eyes on a child. Hunter knew that he had no choice; he must go out to meet them. *Hell, he'd known it the instant he'd seen the smoke, but he would* damn sure *be careful!*

CHAPTER TWO

FLIGHT INTO DANGER

ELISE AWOKE LATE and immediately noticed the smoke. She roused her younger sister, Anna, to help collect dry kindling to get the smoldering fire going. Elise gathered what tinder she could find nearby and knelt at the edge of the fire, adding the driest sticks and twigs, and cursing herself for not making sure the coals were out before bedding down for the night.

Shading emerald eyes against the sun's mean glare, she surveyed the gray-white column floating high above the camp, and anxiously scanned the horizon feeling vulnerable. Leaning forward, she blew evenly on the stubborn embers, nurturing the growing flames beneath the suspended teakettle. Glancing at the height of the sun above the hills, small furrows formed across the young woman's forehead, betraying her troubled mood.

They should have been packed and moving by now, but she hadn't the heart to wake Sarah, her fragile sister-in-law, whose vitality seemed to be ebbing away with each passing day. Enduring a difficult pregnancy and delivery, Sarah never fully recovered her strength. However, the rigors of new motherhood were nowhere near as devastating as the recent disappearance of her husband, William, Elise's older brother. He was the light of Sarah's life, and his unexplained absence had caused her to withdraw, even from Elise, her best friend since childhood.

With Sarah and the baby asleep, Elise boiled water for tea and waited. Anna joined her at the fire with an armful of sticks to fuel the growing blaze. Elise placed a comforting hand on her sister's shoulder, mindful that the normally cheerful girl was uncharacteristically somber this morning. "It'll be alright Anna, everything will be fine—don't you worry!"

Elise gave her a big hug, and the anxious girl held on tight, drawing courage from Elise's strength. At almost seventeen, Anna implicitly trusted her older sister, who all but raised her when their mother was suddenly taken from them the day after Anna's eighth birthday. She looked up to Elise, admiring her ability to handle people and situations, and was especially impressed at the heroic job she'd done in bringing them safely across the trackless wilderness.

"I know, Elise. I don't mean to be down," Anna paused and looked around at the vast emptiness of their surroundings, "but I'm just so worried about Sarah." She held back the tears threatening to cascade down her pale cheeks, "and without knowing what's happened to William or what's going on back home with Father and the rest, I just..." The distraught girl had reached her emotional breaking point. "You know I've been positive all along until now." She braved a smile at Elise. "But ever since the horses ran off and now that we're running out of time..." Overwhelmed by the situation, Anna broke down and began to quietly weep, her face buried in her sister's chest. Elise just held her as she sobbed, gently stroking her beautiful, golden hair.

"There, there, Anna, it's okay. I know how you feel... I feel the same way myself sometimes." She spoke in her most soothing voice, hoping they wouldn't wake Sarah or little Jamie just yet. After a minute, Anna pulled herself together, drying her wet cheeks on the sleeve of her cloak. Elise maintained eye contact, smiling and speaking calmly in a determined effort to bolster Anna's forlorn spirits. "Besides, we've still got each other and we're nearly there now!" She smiled warmly, encouraged to see the mist clearing from Anna's red, swollen eyes and a hopeful countenance return to her innocent face.

"We'll make it back home to Father, and find William, and Sarah and the baby will be just fine! Everything will work out somehow, I just know it will!" She stood before Anna, clasping her sister's hands and exuding a conviction that was beginning to wear thin. "You'll feel much better after a cup of herb tea and a bite to eat." She smiled with an air of confidence and serenity that belied her hidden worries, and Anna managed a small smile in response, drew a deep breath and left to gather more sticks.

Elise placed three ceramic mugs on a flat rock and opened her small leather pouch containing the last of their precious tea. Keeping back one final pot for later, she only half filled the ball, suspending it in the boiling kettle. Replacing the lid, she set the pot off to the side to steep and focused on their immediate dilemma. Though careful to keep her feelings hidden from the others, she was beginning to have grave doubts about the outcome of their mission, painfully aware that they were rapidly running out of options. If they were going to succeed, they must quickly locate the person that Father had sent her here to find.

The days were getting shorter with overnight temperatures just above freezing. Elise knew that there was absolutely no way to make it all the way back to Colorado on foot before the merciless Rocky Mountain winter stranded them in the open. Faced with these growing concerns, she reflected on the events leading up to their journey that began on a moonless night more than three hundred miles to the southeast.

Back home in New Eden trouble had been brewing for months. The community founded by her parents had always been her safe haven and a steady source of strength and inspiration to the three hundred or so settlers living on the several hundred acre retreat. However, since they'd stopped accepting new members, things had taken a drastic turn for the worse.

Faced with a rapidly deteriorating security situation, her father devised a desperate plan. Elise would lead the others from the swiftly eroding safety of the compound and travel north on horseback under cover of night. They slipped out during a midnight storm and, over the next ten anxious days, covered nearly eighty miles of rugged terrain. To avoid roving patrols, they rested during the day, moving only after sunset.

After two challenging weeks of scant sleep and the constant fear of discovery, they put the immediate threat of capture behind them and were able to switch to daytime travel.

On a good day, depending on the weather, they might cover twenty miles over fairly level ground. During the occasional thunderstorm, they made no progress at all while huddled inside their tent waiting out the deluge. In rugged topography, they were lucky to get ten miles before being forced to seek shelter.

For weeks, they pushed north, grazing the horses during the halts and following the natural lay of the land as much as possible without deviating from their course. Every few days, a new mountain range appeared on the horizon, and they sought out river valleys and passes to help negotiate the foothills and ridges as necessary. Crossing into southwestern Wyoming, they kept the Rockies on their right and pressed north as their precious supplies slowly dwindled.

Masterful at both the bolo and spear-thrower, Elise supplemented their provisions with fresh antelope or deer. They camped with backs against boulders or in defensible rock shelters with large bonfires out front to ward off passing carnivores that mostly hunted at night.

Anna brought more sticks, breaking her reverie, and went to find more. Elise watched her go and checked the horizon again. According to Father's map, they must be very close to their destination. After six weeks of rigorous travel, she'd brought them through intact—well, almost. Two nights back, a pack of wild dogs ran off their horses and pack mule, forcing them to continue on foot, with Anna and Elise bearing their necessities on their backs in makeshift packs. Since then, after only two or three miles, they would collapse to the ground, unable to proceed without rest.

Looking around now at the vast panorama swallowing their tiny camp, Elise knew that they were at the end of the line. The crude map, thrust into her hands on the dark night of their departure, guided them faithfully north through steep shadowed canyons, across wild rivers and into the foothills of the Rockies themselves. As the terrain rose to meet the peaks to the east, the passes were harder to distinguish on the map, which showed fewer landmarks and details the farther north they went.

Elise stood and turned aside so Anna wouldn't notice her distress. A single tear balanced on the rim of her lower eyelid, threatening to spill onto her translucent cheek. Deeply concerned about the fate of family and friends back home, she was uncertain of what they might find upon their return.

Scanning the open horizon for answers, she fought the overwhelming sense of despair, settling over her mind like a shroud. Drawing on deep inner reserves, she pushed back fear and willed her heart to be strong. As the eldest and leader of this expedition, she recognized her responsibility for its ultimate success or failure. She was up to the task. She'd promised her father. However, after many arduous weeks in the wilderness, traveling hundreds of difficult miles from home, Elise was beginning to fear that she might now fail them all.

CHAPTER THREE

UNEXPECTED GUESTS

HUNTER CROUCHED BENEATH a thick stand of crimson sumac at the edge of the open plain. Here, on the flats, concealment was a bit more challenging, but he knew that looks could be deceiving. While the landscape appeared level, it was scarred by hidden gullies and ravines sculpted by centuries of erosion.

Moving forward through waist-high grass and sagebrush, he soon bisected a shallow wash heading in the general direction of the camp and followed it for several minutes. When the gravel-bottomed gully eventually veered west, he abandoned it, pushing ahead as silently as a ghost. Minutes later, he slipped through a thin screen of willows a hundred yards from the camp. Taking a long pull from his canteen, he reviewed his plan, preparing to circle around and make his approach in plain sight.

As he started forward, he immediately became aware of the unmistakable sound of fast-approaching hoofbeats, followed by a woman's frantic cry of alarm. Instinctively, picking up the pace, he swept his primary weapon from his shoulder and loaded it in one well-rehearsed movement. Sliding to a halt beside a fallen tree, he crouched on one knee, peering through a ragged wall of brush and nettles not eighty yards from the commotion. Several more cries ripped the air as a mob of horsemen charged through, raising fine clouds of dust and hollering like a tribe of Banshees. He dropped noiselessly behind the bleached trunk, slipped out of his backpack and witnessed the unfolding drama through binoculars.

Through the haze, he counted at least a dozen heavily armed men tearing the camp apart. They were a rough lot, dressed in ragged clothes and poorly-tanned hides. Someone shouted orders, and they gathered their spoils into a small pile near the collapsed shelter. The baby's cry rose above the din and confusion. Hunter slipped across the log and crept closer as adrenaline flooded his bloodstream, readying his body and brain for battle.

In any halfway-civilized society, the raiders before him would be considered criminals and parasites at best. However, here in the wilderness—far from any law or justice—they were much more dangerous than that. Hunter viewed them as he would a vicious pack of dogs; though in defense of the four-legged species, canines acted purely out of instinct, not having the benefit of a human conscience.

In stark contrast, these men terrorizing the camp obviously existed solely at the expense of others, taking what they wanted by force, regardless of the misery left in their wake. He could only imagine their long legacy of victims waking in the night with throats slit, their terrified loved ones desperately begging for mercy from men whose dark souls knew none.

Years earlier, during his migration, Hunter had buried several such victims when it was too late to do anything more. What of his own fate had he not been patient in approaching the camp? He blessed his intuition and sense of timing for once again keeping him alive. At least now, he had a fighting chance to live out the day.

Creeping forward to a position within earshot enabled him a better view of unfolding events. As the raiders quarreled, a single voice rose above the bickering and, but for the muffled cries of the child, the camp fell silent. A giant bear of a man, dressed in matted furs, climbed down from his lathered black stallion to tower over the others. He was an impressive figure, with muscular arms folded across a broad chest and legs like tree trunks spread in an arrogant stance. Long, raven hair was divided into two thick braids framing a face all but hidden by a full black beard.

The women were brought before him, flanked by two of the raiders. The child, sensing his mother's fear, cried in her arms despite all efforts to calm him. As the bandit chief took a stride toward Sarah, she shrank back and twisted away, trying to protect her baby from the hideous person before her.

Cruel obsidian eyes glittered in their dark sockets, despising all within their field of vision. Foul breath and an unwashed stench assaulted her nostrils as he grabbed Sarah by the arm and hoisted her close to his face. He grinned at the frightened woman, exposing broken, decayed teeth and lifted the covering from the infant's body. "It's a boy!" he declared to his leering men, "A beautiful son you have there, ma'am."

She blanched as he jerked her towards him, lifting her off the ground and drawing her close. A sawed-off shotgun dangled from his belt, and his massive right hand held an axe.

"And where would his daddy be, my fine little lady?" He shook her around like a rag doll, nearly causing her to drop her son.

"Please don't hurt my baby!" the frantic woman begged, eyes wide with fear.

The giant man mocked her with a huge voice: "Please don't hurt my baby, please don't hurt my baby!"

His men found this comical and joined in, jeering and mocking her until their leader raised his hand for silence. He lowered the panicked woman to the ground and threatened, "You will tell me how many men are in your party and where they have gone, and I will let the child live. Now! Or I'll split him in two like a soggy piece of firewood!" He raised the axe above his head and reached out to pull little Jamie from Sarah's arms.

"Touch that child and die!" The words pieced the air like bullets. The savage brute's mind froze, stunned that anyone would dare defy his iron will. He turned his head slowly and all eyes were upon the speaker.

Elise stood tall and unafraid. She stepped forward with confidence, placing her hands on Sarah's shoulders and spoke in a cool, even voice that commanded attention. "I don't care who you *think* you are, barging into our camp and behaving like this, but we are a free people here and have every right to remain so. Where our companions go and when they return is no one's business but our own. And

I would suggest to you and your *men* that, if you plan to see the sunset, you withdraw yourselves at once!"

Lightning flashed from the slender woman's eyes, and a dynamic quality could be sensed in her voice. Visibly shaken, the bandit leader returned her unyielding gaze; their two wills locked in psychological combat under the bright afternoon sun. After several awkward moments, he flinched and lunged forward, striking her hard across the mouth with the back of his clenched fist.

Up to this point, Hunter had been transfixed by the rapidly evolving chain of events. The woman's surprising courage, in the face of such overwhelming odds, held him in awe. Now, as the situation rapidly escalated out of control, and being well acquainted with the bestial nature of Man, he silently moved forward, rapidly closing the gap.

As two lackeys pinned Elise's arms behind her back, their leader reached out with both hands and grabbed the front of her tunic as if to rip it from her body. The crowd shouted its approval and drew closer, urging him on.

Without warning, Elise struck with booted feet and immediately her two guards went down, writhing in agony. In a fluid blur of motion, she brought both fists up hard, breaking the grip on her blouse. From somewhere within her clothing, she suddenly produced a dagger and, slashing upward, sliced deeply into the brute's cheek just beneath his right eye!

Stumbling back out of range, the goliath's shock quickly turned to rage as he touched his stinging face, and his hand came away covered in warm, sticky blood! Discarding the axe, he leveled his double-barreled shotgun at the she-devil and, for a split second, seemed to hesitate, thrown completely off-guard by her vicious attack; but he'd surely have his revenge. The cruel eyes gleamed with murder as his finger closed on the dual triggers.

Elise crouched low and prepared to hurl herself at her adversary. She realized the futility of her desperate stand, but would do her best to disable as many as possible before being inevitably overwhelmed. As her enemy prepared to fire, a silent feathered object flashed brightly across the camp, entering his half-opened mouth and embedding itself deeply in the soft tissues at the base of his brain.

Twirling about in spasms, the bearded tyrant involuntarily tightened his trigger finger, blasting one of his cronies nearly in half. The savage recoil sent the scattergun cartwheeling off into the grass as the mortally wounded leader clawed at his face and pitched heavily forward, dead before his body hit the ground. For one frozen moment, everyone stared in disbelief as the impact drove the steel point out through the back of the giant's skull! With that, instant pandemonium erupted as the raiders scrambled for whatever cover they could find.

In the confusion that followed, Elise suddenly found herself unguarded as the bandits scattered into the grass. Leaping over the repulsive chieftain's still twitching corpse, she rescued the fallen shotgun and wrestled the heavy body onto its side to remove a bandolier of shells. Struggling with it, she noticed a beaded leather pouch tied around his neck, identical to one her brother William had worn for as long as she could remember! She quickly slashed its cord and stowed it deep inside her cloak. Hugging the ground, she rejoined Anna who had managed to rescue two of their backpacks and, together with Sarah and the baby, they melted into the dense underbrush.

As Hunter had anticipated, an immediate counterattack never materialized. History was rife with examples of despots failing to appoint a second-in-command, and today was just another case in point. When waging war he preferred to hit first, hit hard and keep on hitting. Being so greatly outnumbered, the element of surprise was his primary advantage. So as his first bolt struck its mark, he backed up and circled around to the opposite side of the camp. Having acted in the travelers' defense, he was now committed to their rescue and forced to design an offensive strategy on the fly.

Consciously slowing his breathing, Hunter defined his objectives: *Rescue the travelers. Destroy the raiders.* It was a simple enough plan, but he wasn't altogether certain that the bandits would cooperate—nor even the women for that matter. Judging from the position of the sun, roughly six hours of daylight remained. It was likely to be a long afternoon. Crouching low, he moved just beyond the grazing horses, keenly aware that, if any of the riders managed to gain their mounts, with or without captives, he would be hard pressed to stop them.

As their enemy circled them, the leaderless outlaws found themselves at an extreme disadvantage. They were effectively pinned down out in the open by an unknown number of adversaries, with only prairie grass, sagebrush and an occasional rock or two for cover. Not that they were ready to surrender by any means—all were hard men, seasoned killers spoiling for a fight, but this was not their usual style.

Though no one dared lift a head above the vegetation, Hunter spotted suspicious movement near a big chestnut gelding with dark mane and tail. The grass seemed to wiggle unnaturally, and the horse jerked his head up, glanced over, and took a couple of steps away from whatever he saw there. Hunter scanned the grass, wishing for higher ground.

Just then, the back of a man's head slowly rose up out of the cover, fifty yards beyond the campfire. He swung his bow up and aimed at a point eight inches below the base of the skull. He pulled the trigger and heard a gurgled shriek before silence once again shrouded the plain. Hunter aimed back toward the grass near the chestnut with another bolt in place. He waited for movement. His third shot left the bow and someone immediately started to scream and thrash about.

"My leg—Somebody help me!"

A carefully aimed fourth shot neatly finished the job, and the day was quiet once more. Reloaded, Hunter slithered forward toward the animals. Someone called out in a hoarse whisper a few yards ahead, and he slowly eased toward the sound. A man with thin, greasy hair was seated with his back to Hunter with a blade stuck in his waistband and some sort of firearm resting beside his hand on the ground. Beside him was a pair of legs belonging to a second man, lying on his stomach and looking off in the same direction as the first.

"I swear I saw one of them, Hank," whispered the balding man, "just for a second, but I know I did."

"Well, I don't want to see any of the sons-a-bitches, Andy," the other whispered back.

"Shit! Bear shot right through the mouth like that—and from a hundred yards out! Man, that guy can shoot I tell ya! Well, I told ya this wasn't gonna be no easy pickins like them last girls we got, but nobody ever listens to old Andy, nope.... Hell, if you and Floyd hadn't used 'em so bad, they would still be ..."

"Shut up, ya old bastard, before I put another hole in your face!"

Hank glared at him, and Andy believed that he would do it. He'd seen some of Hank's work, and the man definitely had a sadistic streak, for sure.

"Now be quiet and stay put. I'm going out to round up the others." Hank crawled away, leaving Andy alone.

Nice guys, thought Hunter as he slipped his heavy throwing knife from its sheath inside his tall moccasin. He hurled it through the air, hitting his target hard between the shoulder blades with the haft. The old man gasped and tipped over onto his side. Seconds later, Hunter was on him, his recovered blade at the stunned man's throat.

"How many…?" Hunter whispered, inches from his face.

"Fourteen," the terrified bandit squeaked.

Hunter struck him hard on the side of the head, and a nasty goose egg formed across the limp man's temple. He tied and gagged Andy, deciding he may need to extract information from this one should any of his partners escape. He collected the knife and revolver and stuck them in his belt.

He ran some figures in his head: four dead and this one unconscious, leaving nine, including the two injured by the woman's kicks. Somewhere off to his left, a man stumbled and a shotgun blast tore the silence. Make that eight.

"You got him, you got the bastard!" a gleeful voice announced, and several figures ran over to the already dead body.

"Shit!" someone said as they all ducked out of sight, "Willie's dead!"

Hunter fired twice into the crowd in rapid succession and two men shrieked, briefly thrashing about in the brush. One of them stopped screaming as a shotgun boomed again. Eight down, six to go.

Suddenly Hunter noticed smoke drifting past. Turning around, he saw a wall of flame ten feet high, fifty yards away and advancing towards him, fanned by the afternoon breeze. The spooked horses whinnied and kicked up their heels, heading north ahead of the fire. Hunter hated to see them go but knew he could track and catch them later.

Backing off, he circled around to where he'd last seen the women. With visibility cut sharply by the smoke, he moved with extra caution. Whoever set the grass fire would be watching, waiting to strike if he showed himself. Soon a second blaze appeared, closing in from the west. He'd need to be quick or they'd all end up trapped!

Passing a large clump of sagebrush, Hunter froze. Detecting a faint rustle, he threw himself sideways as Elise lunged forward. They collided in mid-air and hit the ground grappling, her lethal blade stabbing the soil just inches from his neck. Grasping her wrist, Hunter twisted, rolled, and pinned her down with his lower body, while pressing his free hand hard across her mouth.

"Easy!" He whispered, his face pressed inches from hers. He held her writhing body down with superior weight and strength but was amazed that a person her size could attack with such fury. "I am a friend—I shot the leader," he whispered, willing his truth into her flashing green eyes.

Noting the crossbow and quiver, Elise stopped struggling. She nodded her understanding, and he removed his hand from her mouth and rolled to the side. Wincing, he clenched his fist, and she noticed the red mark where she'd clamped down hard with her teeth. She looked sheepish but, with a wave of his hand, Hunter indicated that it was nothing, just a scratch.

Replacing the dagger inside her waistband, Elise unconsciously rubbed her wrist where Hunter's vice-like grip left an angry welt. He pretended not to notice and, using sign language, asked about her companions' whereabouts. She motioned for him to wait and disappeared into the brush. After a long minute, she returned, leading the others. Hunter noted with interest the bandolier slung across the blonde girl's chest and the familiar way she held the shotgun, as if she knew exactly how and when to use it. *Who are these women?* He wondered, unavoidably impressed.

The growing prairie fire closed in from two directions as wind-whipped flames reached fifteen feet into the air. Waves of stinging smoke reduced visibility to almost zero. Hunter panned the tops of the grass for sign of the enemy. Across the camp, Andy became a human torch as supercharged flames painfully ended his miserable existence.

Veering away from the approaching inferno, Hunter led the women from the smoke-filled plain, backtracking along his original path, recovering his pack and continuing on until reaching the game trail that crisscrossed up into the hills. When the breathless group reached the mixed stand of trees, he had them wait beside the spring while he made another brief recon before guiding them quickly through the small glade and into the higher hills beyond.

On the way up, Hunter thought he heard something on their back trail, and they took cover behind a large boulder while he went to investigate. A few minutes later, he reappeared, wiping fresh blood from his knife on a scrap of dirty cloth before casually discarding it in the brush beside the trail. He smiled grimly, mentally adding another corpse for the vultures to pick clean. In a hushed voice he said, "I don't think we will be followed again. Come, the sun's getting low, and we've still got a long way to go before we can rest." Bristling with adrenaline, crossbow at the ready, Hunter pushed off briskly up the hill, his newly rescued charges following in strained silence on his heels.

CHAPTER FOUR

HUNTER'S LAIR

AS THE FINAL rays of sunset brushed the snow-capped peaks to the east, the silent guide and his weary companions rounded a spectacular rock formation and came to a sudden halt beside a tiny stream. The exhausted women knelt and cupped icy water to their lips, thankful for a moment's rest. The trek up the mountain had been brutal.

Not long into the steep uphill push, their legs began to cramp, requiring extra effort just to keep up. Hunter passed out rations of pemmican—compressed food bars made from dried berries and smoked venison with bear fat added to hold it all together. Within minutes, they experienced welcomed relief and a sustained energy level lasting for hours.

As the afternoon progressed, they ascended the mountain, shadowing the ridgeline, with Hunter maintaining a nearly unbearable pace. The scenery here (had they time to appreciate it) was spectacular, with massive jagged peaks reaching high into the unspoiled sky, ice and snow ever clinging to their upper flanks. Below them on the plain, the fire burned itself out on the periphery of a distant riverbed, and a thick, rusty haze hovered in the lower elevations. During their narrow escape, smoke permeated their clothes, and the smell of burnt prairie remained, clinging to skin and hair.

Their journey up and across the rugged alpine landscape was closely observed by numerous species of wildlife. At lower elevations, herds of deer and elk looked up momentarily and returned to their grazing on dry grass and brambles, while solitary moose browsed among willows or waded in the shallows of lakes and streams. Above the tree line, family groupings of mountain goat and bighorn sheep watched from on high as they roamed the craggy ridges. Along the way, reclusive predators spied from the shadows—wolves and coyotes, cougars, bobcats and lynx, black bears and grizzlies all paused what they were doing to stare at the curious human entourage trespassing through their habitat. Above it all, winged raptors plied the azure skies, noting the unusual human intrusion with casual indifference.

Hunter led them on through an ever-changing panorama, along narrow game trails winding through high alpine meadows and around crystal lakes mirroring the surrounding peaks—edged with dark green stands of stunted juniper and hemlock. They crossed treacherous talus fields layered with chips of broken rock, where a careless step could cause a thousand foot slide into a river-filled gorge, well beyond hope or need of rescue. In the more hazardous sections, Hunter linked them together single file with a safety line from his pack.

Throughout the trek, Anna and Elise were strong enough to bear up, but Sarah would not have made it without their tireless guide who carried her piggyback through most of the truly difficult parts. The sisters took turns bearing Jamie in his papoose-like carrier and, thankfully, the steady rhythm of their steps lulled him to sleep or quieted him during most of the journey.

Resting now in the fading daylight beside the modest stream, Elise sat and caught her breath, refreshed by the icy water. She peeked down inside her cloak to check on baby Jamie, who was fast asleep against her breasts, tucked in and protected from the brisk Canadian wind that brought a chill to the air and turned everyone's breath to steam. Anna and Sarah huddled a short distance away, backs against a steep cliff wall rising another five thousand feet into the clouding sky.

Elise glanced around for a sheltered overhang or anything that might offer some degree of protection from the wind. Not thrilled with this barren location as a campsite, she turned to look for their rescuer. Unseen at first, Hunter appeared suddenly, materializing out of the shadows, returning from scouting their back trail as he'd done several times since leaving the plain.

She watched him kneel and cup cold water to his lips in silence and, for the first time, took a moment to appraise their strange benefactor. The man was rough, yet handsome, and wild though steady, with gray eyes that could be kind, but were mostly hard like the granite forming this unforgiving land. Intuitively, she felt she could trust him but couldn't quite put her finger on the exact emotion he extracted from her soul. "How much further?" she asked quietly, standing and wiping her damp, chilled hands on her travel-stained cloak.

"We have arrived," he stated plainly. Puzzled, she looked around again for some form of habitat or shelter from the elements. Seeing nothing obvious in the half-light, she turned back with a questioning gaze on her oval face and watched with growing interest as Hunter wiped some gravel from the path with his foot, clearing off a space about a yard square. Reaching down, he gripped the edges of a trap door cunningly concealed in the ground and lifted the heavy iron panel back on well-oiled hinges. Without so much as a word, he grasped the sides of the opening, lowered himself down and vanished into the earth! The sisters glanced at one another in amazement as Hunter reappeared half a minute later with a glowing lantern that he hung on the top rung, causing the swaying lamp to cast eerie moving shadows against the stone walls of the tunnel below.

"Hand me the child and follow me down, but watch your step, it's slippery," he said, hands outstretched for the baby. Sarah was reluctant to pass her infant son to this stranger who was about to disappear into the abyss.

"Elise?" She looked to her sister-in-law, who nodded her head.

Hunter held the sleeping boy gingerly in one arm and disappeared into the opening while the others followed, one at a time, on narrow iron rungs descending into the blackness. With everyone safely at the bottom, he returned the still sleeping child to his anxious mother and climbed up to secure the entrance, concealing it from anyone who might be tracking them. Lowering the hatch, he slid two iron bars into place.

Climbing down with lantern in hand, he set off into the thick darkness, leading his troupe down a long, gloomy tunnel that twisted and turned for what seemed like miles through the very core of the mountain. Without an experienced guide, visitors here would quickly become disoriented in the subterranean maze. Along the way, numerous side tunnels and shafts joined the main passageway, and there were no visible markings to distinguish the correct route.

Hunter warned everyone to follow closely and not to stray or take a wrong turn in the dark. To illustrate his point, he halted at the edge of one such side opening and stooped to pick up a fist-sized rock from the chiseled floor. Tossing it into the void, it fell for several long seconds before striking the walls of a deep chasm. He searched each woman's eyes and smiled wryly as it landed with an echoing "whack" hundreds of feet below. Needless to say, everyone kept well to the center of the passageway from that point on.

Seemingly hours later, Anna plodded along on the verge of exhaustion, worn out from the stress of the day's events and Hunter's forced march. She walked arm-in-arm with Sarah and could tell from her sister-in-law's ashen face and stumbling steps that the new mother was nearing collapse. Elise walked behind as rearguard holding the second lantern, with the sleeping baby resting on her chest. Several times during their gradual descent into the bowels of the Earth, she beseeched Hunter to stop so they could catch their breath and allow Sarah time to gather her strength.

The difficulty of the trek through the dark heart of the mountain was no accident. Hunter was taking no chances at being followed or that one of the strangers might try to memorize the path through the maze. After claiming this territory for himself—and knowing that he would be required to protect and defend it alone—he took every precaution to ensure that his mountain base camp was nearly impossible to infiltrate.

Using a dog-eared United States Geological Survey map, Hunter spent the better part of a year exploring every inch of the abandoned mine's web-like labyrinth. Using underground passageways, he could travel undetected beneath miles of nearly impassable terrain above and appear on the surface in various locations throughout the region.

Concealment and ease of movement were not the only benefits to traveling underground. With the tunnel system's lower levels more than a mile beneath the Earth's surface, thermal transfer from deep within the planet's mantle kept temperatures within the core of the tunnel system comfortable even in February, when the outside mercury could register minus fifty degrees Fahrenheit.

Noting Sarah's rapidly deteriorating condition, Hunter again insisted on transporting her piggyback style, which she feebly refused, whereby he simply shrugged, smiled, picked her up and headed off down the tunnel. Soon she, too, was fast asleep, draped over his broad back and shoulders. Behind them, Elise walked beside Anna, marveling at this complete stranger who was obviously willing to do whatever necessary to handle the situation.

After what seemed like an eternity moving forward into the muffled dark, the worn out party rounded a bend and stopped before an apparent dead-end. Perplexed again, Elise and Anna looked to their rescuer for an explanation. Slipping Sarah gently off his back, Hunter pushed hard on a low portion of the wall and, to everyone's astonishment, a section of rock swung noiselessly away on invisible hinges, revealing a large, dimly lit chamber beyond! Retrieving his lamp, Hunter beckoned them inside. Stepping into the grotto, they gazed in wonder as their host silently secured the door behind them.

They stood in a dimly lit, auditorium-sized cavern. High above them, an uneven ceiling soared out of sight into the blackness, its lower portions just visible in the flickering lamplight. The floor was surprisingly level and the rock walls nearly flat. Half a century earlier, the entire complex had been hewn out of solid granite by massive mining machines hungry for gold.

The walls at the near end of the enormous room were lined with sturdy wooden shelves stocked with all sorts of equipment and supplies. Having entered the mountain hall through a seldom-used back entrance, they were led single-file between stacks of crates, past overflowing shelves, and around benches and tables containing a hodgepodge of interesting and useful items, all neatly arranged.

Making their way to the far end of the vast cavern, they passed through a broad arched doorway into a smaller, more lived-in looking cave with a lower ceiling. A startled mouse scurried for the shadows as Hunter placed his lantern on a sturdy table. He turned up the lamp, and warm, welcomed light revealed a meticulously tidy kitchen, complete with antique cast-iron cook stove and insulated food cooler.

Hunter side-glanced his guests' reactions—the first outsiders ever allowed inside his subterranean domain—as they curiously explored his home in open amazement. Anna immediately noticed the generous walk-in pantry stocked with hundreds of canned foods and dried goods of all kinds. She reached out to touch a glass jar of bright yellow-orange peaches, recalling the last time she'd enjoyed some back home a month before their journey.

Turning from the kitchen, Hunter motioned to Elise to follow him down a short hallway into an adjoining room where he lit another lamp and turned it up high. Its bright glow revealed a cozy bathroom built out of stone and timbers, with a real commode, sink, and claw-foot tub! In one corner was a large copper boiler for pre-heating bath water and she stared in wonder as Hunter opened the tap and hot, steaming water poured into the tub! Soap and candles rested on a nearby shelf. He opened a tall wooden hutch and picked out four thick, soft towels, passing them to the bewildered young woman. Without a word, he headed back to the kitchen followed by a shocked Elise, who quickly ushered everyone down the hall and into the bath.

In the kitchen, Hunter opened the cooler and withdrew several ceramic containers. In minutes he had a roaring fire going in the cook stove and a hot, savory supper underway. As the food cooked, he moved to the adjoining sitting room, fitted with thick sheepskin rugs and pillows and started a cheering fire in the freestanding fireplace.

An hour later, three utterly refreshed travelers and one shiny baby boy emerged from the bath. They relaxed on cushions covered with soft furs and sipped hot, spicy tea from ceramic mugs while talking softly among themselves. From time to time, Hunter would catch one or another of them covertly watching him as he busied himself around the kitchen. A few minutes later, he stood poised in the archway, his guests grouped together in conspiratorial discussion about what he could only speculate."Now," he said finally, gently interrupting them, "time to eat." They moved into the kitchen and took their seats without delay. Hunter wondered how long it had been since the famished women had eaten a proper meal. He filled the wooden table with venison tenderloins broiled to perfection, along with fresh baked sweet potatoes and canned corn. In the center was a bowl of the peaches Anna admired earlier. He looked on as his hungry guests passed the serving bowls around and attacked their plates, eating in silence but for an occasional moan of pleasure or exclamation of delight.

Hunter did not join them but left the room, returning a few minutes later. "Elise," he motioned for her to follow him, walking her into the next room. "I have to go out. You sleep here in front of the fireplace." He motioned to mats spread out on the floor and pillows. "Keep the door locked and DO NOT OPEN IT unless you hear three knocks and a whistle like this," he let out a low trill. She scrutinized her rugged rescuer and started to ask a question."Not now, plenty of time for questions in the morning," he insisted. His gray eyes revealed a hint of kindness, and a barely perceptible smile graced his trail-worn face. He showed her how to bolt the massive oak and iron door and vanished into the chilly night.

After devouring two helpings each of the wonderful food, Anna and Elise cleared the table and put everything away while Sarah put the baby down in the next room. Hot water to wash dishes was another welcomed surprise, though not nearly as appreciated as the warm, oil-scented bath water they had luxuriated in earlier. After supper, they relaxed in front of the fire, and Elise helped everyone settle in on comfortable sleeping mats piled high with furs. Within minutes, Sarah, Jamie and Anna were all sound asleep.

Though exhausted herself, Elise felt compelled to discover what she could about their quiet host. She explored the main grotto and several smaller adjoining caverns to satisfy her curiosity. Afterwards, she was certain that he lived alone and was surprised more than once by the many unusual, interesting and unexpected items she discovered. Most curious of all were the books! There must be thousands of them stacked in wooden crates, while others filled row after row of shelves lining the walls throughout the connected caverns. *He must have one of the most complete libraries left on Earth! Father would love to see it.* A deep foreboding settled over her at the thought of him, working so diligently through the years to keep them all safe, only to have his world unravel around him now.

She gathered some cushions, a pillow, and a handful of soft animal furs and made her bed atop a giant bear rug stretched out in front of the huge castle-like door. She lit one of the large beeswax candles and placed it on the floor beside her. The instant she lay down, her travel-worn body melted into the luxurious elk robe beneath her, almost aching with relief. She was physically and emotionally spent and fell at once into a deep, dreamless slumber.

Several hours later, Elise woke abruptly from a dead sleep. She lay still in the dark, not daring to move, temporarily confused by her unfamiliar surroundings. The candle had gone out and the darkness of the cavern was palpable. Slender fingers unconsciously slipped around the haft of the dagger at her waist, and she listened, straining her ears, breathless in the night—three quick knocks on the door followed by a low trilling whistle! With the deadly blade poised, she unbolted the heavy door. Hunter slipped through the partially opened doorway, passing a bundle to Elise on his way in.

Noticeably relieved, she sheathed her dagger and gratefully accepted the familiar implement bag she'd carried with her on the long journey north. As he swept past her, she noticed the smell of smoke mingled with his pleasant earthy scent. Through the opened door she caught a glimpse of Venus hovering above the horizon as numberless stars twinkled in the dark expanse above.

Hunter lit a lantern and bolted the door, quietly sliding the heavy iron crossbar into place. Her gaze followed him into the next room where he turned toward her, his weathered face revealing a hint of weariness. "Go join the others, Elise. I'll see you in the morning."

She stood still, staring at this soft-spoken, resourceful man who appeared out of nowhere to save and escort her family to his home deep inside the mountain. He watched her with an expression that made Elise think for a moment that he could read her thoughts. She blushed, and he started to move towards her. Instantly, she was on guard. *Here it comes,* she thought, her hand unconsciously moving to the dagger, but he walked straight past her into the next room where her sisters and the baby slept soundly. He carefully placed another seasoned log on the fire in the stove and stoked it with an iron poker. Elise brought her furs and pillows back into the sleeping room and made up her bed. She suddenly realized that she and her family were using all of the available bedding, so where was he going to sleep?

Hunter noticed her curious look and smiled, pointing up. Her eyes followed and, for the first time, she noticed a slender object hanging down just out of reach a few feet above her head. The thick braided leather rope knotted every couple of feet or so had completely escaped her initial scrutiny. It led up to a high ledge overlooking the room. Leaving her with an expression of surprise on her face, he was up the rope before she could formulate a response.

Leaning over the edge, he peered down at her and whispered, "Back to sleep now, Elise. Tomorrow is another day." The rope vanished as he turned toward his bed.

"That's not fair," she whispered indignantly.

"Not fair?" he asked curiously, turning back. "How do you mean?"

"I mean that you know *my* name, but I don't know yours."

He looked at her thoughtfully, gray eyes twinkling in the lamplight. Alone these many years, he'd apparently forgotten his social graces. With all they had been through, formal introductions had slipped his mind. "You can call me Hunter." He turned to go.

"Hunter," she whispered.

He turned back, the upper half of his face barely visible in the lamp's glow.

"Thank you... for everything today... we are... very grateful..." She stumbled over her words, glancing about for help and feeling suddenly unable to adequately express herself. She looked up at him, perplexed at her unusual loss for words. Hunter's eyes smiled into hers for a long moment and he was gone.

Slipping beneath the furs, she closed her eyes, silently mouthing his name and smiled. Pulling the elk robe to her chin, she soon drifted off, certain beyond question that he was indeed *The One* Father had sent her hundreds of miles through the wilderness to find!

CHAPTER FIVE

BITS OF THE PUZZLE

AN EXHAUSTED HUNTER slept as his head touched the pillow. He had covered many miles since preparing supper—returning to the plain and the scene of the battle. He went back for several obvious reasons. He needed to recover his bolts, since accurate crossbow ammunition was difficult to manufacture from scratch. Even with some fire damage, such as singed fletching, the bolts could be refurbished as good as new, as long as the shaft wasn't bent out of true. His dwindling supply of alloy shafts was extremely precious and each bolt was definitely worth recovering.

He also wanted to salvage any supplies and other items, such as tools or weapons that might have survived the fire, both from the travelers' burned out camp and the corpses. Also, he wanted to track the horses, as it was vital that the bandits didn't use them to escape his coming justice. He hoped, as well, to discover something more about the mysterious travelers themselves who had so suddenly disrupted his solitary life.

* * *

ARRIVING AT THE burned-out campsite in the revealing light of a harvest moon, Hunter found it necessary to drive off a hungry pack of coyotes who perceived the scent of death on the wind and were hard at work, apparently starting with old Andy. He sensed them roaming about, impatient for him to move on, so they could resume their grisly feast. He knew they would return to feed as soon as he was gone. The insects, too, had already staked their claim, and fly larvae, by the tens of thousands, hatched, wriggled and fed.

He was glad he hadn't postponed his return. In another day or two, all that would remain of the fallen would be stripped down, dismembered skeletons with the larger bones cracked open to access their iron and protein-rich marrow and his bolts scattered and nearly impossible to find. Making a methodical sweep of the battlefield, he located several charred bodies in the blackened stubble. As anticipated, the surviving bandits made a hasty get away without bothering to bury their dead. He recovered his bolts and rummaged through their smoldering remains, recovering two handguns, several knives and a combination compass/altimeter in a brass case. Half-hidden beneath the leader's charred carcass, he discovered a thick leather satchel containing several items worthy of closer inspection in the light of day.

After recovering some salvageable cooking utensils and other miscellaneous artifacts from the burned out shelter, he set out after his quarry at a brisk pace. Starting from the center of camp and circling out in a widening arc, he picked up their trail in the moonlight—several sets of tracks headed north, shadowing the horses. He tracked them across the blackened prairie to the edge of a dry riverbed where the fire had eventually burned itself out. Beyond this, the bent grass made the trail easier to follow, and plentiful blood sign revealed that at least one of them was badly wounded.

A little further on, the horses turned off into a box canyon, but the fleeing bandits missed them and kept right on going. Hunter wasn't surprised at the horses' choice. He knew that back in that draw, a stream surfaced in a large pool. He figured the thirsty horses probably smelled the water and pushed in for a drink, a positive development since the narrow canyon bottom would make rounding them up that much easier when the time came. Leaving them for later, he continued following the blood-flecked trail, moving quietly and keeping to the shadows in the bright moonlight, ever conscious of the possibility of ambush. As the night progressed, temperatures dropped, but the tracker felt neither cold nor fatigue. He steadily dogged his enemy, reading the abundant sign left in their wake.

Their wounded man was hemorrhaging badly. Dark rivulets mingled with earth and disturbed grasses where he was half-carried, boots dragging along the ground. A mile later, Hunter came upon the chilled corpse propped against a twisted tree in a thickening puddle of blood. With some effort, he removed the bolt point from the dead man's pelvis and with it, accounted for all of his shots.

Doing some quick calculations, he concluded that five bandits still remained alive, as this one was previously counted as mortally wounded. With the night far spent and the moon beginning to sink below the western horizon, he headed back to get some sleep. He would have to return very soon to hunt down the survivors and finish them off. Allowing any of the raiders to escape was simply not an option.

* * *

LATE THE FOLLOWING morning Elise awoke slowly, becoming conscious of the new day in several blended stages. Lying on her back with eyes closed, she became aware of the gentle support of the down-filled cushions beneath her. Shifting slightly, she distributed her weight more evenly upon the comfortable bedding and pulled the soft elk-hide covers up around her neck, settling further into the pillows.

As far back as she could remember, she had savored the detached tranquility in that marvelous state-of-being halfway between waking and deep sleep. Vaguely familiar sounds and scents drifted through her growing awareness. There was a ceramic scraping, the stirring of something liquid, muffled footsteps of someone moving purposefully about in an adjacent room. Raising her arms above her head, she arched her back and stretched, and, in so doing, her right wrist brushed against cold, hard stone.

Her eyes flew open as she sat upright, staring suspiciously about the unfamiliar room. Seeing Anna, Sarah, and Jamie sleeping contentedly nearby, she suddenly remembered where she was and her expression softened. Reaching back, she freed her long, brown braid and shook it out, delighting in the luxury of clean, scented hair. Last night's bath was pure ecstasy; she hadn't experienced such physical comfort since leaving New Eden six weeks earlier. Then, like a cloud, the ever-present sense of foreboding pressed in on her once again. Combing her fingers through her dark, gently curling locks, Elise brushed an errant wisp from her pale forehead and gathered her sobering thoughts. Reviewing the previous day's remarkable events, she was certain that she and her family would have been killed or worse had Hunter not shown up to save them when he did. Grateful for his dramatic rescue, she now understood what Father meant when he said there was one man who could make all the difference to their survival.

Elise recalled the stormy eve of her departure from New Eden, when she'd inquired again about her older brother, unwilling to accept that something terrible may have happened to him. "But what of William.... is there still no word?" The furrow on Adam Planchet's brow had deepened and a verbal reply was unnecessary. It had been twelve weeks since he'd last heard from his son. In spite of his faith in William's strength, courage, and resourcefulness, even he now began to fear the worst.

"Had he been successful, he would have returned by now." The weary patriarch let out a long, unconscious sigh. He turned and looked into his eldest daughter's worried eyes. "*You* will have to go." Registering the finality of his words, she realized that there was no one else to send. With William unaccounted for and her younger brother, Robert, recovering from wounds received in an ambush, the responsibility fell on Elise, who willingly accepted the task, clearly aware of the gravity of the situation. "It won't be easy to convince him to come back with you. He distrusts people and prefers solitude to human companionship," continued her father.

"But if he is so isolated, how will I find him?" she implored, unsure of what to do once she arrived in Hunter's territory.

"Do not worry, daughter, approach his domain, and he'll find you! This map will get you close. When he appears, give him this letter. He will know what to do." He handed the map and letter to Elise, embracing her before she hurried off to pack.

Looking back now, it all seemed surreal—the six-week journey through the wilds, the near disaster of losing their horses, yesterday's attack and miraculous rescue. Life, she reflected, was a constantly evolving challenge. Today she would present the mysterious Hunter with Father's letter, doing her best to convince him to return to New Eden and save them from their enemies. She dare not consider his refusal. In this task she had no choice but to be successful. Otherwise, all that she loved would surely be lost.

* * *

HUNTER AROSE EARLY, despite his few short hours of sleep, and was dressed again in sheepskins and moccasins as he made preparations to deal with the five remaining marauders and round up the horses. He rustled up a quick breakfast for his guests and packed a small bundle for himself before rousing the others. The previous day's events had left many unanswered questions and what he needed this morning, before heading out, were some answers.

Immediately after breakfast, he escorted Elise into the large grotto behind the living quarters where they could be alone. He preferred to question his guests separately in the event he needed to cross check some of their information later. They sat across from each other on simple benches at a rough-hewn table adorned with beeswax candles.

Hunter confronted Elise, demanding answers to the obvious questions and carefully observing her reactions. As she began to speak, he tuned in with more than his physical senses, seeking the message beyond her words and body language, to discern the truth in her story.

"Perhaps you can explain this," he stretched out his hand, placing a shiny metal object on the table between them. She looked upon the familiar medal, identical to the one she'd seen displayed on the wall of her father's study ever since she could remember. It was a Silver Star, but was not her father's. Beneath the red and white striped ribbon hung a bronze, five-pointed star with a smaller silver star embedded in the center. On the reverse side, engraved beneath the raised letters "FOR GALLANTRY IN ACTION" she could clearly make out "SGT. H. J. Macintosh" in the gold-colored metal.

Hunter Joshua Macintosh.... How long had it been since he'd considered his full legal name? Until last night, he hadn't laid eyes on the military award in over a decade and a half. He shot a hard look at Elise. "How is it that a bandit chief was in possession of my medal given to a friend more than sixteen years ago?"

"It was entrusted to my brother, William, by my father—Adam Planchet. He sent William out nearly five months ago to find you. The bandits must have come across his party. I don't really know." Hunter's busy mind screeched to a halt.

"Would that be *Colonel* Adam Planchet?"

"Yes, father was a colonel in the Army in Africa."

"And you are Colonel Planchet's daughter?"

"Elise Planchet," she stood and formally introduced herself, offering him her hand. Hunter stood slowly and leaned forward clasping it, still stunned by this sudden disclosure. *Colonel Planchet in contact after all these years...they had served together in the African Campaign.* Elise knew little of her father's time in service; he never really talked about it much. She understood from her mother that he was a highly decorated field commander in the Army's Airborne Infantry and was badly injured. "My father said you would remember him," Elise said hopefully as she handed Hunter a small parchment scroll. It was the letter from her father.

Remember him? Hunter asked himself incredulously, unrolling the scroll. *How could I possibly forget the man who risked his own life and military career to rescue my unit pinned down by enemy forces and written off by higher-ups in the chain of command?* He read the words with intense interest, still reeling from Elise's unexpected revelation:

2nd New Moon after Summer Solstice, Year 14

Sergeant Hunter Macintosh,

If you are reading this, then you are still alive in Wyoming and my daughter was successful where my son was not. I had rather hoped never to have to write this letter, but the situation here in Colorado has turned suddenly grave, and I am afraid that, without your expertise, all may soon be lost. You once offered me your services in a sand-filled, God-forsaken place far from the comforts of home, and I would be very much obliged if you could manage to provide some much needed assistance, should you still have the inclination. I trust that you will do the right thing by my family. They are everything to me.

Sincerely,
A. Planchet

Colonel Adam Planchet, (retired)

Looking up from the letter, Hunter explained, "Your father was the commanding officer of my military unit in Africa." He recalled the day they'd saved each other's lives more than once. "Colonel Planchet bailed me out of a couple of tight spots." He smiled grimly as the memories came flooding back like a distant tsunami swamping the shore and dragging Hunter out into the past with it....

The night was black, the air heavy with the acrid smell of smoke and gunpowder. The 5th North African Expeditionary Force was pinned down behind enemy lines. They had night dropped into the bush surrounding a small regional airport near the north-central Moroccan coast that was being used by Islamic extremists to interrogate captured Allied soldiers and local Moroccans suspected of aiding the Infidels.

Known back then as Sergeant Hunter Macintosh—Sgt. Mac for short—Hunter was attached to a company of special warfare operatives with orders to rescue all POW's and Friendlies and destroy the enemy's HQ and airport facilities.

The seventy-five member joint force, consisting of special warfare combat infantry units from the U.S., U.K., and EU, successfully dropped in undetected in a flawlessly executed H.A.L.O. night parachute jump. Regrouped on the ground about a mile from the airport complex, individual units began moving toward their objectives. Thirty minutes later, as the allied forces were moving forward along a brush-covered fence line, the lead scouts stumbled into a deadly minefield fifteen hundred meters from the airport terminal complex, instantly killing four U.S. Army Rangers and two Scottish Black Watch (Royal Highland Regiment) recon scouts, and seriously wounding nine others!

Immediately, all hell broke loose as the four-hundred-man enemy garrison guarding the airport quickly responded, firing illuminating mortar rounds above the surrounding area, and detonating scores of antipersonnel mines hidden throughout the rocky, inhospitable terrain. In less than five minutes, the allies had suffered a sixty-percent casualty rate. The shell-shocked survivors, dragging their dead and wounded with them, scrambled down into an adjacent drainage ditch where they found themselves effectively pinned down by enemy snipers guided by overhead flares.

"Return with us and help my father set things right." Her words were true and powerful, returning him fully to the present. Elise leaned forward, emerald eyes willing the quiet stranger to agree. Sitting across from her in silence, Hunter appeared calm and detached, yet, behind his carefully constructed defenses, he was rocked by the immensity of this news suddenly smuggled into his insulated world. He reread the letter for the third time. After a long minute of silence passed between them, Elise calmly insisted, "I speak the truth and…"

"I believe you," he interrupted, convinced of her sincerity and persuaded by the evidence she presented. He sighed and closed his hand around the silver star, caressing it gently with his fingertips. He leaned back, taking a moment to reflect on the far-reaching implications of her words. Without warning, the past had infiltrated the present, calling him out of his comfortable solitude and into a far-off conflict, not of his choosing. In North Africa, Planchet had risked everything to rescue what was left of his pinned-down unit. Now, more than sixteen years after Morocco, their roles were reversed and Hunter was duty-bound to ride to his former commander's aid. "It would be an honor to help your father. Please tell me everything I need to know."

He postponed his trip down the mountain to spend the balance of the day with Elise, who brought him rapidly up to speed. She began with a brief history of New Eden, though before the End War, Hunter and her father had stayed in touch from time-to-time via email, and he vaguely remembered a few sketchy details about the community his former commander was so proud of. Planchet had even once invited Hunter to visit New Eden, telling him he was always welcome and could fort up with them "if the shit ever hit the fan." Hunter thanked him but explained how he preferred to be in the wilderness away from other people, especially in times of trouble. He remembered sending Planchet a Google Earth map of the primitive hunting cabin and forty acres he purchased in the Wind River Range just a few miles from the cave where they now sat.

Elise continued, describing the present situation at New Eden and the strength of their adversaries from New Hope. She answered his many questions, sharing the details of her journey north from Colorado, offering, as well, what little she knew about the disappearance of her brother William. From time-to-time during her narrative, Hunter pressed for further clarification, jotting down notes in a journal. He wanted to know everything he could about New Eden: its history, its people, its relationship with New Hope, all of it, from its inception to the time Elise and her sisters left. He asked for a detailed schematic of the buildings and grounds, which she reproduced in charcoal on the back of an animal hide.

Though surprised several times by his line of questioning, Elise answered everything honestly without reservation. Based on her father's faith in the man and her own personal experience and observation, she elected to trust him completely. Later that evening, however, Hunter offered her his plan and she became dismayed. With the setting sun sending pink and orange rays across the cloud-layered horizon, she reacted strongly to his words."But we can't just leave them behind!" She was shocked at his suggestion that Anna, Sarah, and the baby should remain here, while she, alone, led Hunter back to New Eden. The idea left her feeling suddenly out of control—an unnatural state that she didn't easily abide. "I don't think it wise for us to split up. We came this far together, and, if anything were to happen to my family, I could never forgive myself." The young woman looked uncomfortable, her arms crossed in a defensive posture.

Hunter measured her with his penetrating gaze, speculating on her ability to handle the challenges facing them in the coming weeks. He was certain that she was determined and capable enough, having witnessed her courage back on the plain, but would she be willing to follow his lead? Only time would tell. "There is no other way, Elise," he patiently explained. "Sarah is much too weak to travel, and the baby would be impossible. Anna can stay here and look after them while we go and assess the situation at New Eden."

They stood on a rocky ledge just outside the great oak and iron door to his bastion. Elise appeared to study the fading sunset, framed by ragged clouds swallowing the snow-covered peaks. Without looking at him she asked, "And what if we don't get back until next spring?" A likely prospect, given the distances involved, the lateness of the season, and the time it would take to return.

"Then your family will be safe here with plenty of food, firewood, and supplies to see them through the winter," he calmly replied. "It's either that, or we wait for Sarah to regain her strength and all make the trip back together, once the passes clear next year." Elise frowned, feeling beset. With the violent attacks upon New Eden becoming more frequent, postponing their return until spring was out of the question. Conditions back home could have easily worsened in the weeks since leaving Colorado, and there was no telling what they might find upon their return.

In the end, she accepted Hunter's analysis. Without bed rest and nursing, Sarah would probably never recover her strength, and then where would young Jamie be, without father *or* mother to nurture and guide him in this world? She realized that leaving Anna here to care for Sarah and the baby was the only realistic option. Traveling light on horseback, she and Hunter would be able to make excellent time and could search for clues to William's whereabouts along the way.

Her thoughts flew again to her brother. *There's still a chance he's alive,* she told herself, desperate to believe it. He'd obviously never reached Hunter's valley; so he must be holed up somewhere between here and New Eden. The fact that the bandit leader was in possession of William's medicine pouch and Hunter's medal only proved that their paths had intersected at some point. At a time when most people would surrender hope to logic, Elise refused to believe that her brother was dead, in spite of the strong circumstantial evidence to the contrary. If anyone could help her find William, she felt certain that it was Hunter.

Elise considered the man she'd come to respect in the few days since their meeting. He was quiet and obviously determined to maintain his usual solitary patterns, despite their intrusion into his private domain. He spoke very little and only then when necessary to convey some important bit of information. He wasn't unfriendly, but kept his thoughts and emotions to himself. A peculiar man in some respects, she mused, but incredibly resourceful and very much in charge of his life.

"He's a lot like you in that way, Elise," Anna teased the next day, while harvesting the last of the summer squash and pumpkins from a stone-walled garden etched into a south facing slope not far from Hunter's mountain home. Elise scowled, wondering why she felt such a strange mix of emotions about this hermit who lived in a cave like a wild beast. Just when she thought she had him pigeonholed, another unique aspect of Hunter's complex nature came to light, such as their pleasant surprise at his small farming operation hidden away in the hills.

Over the years, he'd painstakingly terraced a fertile strip of land between two rock outcroppings and successfully grew fruits, nuts, vegetables and herbs. He even had two beehives and a small glass greenhouse! In a well-concealed stone and log coop, built into the side of a limestone overhang, he kept a handful of laying hens, a couple of roosters, and a pair of prolific rabbits. But the greatest shock of all were the horses!

When the end of civilization arrived fourteen years earlier, Hunter retreated to his nearby cabin, swapping his off-road truck for two good riding horses and a mule that a local rancher—who believed that things would be rapidly returning to normal—was more than happy to provide. As the years passed, he replaced his aging mounts with younger animals captured from the mustang bands that freely roamed the Wind River region. From spring to late fall, he stabled them within earshot of his cave at the top of an alpine meadow, cordoned off with a split-rail corral. Prior to winter, he'd let them loose to fend for themselves down in the valley with the rest of their kind. Every spring he'd capture and break two or three to ride throughout the rest of the year before releasing them back into the wild at first frost. The mysterious Hunter was full of surprises.

Today, he'd left before dawn, saying only that he might not return until the following evening. He showed them the garden, the spring and small greenhouse, and showed them what to feed the livestock. He took Elise aside and handed her a compact pistol and a handful of cartridges he'd recovered from the plain. "I assume you know how to use one of these?" She casually accepted the small-framed .38. Releasing the cylinder, she loaded six bullets, snapped it shut, and spun the nickel-plated pistol around on her finger like a wild-west gunfighter! As he rode down the mountain to round up the horses and take care of loose ends, Hunter had trouble keeping the smile off his face.

CHAPTER SIX

AN UNEXPECTED ALLY

RETURNING TO THE plain on horseback in the uncompromising light of day, Hunter discovered the carcasses of the dead already stripped down to bone and hair. It was amazing what Mother Nature could do in just three days! Here and there, a few scattered bones were all that remained of the tough marauders, a fitting end without headstone or remembrance to commemorate their ill-spent days.

Retracing his three-day-old trail, he guided his mount north, this time entering the canyon where the horses' tracks led. Once inside, he dismounted, leading his mare in on foot. The walls were steep and the canyon long and narrow with a slice of sky above. He figured the animals would be fairly easy to catch and brought along a rawhide lariat and some treats to assist him. Cautiously moving deeper into the rift, he scanned the high walls and surrounding rocks and brush, keenly aware of his vulnerability. Seeking fresh tracks, he saw only where the horses had casually moved about, alternately grazing and drinking from the shallow creek that tumbled through the rocky bottom.

On either side, near-vertical sandstone walls in countless shades of red, yellow, and orange, rose eight-hundred feet into the cloudless blue. The canyon itself was about three miles long and shaped like an hourglass. A thousand yards across at the widest point, it narrowed to a few hundred about halfway along, and then widened back out for another mile and a half or so. The ground was covered in sand and gravel, and dotted with gray-green bunches of sagebrush, with thin tufts of grass flanking the creek. Scattered here and there along the bottom, sharp, solitary boulders dotted the broken floor, offerings from the towering cliffs above. A few solitary cedars and junipers, with intermittent glades of willow, aspen and poplar, traced the watercourse.

Hunter spotted a game trail leading up and across a red-washed canyon wall, offering a better look at the lay of the land. He tied his mustang to a shrub and scrambled up, as the trail switched back and forth across the side, angling for the top at a fairly steep grade. About halfway along, he gained enough altitude to see all the way to the back.

Pausing beside a skewed limestone slab, he looked out over the shadowed canyon floor hundreds of feet below. As he surmised, the horses were bunched together toward the back through the narrows. Scanning with his binoculars, he spotted half-a-dozen or so, grazing a couple hundred yards upstream. He located two or three more in a clump of cottonwoods a short distance beyond the rest. From here, they looked to be doing fine but would no doubt appreciate being relieved of those annoying saddles and bridles.

He headed down and soon rode his horse out into a small clearing in plain sight of seven of the animals. They were all heads up and wild-eyed, flaring nostrils testing the wind. Their ears cocked forward as he approached, snapping back and forth like miniature radar dishes as he drew near. Speaking softly, he slid easily from his horse and walked calmly towards them, offering a handful of something from his saddlebags as he went. While the nervous animals bunched up and tried to decide whether to run or stay, a blaze-faced mare snorted as she caught a whiff of wild oats and honey. Whinnying with interest, she took a few cautious steps towards Hunter, while the rest of the herd held back and looked on, not yet convinced.

He offered her a bit of the grain, which she nosed right into and immediately settled down, allowing him to right her saddle, which had slipped badly to one side. With soothing words, he loosened her cinch and removed the saddle and bridle altogether, patting her gently with gloved hands. He rubbed her damp, matted fur back and forth in long clawing motions as she crunched the grain and leaned into his hands, occasionally swishing her long tangled tail, obviously appreciating the back rub.

Producing a well-used currycomb from his pocket, Hunter brushed down the grateful animal and recalled Elise saying she thought she recognized a couple of her lost horses among the bandits' mounts. As he groomed the happy horse, he was pretty sure that this was one of the beauties she'd referred to. Witnessing the mare's relief, a couple of others nosed in looking for grain, and Hunter removed their saddles and bridles, rubbing them down as well. Before long, they were all taking an overdue roll in the dust, relieved to be free from their constricting tack. Afterwards, he led them to the stream to drink before tying them close to a small clump of willows in the shade. He left them there, looking sleepy and content, and went off to find the rest of the bunch.

He collected a total of five more when he came upon the corpse. Hunter was stilled by the macabre scene. A man had been stripped naked and staked out over a fire pit. Most of the skin on his arms and legs was missing. Hunter went instantly into combat mode, loading his crossbow and quickly scanning the area. He found nothing but a few faint tracks, the ground here being mostly rock with little topsoil covering the granite substrate. Careful examination of the body revealed that the victim was strung up alive and skinned while a tightly focused fire toasted his sexual organs to a blackened crisp. Sometime later his face and scalp had been removed, perhaps as a trophy, or maybe the killer was simply signing his work; it was impossible to know.

Hunter was unsettled. He hadn't seen anything like it since Africa, where ritual killings involving witchcraft and torture were commonplace among warring tribes. There, such mayhem was practiced not only to terrify and destroy an enemy, but to capture his soul, thus preventing him from entering the afterlife. *But who here would commit such barbarism and why?* Hunter shook his head. Whoever did this had effectively eliminated one of his enemies, but created an entirely new set of problems. With four bandits still at large, it seemed that someone else was hunting them, and he needed to find out who that was and fast. Troubled that he'd failed to distinguish the killer's tracks, he scanned the shadowed canyon walls, half-expecting a bullet to come crashing into his unprotected flesh. Driven to quickly unravel this newest of mysteries, he melted into the sagebrush at the base of the cliff and vanished.

* * *

CAUTIOUSLY MAKING HIS way deeper into the canyon, Hunter soon found what he was looking for: *hoof prints entering from the opposite direction of the burned out camp!* He'd dangerously assumed that all tracks in the canyon belonged to the runaway horses, but those all entered the canyon from the south. Carefully examining the hoof prints, he determined that one rider, leading a pack animal, entered the canyon from the north as recently as this morning, returning back the same way. He hadn't previously considered the possibility of another exit!

After a mile or so, another break in the hills appeared, and a second entrance opened up. His hunch about there being another way out of the canyon was correct! He continued following the tracks as they curved around towards the northwest. The rider's trail merged with the footprints of the fleeing bandits who were still heading north on foot. A short time later, he spotted where the rider came down through a thick stand of Douglas fir. *How strange.* It appeared that the rider followed the raiders, took one alive, packed him down to where the horses were gathered in the canyon, and killed him there before returning to the remaining bandits' trail. *But why?*

Hunter guided his horse cautiously up the hill following the bandits' obvious trail and scouting for the faint sign of their stalker. Passing through some particularly rugged terrain, he paused, noting the usual wilderness sounds: the high-pitched cry of a bird of prey, wind rustling through sagebrush and whisking through the boughs overhead, noisy jays and crows warning of his approach. The intermingled tracks of both predator and prey wove in and out of the trees and around boulders on a gradual incline up a sparsely forested shoulder of land.

The day was already half spent and the sky clouding up, like it might rain, when the afternoon breeze picked up, and Hunter noticed the faintest odor of wood smoke in the air. He tested the wind, determining the direction of its source. Dismounting and sticking to cover, he painstakingly followed the scent of the smoke on foot, scanning the surrounding landscape and moving silently from tree to bush to rock, always keeping to the shadows when possible. Pausing at a seeping spring to refill his canteens, he spotted something out of the ordinary among the jumbled bird and animal tracks at the water's edge: a single set of moccasin prints in the mushy ground!

Widening out in a circle, Hunter located the well-hidden remains of a tiny camp with its recently extinguished fire. Squatting beside the bits of charred sticks, he carefully swept the vicinity of the campfire with piercing gray eyes. Noticing something curious, he reached down and picked up a small, partially burned bundle of crumbling, reddish-brown, plant-like material. Holding it under his nose, he rubbed the substance between his thumb and forefingers and sniffed. The aroma was unmistakable—tobacco! He hadn't seen any in years because it didn't grow naturally within several hundred miles.

Hunter figured that the killer probably traded with people from down in the southern part of the country or was perhaps from there himself. Poking through the ashes with his knife, he soon came across something even more unusual... a small number of dark brown coffee beans! Hunter was duly impressed. After tobacco, coffee was one of the first items to be pillaged and depleted following the End War. In fact, tobacco and coffee, along with sugar, salt, and cooking oil, were considered primary means of exchange in lieu of money. Whoever camped here was extremely well supplied and lacked none of the few remaining luxuries that this world had to offer! He placed the items into his shirt, returned to his horse and picked up the trail with more questions than answers.

By late afternoon Hunter's keen mind and sharp eyes were completely engrossed in tracking the mysterious horse canyon killer. Following the easily discernible footprints of the bandits, the killer's trail was nearly invisible, and Hunter was becoming increasingly disturbed. Never before had it been so difficult to track a human being through the wild. In fact, humans, without question, had always been the easiest species to follow until today. Now he was forced to draw upon every bit of skill and experience he possessed to decipher the extremely limited sign, getting the distinct feeling that, if this person wished not to be followed, there would be no sign at all. Whoever he was, the man he sought knew how to pass through rugged, broken country as if he were a ghost, and Hunter began to have grave doubts about ever catching up with him.

Crouched down beside the faint trail, he moved forward, tracing where his quarry left the hilltop and crossed into a ravine with a fast flowing creek running through the bottom. As he cautiously worked his way up the steep opposite bank, an unmistakable odor assaulted his nostrils and suddenly Hunter knew what he was about to find. Two large shadows swept over him, as vultures angled in for a meal. Peering over the top of the bank, the horrific scene assailed his senses, stopping him in his tracks. A few yards beyond the ravine, two more of the former raiders, or, more specifically, some eighty-five percent of their remains, were stretched out and hung upside down on makeshift wooden frames, constructed of small flexible tree limbs tied with vines. Again, the dead were void of clothing and mutilated, with much of their skin missing. The vultures had done a rather thorough job of further disfiguring the gruesome corpses. Thanks to the cool September weather, the bodies had not had time to begin decomposing; so the reek wasn't as foul as one might expect.

Warily circling the site with crossbow poised, Hunter spooked the irritated scavengers who squawked and flew into a snag a dozen yards away. The bold opportunists certainly had no plans to give up their feast so easily. Hunter examined the kills. This time, a cairn of rocks was built up into an altar harboring the remains of a fire used to heat some sharp sticks. Above the fire altar, a spit contained what appeared to be internal organs roasted to a crispy blackness.

Further disquieted by the pattern revealed in this new discovery, Hunter was struck by the contradiction it represented: Why would the executioner leave virtually no sign between kills, yet position his victims out in the open, as if to invoke admiration for his handiwork. Again, both carcasses had been expertly skinned, with face and hair removed, leaving only muscle, bone, and skull. From the evidence, the victims were alive at the time of their ordeal. The extreme nature of the murders spoke strongly to Hunter of revenge.

CHAPTER SEVEN

AS YE SOW....

SEATED COMFORTABLY ATOP a flat rock, a few miles due west of the grisly altar where Hunter crouched, sorting through signs and symbols seeking answers, Dr. Constantine Sirocco peered through a fine pair of German binoculars at the exhausted fugitives scrambling up the far slope of a steep, wooded ravine. He smiled at the miserable remnants of the once proud band of mounted marauders, desperately seeking to escape the terror that had shadowed them for the past three days. The patient executioner, methodically stalking his final victims with singleness of purpose, watched them struggle a while longer before mounting up and heading down their trail.

Hanging from the pommel of his native-style saddle were the grisly trophies of his three previous kills: the complete face and head skins of his victims with hair attached. Soon there would be five and he could begin the process of "shrinking" them, a technique perfected centuries earlier by the Shuar tribe from the Amazonian Basin in Ecuador.

With an Ivy League Ph.D. in Cultural Anthropology, Sirocco extensively traveled the globe in the two decades before the End War, systematically cataloguing the cultural and religious rituals of the last remaining primitive societies on Earth.

He'd been tracking this group for nearly a month now, picking up their cold trail at the burned out homestead of a settler friend. He'd found Mason Cole, his wife, and young son brutally murdered, and their two teenaged daughters nowhere to be found. Sirocco tracked the horsemen for eight days before finding the girls. He stopped just long enough to bury their battered bodies before continuing his pursuit with a renewed vengeance. The men he hunted were beyond evil. Sirocco was just making sure that they would never have the opportunity to commit such atrocities again.

* * *

HANK'S ANKLE HURT every time he stepped down, but he dare not stop. The phantom chasing them was closing in, and he knew what would happen if he were captured. He and Kendal were all that remained of their gang, and Hank was determined not to end up like the rest. His younger companion slipped suddenly, falling face-first into the steep hillside. "Get up you dumb piece of shit," Hank urged as he rushed past, "before you get roasted alive on a spit just like Charlie and Glen was!"

Kendal watched Hank streak by, his mind frozen in terror, eyes bulging. He got back up to his feet and scrambled for the top of the ridge. *Almost there,* he told himself. Just a little further and then down to the river where the current would carry him safely away, wiping out any trace of his passing. He took another step and was stung by a wasp. He slapped at it but felt something else. Confused, he plucked a slender, feathered dart from the back of his neck. *What the...?* His head started to spin as he lost his balance, collapsing to the ground in a heap. Paralyzed and helpless but fully conscious, he tried with all his might to get up, but couldn't move his muscles. Up ahead, he saw Hank stumble on, getting smaller and smaller and never looking back.

Sirocco moved purposefully up the hill, loading another dart into his blowgun. He slipped past Kendal who was already lying motionless but for the very faint rise and fall of his chest. The *curare* acted fast, he observed, always impressed with how quickly the potent muscle relaxant moved through the bloodstream, causing rapid paralysis. The toxin was a prime choice of the Peoples of the Amazonian Basin who traditionally employed it in both hunting and warfare. The primary active ingredient of curare, *tubocurarine*, was an alkaloid extracted from *Chondodendron tomentosum,* a south American vine, and several other plant species. The poison produced muscle paralysis by interfering with the transmission of nerve impulses at the receptor sites of all skeletal muscles. Muscles with many nerves were affected first. Sirocco had been cultivating the vine for many years and had always maintained a more than sufficient supply of the substance to meet his distinctive needs.

Cresting the ridge, he spotted Hank thirty yards downhill. Hoisting the seven-foot weapon to his lips, he puffed his cheeks and sent a dart flying through the air towards his target. The tiny missile arced in a perfect trajectory, dropping dead center between Hank's shoulder blades as he raced for the river. By the time he took three more steps, he was down on his knees and pitched forward face-first into the dirt.

Half an hour later, Sirocco hoisted the second man into the air where they both dangled helplessly, hogtied above stacks of dry kindling and sagebrush, naked bodies covered in strange symbols and pictographs drawn in charcoal. Sirocco had decorated his own face, arms, and chest, employing a brownish-red pigment base and highlighting certain areas with black and white stripes and dots. With bright bird feathers in his hair and a jaguar-claw necklace around his neck, he chanted in an ancient native tongue as he shuffled his feet in a slow, rhythmic dance, adding sticks to a small fire.

Leaning in close, he peered into his victims' eyes and saw the horror. He knew they could see, hear, and feel everything that was happening to them, but had no way to physically respond or resist. He worked quickly, lest their respiratory systems fail too soon. He'd learned to use just enough curare to nullify a person's ability to react, yet prolong their agony as long as humanly possible. It was an art, really, more than a science, requiring years of experience and experimentation to perfect.

"Payback time, pieces of shit," he announced, deftly removing one of Hank's testicles and stuffing it into Kendal's open mouth with the haft of his knife. He gave Hank one of Kendal's freshly severed testes in return and chuckled. Faint gurgling sounds leaked from the two drooling miscreants as the horrifying predicament overwhelmed their shattered souls.

Fondly caressing his favorite skinning knife, he suddenly traced a line around Hank's ankles with the razor sharp point and began tugging on the skin, peeling it inside out toward the knee. He knew Kendal was fully aware of Hank's agony—the terror in his eyes unmistakable. Sirocco spoke in a low methodical voice as he worked, carefully detailing each step of the excruciating process they were about to undergo. As he got busy with his blade, he recalled the desecrated bodies of the young sisters. His eyes took on a curious gleam, a faint smile appearing at the corners of his mouth. Skinning their legs to the crotch, he left the stretchy material attached and dangling. Suddenly, he spun them around to face each other, eyes bulging from their sockets as he dangled his trophies before them, slapping them with the face skins of their former comrades.

Stepping back to admire his handiwork, Sirocco lit his pipe with a stick from the fire and inhaled deeply of the rich tobacco. Slowly releasing the smoke, he casually dropped the burning twig onto the dry kindling and watched as the hungry flames spread, caught, and began climbing the hanging shreds of leg skin. The coals smoked and hissed, as melting fat dripped into the fire, and the aroma of burnt flesh filled his nostrils. As a sign that the gods had accepted his sacrifice, he felt *the anointing* rise within his chest and so lifted his mouth to the sky, piercing the air with a primal scream that echoed from the neighboring hills.

A deep sense of peace settled over him as bright orange flames caressed the blistering bellies of the condemned, and he realized that his work here was nearly complete. While still alive, he removed their faces and scalps in one piece, reflecting on the glory of his calling. It was moments like this when he felt truly inspired—God's avenging angel cleansing the world of evildoers!

* * *

HUNTER ARRIVED AT the top of the rise and paused, taking in the beauty of the panorama before him. The sun was low on the horizon, painting the cloud-flecked sky with a kaleidoscope of red, orange, and purple. As far as the eye could see, forested, snow-capped mountains spread out in every direction. On the ridge top, the cold north wind gusted, prompting him to don his sheepskin parka and mitts. Up here near the tree line it was strong and constant, stunting and deforming any vegetation unfortunate enough to take root. Entire trees, sixty to seventy feet in length, lay sprawled across the landscape, their trunks hovering a foot off the ground like lignin-shrouded supplicants begging mercy from a relentless wind god who offered them no quarter.

Dismounting in the waning light, he knelt to read the now plentiful sign. Since leaving the smoldering remains of the final two bandits a few miles back, tracking the killer had suddenly become easy. It was as if he'd decided that, with his work complete, it was no longer necessary to cover his tracks. *Or maybe,* thought Hunter, *he is fully aware of my presence and is purposefully leading me into a trap!* Either way, the entire experience was unnerving.

Hunter knew that he would eventually have to face him. What would transpire between them was anyone's guess. While not looking for a fight, he obviously couldn't allow such a dangerous person to remain in his territory with Anna, Sarah, and the baby wintering here alone. He mounted and moved down the opposite slope, loaded crossbow across his lap, roving eyes seeking a target. Rounding a small knoll in the gathering dusk, the distant fire was impossible to miss.

Half a mile away, a warmly bundled Constantine Sirocco, with ceremonial dress and paint removed, banked kin-

dling against a wide, flat boulder and piled on logs as if he were preparing a signal fire. In fact, that's exactly what he was doing. He was counting on the man who lived in this land to follow him, and he was not far behind. He, who had killed so many of his enemies, was very conscientious and would return to finish his task. Luring the woodsman in, by leaving intriguing clues, was really quite simple.

Sirocco admired the man's remarkable tracking skills: very few were able to follow the little he left behind. His own oneness with the wilderness was in his blood, inherited from his mother's people of the Amazon Basin. He was curious how Hunter had acquired his.

* * *

A QUARTER MILE out, Hunter hobbled his horse and moved closer to survey the camp. The fire was obviously a beacon, not typical of a man wishing to avoid detection. He was intentionally disclosing his position to the world, and Hunter was troubled by it, knowing something of the talents and nature of the man. He weighed his options. He could always move in close and take him with his crossbow from the shadows, but that was not his way.

The stranger had done him no harm. In fact, he'd saved him the trouble of finishing off the remaining bandits. As to the unorthodox executions, they were obviously revenge killings, mixed with elements of witchcraft or voodoo, but, as weird as that seemed, it didn't necessarily prove that the man was mad—definitely different, but not necessarily certifiable. Besides, as gruesome as their deaths had been, Hunter was sure that the bandits simply got what they had coming—*Karma.*

With the cold September sky awash with stars and a bright moon rising over the eastern peaks, Hunter decided to wait for daylight to make his next move and resigned himself to a fireless camp. Sheltering his horse in a protected wash, he picketed her where she could nibble sedges along a tiny creek as she pleased. Climbing up to a bowl-like depression near the top of the ridge, he wrapped himself in warm sheepskins, wedged his body into a shallow rock crevice out of the wind, and waited for the dawn.

* * *

HUNTER AWOKE IN the cold, damp mist of first light, immediately sensing a foreign presence. His hand moved to his knife as he scanned the rocks and scrub surrounding his camp. The unmistakable odor of tobacco smoke lingered in the air as he rolled out of the crevice and hugged a nearby boulder. Spotting something curious lying near his pack, he reached for the small woven-reed basket placed there sometime during the night. Inside, he found a scrap of deerskin pinned together with a three-inch, feather-backed dart. Careful not to touch the tip, he withdrew and examined it. The tiny missile, designed for use in a blowgun, was expertly crafted. Opening the hide wrapper, he smiled, relaxing at the discovery of a handful of dark brown coffee beans along with a fat wad of dried tobacco in a little pouch.

Breaking camp, he discovered what he already intuitively knew: the killer had gone, his campsite was empty; yet no tracks led from the place. Within a circle of stones, ashes were warm to the touch, but there was nothing beyond that to prove that anyone had been here. It was as if he'd simply vanished into thin air.

Riding back to the canyon to round up the horses, Hunter pondered the improbable events of the last few days, reminded of how mysterious and unpredictable the world-at-large could be. Much that occurred was unexplained. Ever since the End War, there was no such thing as *normal.* He could expect the unexpected at any time and place and remained constantly on his guard.

Later that evening, when he arrived home on the big black stallion, leading a string of eleven horses, his guests were overjoyed to discover their mounts safely among them. How they ended up in the possession of the bandits was yet another mystery, but it was wonderful to have them back again. Only the absence of Rocky, their trail-steady mule, dampened Elise's spirits. She had raised the loyal animal from a foal, and his strong, even-tempered presence would sorely be missed.

* * *

THE FOLLOWING DAY at the corral, Hunter and Elise picked out suitable stock for their passage to Colorado. With the harsh winter looming, they selected six for the journey: four of Elise's favorites to switch out as mounts and a strong pair of Hunter's mustangs as pack animals to carry their gear. The rest were released into the wild with the large black stallion to lead them; they quickly galloped off, hooves thundering out their pleasure, manes and tails tossing in the wind.

Those left behind whinnied and darted around the corral with ears erect and longing eyes yearning to join the others.

Elise watched them go with mixed emotions. Come morning, she and Hunter would leave the safety and familiarity of these mountains and set out for New Eden, some three hundred-odd miles to the south. She was still a bit apprehensive about leaving her family here alone, but could already see some improvement in Sarah's condition. With proper rest and Anna's help with Jamie, she would likely be back to her old self in a few week's time.

"Sarah and Jamie will be fine, Elise," Anna asserted in her most self-assured voice. "We have everything we need here and next spring you can send someone back for us. You must travel light to get back home as quickly as possible." Elise had always admired her younger sister's courage and positive attitude and gave her a warm hug, promising to return for them as soon as the passes were open.

While Hunter packed and prepared for their departure, the family spent their final evening together seated before the cozy fire, wrapped in furs, with little Jamie dozing contentedly nearby. As the dancing flames licked the seasoned oak, they laughed and cried, sharing their hopes, fears, and memories of a good life well-lived in the magic that was once New Eden.

* * *

Dawn of the forty-fifth day of the siege broke slowly. The smell of burnt wood and gunpowder drifted up the hill to New Eden's southern guard tower where Robert Planchet, his injured left arm in a sling, swept the ghostly vale below with glasses. A heavy fog had rolled in during the night, blanketing the ground in a thick, eerie haze. "What do you make of it, Spencer?"

"I'm not sure, Robert," Spencer Wells, the slender, deliberate Commander of the Night Guard answered in his measured cadence, "they just broke off the attack and vanished about an hour ago." Robert stood on the recessed roof looking out over the thick stone wall towards the far hillside. Through the fog, he could just discern moving silhouettes against the dim orange glow of distant bonfires, as night watchmen were relieved by the day guard. A thin band of rose broadened on the eastern horizon as the sun made a timid appearance over the mist-shrouded land. Wrapped in a thick bearskin parka, the youngest Planchet son resisted the creeping chill sinking down into his bones. His breath was expelled in great clouds of vapor that momentarily wrapped around his thinly bearded face, before being briskly whisked away and scattered by the wind. Winter was coming early. He could smell it on the squall blowing down from the Arctic Circle, bringing with it the promise of snow and sub-zero temperatures.

"We were lucky last night." Spencer continued his report. He spoke as a man of duty, not allowing emotion to pervade his voice. "Zero fatalities, two minor burns, and one shrapnel wound to the leg."

"Livestock?" Robert inquired, almost casually, both men knowing that, if the herds and flocks continued to dwindle, the community would be hard pressed to feed itself through the long winter ahead.

"Three ewes and their lambs taken during the fire and commotion at the cattle barn." They were interrupted by rapid footsteps pounding the flagstone floor. "Robert, Spencer, come quickly!" It was Donnie Curry, the blacksmith's son. "They're tunneling under the wall!"

CHAPTER EIGHT

THE RIDE SOUTH

JUST PAST NOON two weeks out, Hunter sat comfortably astride a fine chestnut mare atop a small rise, studying the surrounding terrain with field glasses. Elise was dismounted beside him, making minor adjustments to her saddlebags and re-tightening her cinch, while their string of pack animals and spare mounts grazed nearby on the sparse, dry grass peppering the rolling hills.

Hunter carefully swept the skyline, scouting the most efficient route across country, mindful of their exposure since leaving his valley. From time-to-time he consulted a well-worn topographic map, referred to his compass, and jotted down notes in a small journal. They were moving steadily southeast, shadowing old roadbeds and keeping the Wind River Range on their left. At South Pass, they struck due east, keeping to the broken waves of foothills along the east rim of the Great Divide Basin stretching from the southern tip of the Wind River Range in Wyoming to the northern Sierra Madre just north of the Colorado border.

This was a wide open country of muted browns and reds, shallow river valleys with patches of bare cottonwoods and willows strung out along streams and creek beds, and low rounded hills speckled with cone-filled pines and junipers. To the west, colossal rock towers and mighty buttes jutted defiantly from the ground—massive stone monuments stubbornly resisting the inevitable ravages of erosion with surrendered slabs of jumbled stone piled unceremoniously at their feet.

The late September sky was blue and cloudless with temperatures in the low fifties and a steady breeze from the north. Checking their back trail, Hunter pocketed his map and looked around for Elise who was back attending the pack animals. He watched quietly as the confident young woman hugged and patted the horses, scratching behind their ears, as one would a dog, and speaking softly to them as she checked over the rigging on their loads.

From the outset, she'd naturally assumed responsibility for the care and well-being of their four-legged companions and, from the beginning, it was obvious to Hunter that Elise was fearless around horses, even when they acted badly. She had the steady hand and confidence with them that came from growing up in the saddle on her father's spread.

By the time she could walk, she'd learned to ride a horse and, over the years, absorbed everything she could about the care and training of this remarkable species—first domesticated by nomadic tribes from the Steppes of the Ukraine around 4,000 BC. Working with the large herd at New Eden, she'd developed a deeply intuitive understanding of these big, gregarious mammals. She even applied the principles of herbal medicine to them. "And why not?" she'd retort with furrowed brow when teased about it by siblings or friends, "horses are people too!"

They had taken an immediate liking to her as well, permitting Elise to readily control and manage them. Hunter admired her competence and was surprised to be growing fond of her companionship. He watched her cajoling the animals and smiled. *Not that her garments would help her win a beauty contest*, he thought wryly.

She was comfortably dressed in wool and sheepskin from head to toe. With most of her clothing destroyed in the prairie fire, she wore a baggy, shortened pair of Hunter's fleece-lined sheepskin pants and one of his heavy woolen sweaters. Around the campfire in the evenings, she crafted a snug sheepskin hat and mitts, a tall pair of fleece-lined moccasins, and a hip-length coat, all from pelts Hunter brought along for just such a purpose.

Finishing her equipment check, she turned back toward her horse and noticed Hunter watching her. She immediately felt herself introvert. Avoiding his gaze, she strode back to her five-year-old horse with the long, crooked blaze on its forehead, aptly named "Lightning." Climbing gingerly onto the young mare's back, she waited out the awkward silence, relieved to be slightly behind and to the left of Hunter's horse and out of the man's direct line of sight.

Though outwardly composed, she was vexed by her reaction. Even as a young girl, she knew that being strong and self-confident, both emotionally and physically, was vital to her survival and so had fashioned her persona as a fortress of self-restraint. Consequently, she failed to understand her discomfort when she noticed Hunter watching her. In those awkward moments, she felt somehow exposed, as if she'd inadvertently let down her guard, and there was no telling what part of her secret self she may have revealed to his scrutiny. After a few moments, the self-consciousness passed, and she became poised and relaxed once more.

Seated comfortably in her native-style saddle, she watched her rugged, silent companion gather in the long, braided lariat attached to the lead pack horse, tighten it around his saddle horn in a quick-release, and start off down the hill toward the valley. He was a good-looking man, she guessed mid- to late-thirties, well-proportioned and strong as steel. She'd watched him move a downed tree out of their path and was impressed by his obvious physical strength.

His jaw was strong with a faint, jagged scar across his chin, but his mouth was kind and filled with good teeth. Piercing gray eyes, like those of a bird of prey, missed nothing. His light-brown, long hair was thick and wavy and worn variously in one or two braids, or back in a ponytail and tied every six inches or so with leather laces. A few day's growth of beard framed his pleasant face.

One day, she inadvertently came up on him as he was getting dressed. He stood with his back to her in leggings and moccasins, unaware of her presence, pulling on his softly-tanned shirt. Her eyes swept his muscle-ripped body, and she couldn't help but notice several scars across his shoulder blades and what appeared to be two old bullet wounds down low on one side.

Before she could stop, she caught herself wondering what it would be like to be held by a man like that. She recalled how his muscular legs and lower body pinned her to the ground as she tried to stab him with her dagger. Just then, Hunter turned around and she blushed and hurried away.

This morning she knew better than to start asking questions about what direction they would take, or anything else for that matter. He didn't say much during the day and especially wasn't into small talk. She knew that he would eventually tell her what the plan was, or he wouldn't, but it didn't matter either way. She was familiar with his silence by now and found it somehow comforting not to have to communicate using words.

Traveling with Hunter was instructive. While the man might be verbally silent, he was by no means dormant. His mind and senses were intently focused on the surrounding environment as its perceptions constantly filtered into his lively consciousness. Hunter really *saw and experienced* the world around him, not as a spectator or a tourist sees, but as one who fully lives in and occupies a place.

He was intimately familiar with every aspect of this land: its history, geography and geology. He could identify the flora and fauna by both Latin and common names. He could explain how each species interacted with the others and knew what to expect from every element in the universe around him. He could predict the weather and tell you the size and gender of deer that passed by this creek last night at approximately what time. Elise instinctively trusted him and noted how unusual that was for her.

Following Hunter and the horses down into the golden, grassy valley, she again pondered the fate of her family and friends at New Eden with growing concern. Each step of their journey south brought her closer to home and to what she might discover upon her return. Not knowing was most maddening, and Elise fought constantly to direct her thoughts and remain positive. Not far beneath the surface, the gnawing mystery of William's disappearance simmered, along with a growing awareness that her safe, ordered world may very likely never again be the same.

* * *

IN A HIGH, secluded valley sheltered by a thick ring of conifers, thirty-one-year-old William Planchet sat on a makeshift bench on the front porch of a rough-hewn, single-story log cabin. He leaned forward, gently loosening the rawhide straps securing a carved hickory brace to his tender right leg.

Somehow he had endured four grueling months immobilized in a body cast, recovering from a near-fatal gunshot wound that fractured his right femur in two places and came within half-an-inch of severing his femoral artery. Left for dead, weak from blood loss, and with a vicious infection setting in, he was brought here by unknown persons who expertly set his badly broken leg, cleansed and dressed his wounds, and stitched his torn muscles and tissues back together.

During the weeks immediately following the ambush, he slipped in and out of consciousness, hovering on death's doorstep, and could later recall almost nothing of what happened during that time. In order to save his life, his mysterious caregivers were forced to restrain the powerful man, using traction to set the bone, while keeping him sedated with potent medicine made from the roots and bark of wild herbs and trees. Weeks of constant attention and treatments using poultices and specially prepared teas healed the tissue damage from the .44 rifle slug enough to allow a full leg and hip body cast to be applied to their slowly mending patient.

During the ensuing weeks, the compound fracture fused nicely and the unbearable clay and mud cast was finally removed. William was relieved to be exercising the healing appendage at last and sensed his muscle strength slowly returning with each passing day.

He appraised the jagged, six-inch scar located on the outside of his right thigh, halfway between his knee and hip and gently rubbed the slightly itching tissue with dry, calloused hands. The visible end-result of the wound and the treatment applied to repair it actually wasn't *too* repulsive, he reflected, considering the hundreds of stitches it had taken to sew up the torn thigh muscle and surrounding damaged tissue! There was an obvious bullet entry wound dimple on the outside of his right thigh, and he'd lost a chunk of muscle and flesh in its immediate vicinity, but, with time and exercise, he should regain full use of the limb.

From a nearby pine, a raven's raucous cry shattered the tranquility of the late autumn afternoon, calling out a warning to a golden eagle twice his size passing uncomfortably close to the bird's favorite perch. Glancing up, William observed the soaring raptor pass overhead, framed against the canopy of dark storm clouds and sensed the coming winter in the air. He scanned the clearing, finding nothing amiss.

Out of unconscious habit, he noted his weapon leaning against the cabin wall: a weathered, fifty caliber *Hawken,* primed and loaded. The long-barreled, black-powder rifle was a classic example of old-fashioned American ingenuity at its best. For the past one-hundred-and-sixty-plus-years, the muzzleloader had served the Planchet family well, handed down from father-to-son, generation-to-generation. Though quite old by firearms standards, the weapon was clean, well-oiled, and in excellent working order despite its constant use throughout the decades. How it wound up here with him was another baffling mystery.

Reaching for his crutches, he winced as he stood and steadied himself, testing the fit of the brace and distributing his weight between the carved wooden supports and his one good leg. Pleased with the results, he crossed the porch to the steps and began a slow descent at a slightly awkward angle. Without warning, he lurched forward, as the tip of one crutch caught in a wide crack, nearly spilling him headlong onto the gravel footpath. Catching himself in the nick of time, he twirled about, bashing his bad leg into the solid wooden post of the handrail.

"Damn this thing!" he cursed, gritting his teeth as a wave of pain and nausea swept through him. He lowered himself down, sitting on the second-to-the-bottom step and with both hands, carefully repositioned his throbbing leg. The calmness on his chiseled face belied the fact that inside he was seething; only his dark brooding eyes revealed the true depth of William's frustration.

From early childhood, Adam Planchet's firstborn son led an extremely active life, to the point of being typified by family and friends as one who physically *attacked* each new day and situation with unfettered zeal. For a man so well connected to, and defined by, his own physicality, the past few months were a hellish nightmare. Sidelined by the severity of his injuries, he was forced to remain here, recuperating on his back, while the people he loved and cared about most faced perilous times on their own, far beyond the influence of his help and support.

He unconsciously reached for the comfort of the medicine bag he'd worn around his neck since he was a boy. The beaded leather pouch held the few sacred, spiritually significant objects he'd collected during his lifetime, but he remembered *again* that it, too, was gone, lost along with everything else he owned, except for his rifle, shot, and powder horn, which were brought here by whomever was helping him. *There can be nothing worse than being stuck in this limbo*, he lamented, cursing his luck and reliving the dark events that brought him to this place.

Trouble with the neighboring community of New Hope had simmered all spring, and an all out war threatened to erupt at any time. With instructions from his father, he rode forth from New Eden with five of his most trusted friends, all seasoned men in their early-thirties, raised together and close-knit as any family. Their urgent quest: locate a man named Macintosh, a former comrade-in-arms of his father, living alone up at the northern end of Wyoming's Wind River Range, west of the Continental Divide.

The trip out should have taken no more than six weeks. Heading north into Wyoming, west of the Sierra Madre, they skirted the Great Divide Basin along the east rim, and drove west over the famous South Pass. Hugging the western base of the Wind, they made excellent time until one warm, sunny morning, three weeks out, when they were ambushed as they prepared to break camp on the banks of a fast-flowing river.

William was standing in the current up to his knees dressed only in leggings, splashing water on his face and upper body, when they were set upon by a dozen or more well-armed and determined marauders. Pinned down in the open on the stoney bank, his men fought back courageously, but it was no use; they were outnumbered more than two-to-one, and the bandits held the high ground.

William raced to his horse, which was saddled and ready to go, but they shot her down as he reached her side. With bullets ricocheting all around him and no time to retrieve boots or other gear, he reached for his bag of shot and powder horn, and slipped his rifle from its scabbard. Sprinting out into the neck-deep river, he made for the far side, holding his gun and ammo above his head while the current pulled him rapidly downstream. Reaching the far bank, he looked back to witness two of his closest friends shot from their saddles. Raising the loaded rifle to his eye, he sighted in on one of the attackers but, before he could squeeze off a round, something slammed heavily into him, knocking his legs out from under him.

Across the river, a sharpshooter had kept pace with William as he reached the far side. Waiting until he scrambled up the bank and stood still to take aim, the marksman squeezed off a deadly round from his .44 Winchester. The report of the shot echoed across the water, and William felt his femur snap as the large caliber bullet slammed into his right thigh. The force of the impact spun him around, causing the rifle to fly out of his hands as he fell, and he slid down the slippery bank into the rushing current below. Fighting to keep his head above water, he reached a series of small falls and disappeared around a bend.

The shooter observed the limp body through his riflescope as the current pulled it down over the falls. The last thing William remembered was dragging himself onto a pebble-strewn sandbar miles downstream before waking up in traction in the cabin, tended by mysterious helpers who somehow managed to remain maddeningly anonymous.

Seated on the porch, he eased his tender leg and only then noticed the snow. Lifting his face, large, white flakes landed lightly, melting as they touched. He frowned again, not wanting to consider the prospect of being snowbound here for the winter. He was determined to get back to New Eden. He started to stand, but froze, as, out under the trees, a stick snapped loudly in the snow-muffled air. Instinctively reaching for his gun, William scanned the tree line in the direction of the sound and waited.

CHAPTER NINE

CONNECTING THE DOTS

THE FIRST WEEK of October passed and, by anyone's standards, Hunter and Elise were making good time, traversing half the distance to New Eden in just twenty-one days. From Hunter's valley, fair weather held with clear, sunny days turning sharply colder at night, when the mercury dipped below freezing and heavy frost dusted the hardened earth.

Each evening at dusk, when the sun slipped below the western horizon, brisk Canadian winds, foretelling of the coming winter, swept through the valleys, chilling the air and causing great clouds of steam to billow from the mouths and nostrils of humans and horses alike.

Their four-legged companions were holding up well under the rolling terrain of the Southwestern Wyoming foothills. Their coats were thick and muscles strong with constant use. As the days passed, they seemed to be enjoying the cooler temperatures and accompanying lack of insects that all were forced to endure during the hot summer months. In the surrounding hills, the vivid colors of autumn peaked and slowly faded as oaks, poplars, and quaking aspens surrendered their leaves, and the short grasses went to seed, turning brittle to the touch.

Life for the humans had fallen into a comfortable pattern as well. Up at sunrise to eat and break camp, then moving steadily southward along crystal streams through game-filled river valleys, always keeping the tall snow-capped mountains on their left, drawing ever closer to the Colorado border.

Midday break was a brief but essential respite for both horses and humans alike to relax, take nourishment, and re-hydrate before continuing south. An hour before sunset, Hunter would lead them up into the hills to a defensible cave or a level shoulder of land, where air temperatures averaged ten degrees warmer, to set up sleeping camp amidst a thick stand of conifers ringed by large boulders, or with a steep hill at their backs, for defense.

By now, the man and woman had developed a largely unspoken system of communication based on body language and increased sensory perception born of the solitude of their surroundings and being together twenty-four hours a day. Elise found herself feeling more at ease in Hunter's presence, though he was unlike any man she'd ever known. She found him physically capable of meeting whatever challenge might arise, but, unlike so many others, was not overly conscious of his abilities.

His strength was understated and he applied only the exact amount of effort or force needed, based on the situation and its requirements, never to flaunt his ability or invite admiration. His demeanor was one of composed intensity, of action born of necessity, with no movement or word unnecessarily wasted. She likened his acute awareness of his environment to a complete immersion in which Hunter's perceptions of his constantly changing surroundings acted almost as a second skin. He was intuitively sensitive to the elements, the sky and the weather, to topography, geology and geography. Animals, plants, and minerals all spoke volumes to him about the presence of danger, game, water, or shelter.

Halfway through midday break, with a bright sun suspended in the blue expanse, Elise sat cross-legged on a lichen-pocked boulder atop a grassy hillock, looking out across the widening valley towards a distant line of rolling hills. She watched a vast herd of pronghorn antelope moving through the valley a half-mile away. Thousands of the graceful North American natives trotted and bounded past in a fawn and white speckled sea of movement, raising clouds of fine, white dust. Looking past them through a well-worn pair of compact field glasses (a gift from Father for her thirteenth birthday), she peered off into the distance beyond the farthest hills, as if, by so doing, she could somehow span the remaining miles to her home. Her thoughts were drawn again to New Eden, and, despite every attempt to control them, of what she might find there upon her return. She imagined she could hear Father's last words as if he were standing here before her.

"Find him, Elise, and he will set things straight. Now Godspeed and watch over the others. And do not worry so, you will do fine! I know you have doubts, but I have never doubted you, and I know that you will find a way." She closed her eyes and willed her thoughts to him. *I am coming back to you, Father. I have found The One who will make things right.*

Just then, a noisy flock of Canada geese brought her back to the present, and she glanced up, shielding her eyes against the sun's glare to admire their effort. Long lines of the migrating waterfowl passed over almost constantly now, making for the warm marshes of the temperate Gulf region a thousand miles south. *They will be over New Eden sometime late tomorrow,* she calculated.

With the air temperature rising into the high forties, Elise basked in the relative warmth of the noonday sun. She turned halfway around to check on the horses as they foraged for dry brush and grasses among the nearby rocks and stunted junipers. Some years ago, a mighty ice storm must have moved malevolently through this place, breaking off the tops of the trees, and now each survivor sported two or three replacement crowns in its stead. Except for her contentedly grazing companions, she was alone.

Following his usual daily pattern, Hunter slipped off the moment they halted and had not yet returned, although she was not troubled by his absence. Elise had grown accustomed to his unannounced comings and goings and had comfortably adapted to his near total silence. Living in such close proximity these past weeks provided surprising insight into the person Hunter had become during his years of solitude in the wilds. The more time spent with him, the more she recognized how truly amazing and completely a part of the wilderness he was. His mannerisms and routine were predictable and even comforting. More than likely, he was scouting out the territory ahead or checking their back trail and would probably return with something for supper, as was his habit. She'd learned a great deal by simply observing him and noting his choices and decisions for each new situation and circumstance along the way.

His apparent anti-social behavior did not confuse her. After all, from what she could gather, he had survived in this wilderness without human contact for better than seven years and was essentially alone many years before that. Thus, she was caught off guard one recent evening when Hunter unexpectedly opened up and offered her a rare glimpse into the private person beyond his usually impenetrable facade.

They sat in their customary places across from each other at the evening fire, wrapped in heavy sheepskins to fend off the biting wind pouring down out of the Canadian Rockies. The air temperature crept below the freezing mark, but the wind chill, driven by thirty mile-per-hour gusts, made it seem much colder. High above their modest encampment, countless brilliant stars and planets stretched across the clear night sky in an innumerable parade of multi-colored lights.

To the east, a full moon crouched playfully behind the snow covered peaks, as if threatening to rise up and bathe the Great Basin with light in mock challenge to a sleeping sun who would someday, in some uncounted future moment, extinguish her reflected glory, plunging the solar system and all life in it into instant cryogenic suspension. From a nearby wolves' lair, an alpha female raised her sensitive voice to the sky, offering a beautiful lamenting *solo* that reached out across the windswept valley, conjuring a far-off reply from her hunting mate. Soon others joined these two up and down the valley in a dissonant chorus that touched a nerve deep in the human psyche, evoking primal emotions drawn from a much earlier period in Mankind's fragile history.

"I remember dreaming of flying as a child." Hunter uncharacteristically broke the silence, speaking in a gentle, melodic tone. His words were cloaked in a wistfulness that Elise hadn't previously recognized, lending a far-off, elsewhere quality to his voice.

He placed another seasoned juniper log from a downed snag onto the well-stacked fire and watched as dancing orange flames hungrily licked the smooth, gray bark. Intense heat from the deep bed of glowing embers beneath quickly caught the added fuel, and tiny fragments of red glowing material swirled up in a super-heated column, cascading high into the night sky. The fire crackled and popped, adding rhythm to the steady swoosh of the wind blowing through the pines and dry sagebrush of the surrounding valley. Elise sat stone-like in her usual lotus position, quietly waiting for him to continue, momentarily unbalanced by his unexpected utterance.

"I don't mean flying like in a plane or using some man-made contraption—I really wanted to fly—like a bird." His angular face with strong jaw line and high cheek bones inherited from his mother's Cherokee lineage was half turned away, and the orange glow from the fire washed over his handsome features in rivulets of wavy, amber light. Hunter stood and began stoking the fire with an oak staff he'd picked up some days before. Its weight and balance were pleasing to the touch and he'd spent several evenings around the fire casually carving the thick topknot into the shape of a howling wolf.

"I don't know why, but in my waking life I could never get close to matching the intoxicating sense of freedom experienced in those fleeting, heady dreams. It was as if I was given a taste or vision of what our feathered brethren must experience as they lift off and soar high above the land, moving horizontally through the air and across the rushing landscape below. I've often wondered, to what end should I be given such vision?"

He paused and sat down, gathering the thick sheepskin robe about his broad shoulders and gazed deep into the dancing flames. Across the fire, Elise was held in suspense. She pondered her normally silent companion's unusual openness and waited.

Suddenly Hunter looked up and straight into her eyes, and she felt as if he were gazing directly into her most secret heart of hearts. He calmly measured her, recognizing her stillness and sensing her curiosity. She felt somehow exposed, like an intruder caught peering through a private window that had unexpectedly opened to reveal Hunter's essence.

"I knew that I could never truly know that joy, that exhilarating freedom as long as I remained earthbound, and upon waking, found myself hoping that perhaps in another life I would be reborn as a bird of prey or maybe a large heron or crane." He smiled. Their eyes met, and his happiness warmed her. She felt a glow deep within and did her best to rebuff the emergent fondness budding in her heart despite her earnest efforts to reject it.

Shrouded again in his usual silence, Hunter recognized that he had clearly crossed over into dangerous territory with Elise. From the very beginning, his attraction to her had increased, from the moment he heard the unflinching confidence in her voice and witnessed her unwavering courage when outnumbered by the depraved band of outlaws on that momentous morning only a few weeks earlier. Ironically, her attempt to run him through with her dagger had further endeared her to him, that being the first time any woman had intentionally tried to kill him that he knew of. And though he hated to admit it, the very act of pinning her body beneath his own sparked a smoldering desire to lie with her again, though, this time, it was an entirely different type of wrestling that he had in mind. Even her bite somehow aroused him; her warm, wet mouth feeding on his muscled hand stirred something dark within him, and he subdued such thoughts and emotions with great effort.

The wind picked up a notch, and the temperature dropped another couple of degrees. His thoughts went to the comfort of the horses, and he silently excused himself from the warmth of the fire to check on them. With his back to the flames, he took a few moments for his eyes to adjust before making his way through the darkness toward the animals. He found them standing huddled in a contented group, tails to the wind, dozing beneath a jet-black sky pin-pricked with stars. As he approached his favorite mount, she nickered a friendly greeting, and Hunter pulled a warm hand from his glove to gently rub the affectionate mare's nose. Great clouds of steam billowed from her nostrils and clung to the wiry hairs protruding from her chin. Moving noiselessly from horse to horse, Hunter checked their pickets and hobbles to ensure that all was well before making his way back to the comfort of the fire.

Pausing just outside the throw of light, he cast his gaze across the flames to where Elise was already fast asleep, a thick elk robe tucked snuggly under her chin. He looked upon her flushed face washed in the glow of the fire and deliberately turned away. Living in such close proximity required that one consciously grant his companions personal space, and Hunter remained ever aware of Elise's need for privacy, especially as she was a woman. However, as far as gender was concerned, he found her to be a cut above all others that he'd known. With Elise there was never a complaint or unpleasant remark, and she could be counted on to always do whatever was required of her without ever having to be asked or told.

She was certainly not a burden in any sense, beyond being an additional person to be concerned for. Having lived alone for so many years, Hunter wasn't accustomed to such additional responsibility, though, in this case, he really didn't mind. In fact, he found that he rather enjoyed her company. Simply knowing that there was someone waiting back at camp gave him an unusual sense of belonging that he hadn't thought much about during his self-imposed exile. It was, no doubt, rooted genetically or psychologically in something deeply primordial, a sense of tribe developed by his human ancestors over some 200,000 years. Intellectually, he rejected the implications of needing someone to be complete. Emotionally, he was enjoying the time and space they shared.

He quietly added a couple of slow-burning oak logs and banked up the coals with his staff, preparing the fire to provide adequate heat until a dawn still some hours off. Turning around, he knelt and manually checked the ground for sharp sticks or stones before spreading out his thick bedroll and crawling beneath the furs. Slipping out of his warm sheepskin clothing, Hunter stretched out on his back with hands cradling his head and gazed up at the wonder of the Milky Way. He exhaled deeply and pondered his earthly existence.

They were passing through a rich and varied land with plenty of fresh water from rivers and springs. Caves and rock outcroppings provided shelter, while downed hardwoods supplied fuel for fires. Abundant upland game, including deer and elk, thrived here, and, in the rolling grasslands, vast herds of antelope and bison were commonly encountered. Moose foraged among marshes and along the shores of ponds and lakes, and, throughout the grasslands, herds of wild pigs roamed the hillsides and valleys. Plentiful pheasant and turkey populations provided a reprieve from heavier fare, and countless flocks of migrating ducks and geese passed constantly overhead. Just today, Elise had taken a trio of plump sage grouse with her bolo that roasted up quite nicely over the evening fire.

The horses also fared well, grazing contentedly on sedges, dried wheatgrass, and wild grains, while drinking from pure running springs or snow-fed streams. The miles slipped past them almost unnoticed, and, by Hunter's calculations, they should be crossing over into northwestern Colorado within four or five more days.

But as pleasant as their journey had been so far, Hunter knew not to let down his guard. At any given moment, this wild country could offer up a life-threatening challenge. He and Elise were constantly coming across predator sign, and nearly every day, a large wary bear or two were seen out on the fringe, keeping their distance. Fierce mountain lions prowled the hills and valleys mostly at night, and were not easily spotted, though he'd caught a glimpse of a large cat at dusk three times since leaving his valley, and, the following morning, he discovered panther tracks circling their sleeping camp just beyond the boundary of the campfire's throw of light.

More often than not, the silent wilderness nights were punctuated by packs of wolves, or their smaller coyote cousins, howling out their melancholy chorus, speaking to each other across vast, unbroken distances in a language evoking fear in the hearts of the uninitiated, yet somehow comforting to those who knew them and were familiar with their ways.

While not strictly classified as predators, wild pigs were of particular concern as adult boars could stand three feet at the shoulder and weigh over five hundred pounds. Armed with razor-sharp tusks, they had been known to disembowel a horse or man with one vicious slice. As potentially dangerous as these animals were, however, it was the two-legged beasts that concerned Hunter most, especially since they were now passing through completely unfamiliar territory. Thankfully, they'd seen no evidence of a human presence yet, though they were constantly on guard, scanning their surroundings for any such sign.

Focused on the immediate moment, he preferred not to speculate about what they might find upon their arrival at Elise's New Eden, though his gut told him that all was not well. The Colonel Planchet he knew would never send precious family into the wilds, away from the protection of his fortified compound, without good reason. He must have felt an extreme urgency to risk so much to summon his help. From what Elise conveyed, the settlement was strategically designed to deny outsiders access unless specific permission from within was granted. Given a reasonable plan in place, and the number of settlers there seemed more than adequate to provide such, New Eden should be able to withstand a vigorous siege for many months by a much larger force without being compromised.

In spite of all that, something still bothered him that he couldn't quite put his finger on. Shrugging off his sense of foreboding, Hunter would deal with the New Eden situation in its own time, but, for now, his body needed rest. With one hand on the loaded crossbow at his side and the other lightly grasping the haft of his knife, he closed his eyes and slept.

* * *

AN HOUR BEFORE the dawn, a lumbering shape emerged from the shadows, growing larger, eyes blazing in the dim firelight, hackles on the hump below his neck bristling, lips pulled back in a frightful grimace. The mature grizzly had identified the scent of horses from a mile off and was closing in for a meal. Awakened by the agitated animals, Hunter slipped silently from his bedroll and pulled on leggings and moccasins. Crossbow in hand, his senses strained, he squinted into the blackness beyond the fire's light.

The horses smelled the bear long before they heard him, snorting and nervously stamping their hobbled feet as he drew near. As Hunter circled around toward the animals he spotted the bear and stopped, shocked by the size of it! He was big, one of the largest Hunter had ever seen! Must be close to twelve hundred pounds and over nine feet tall! It was unusual for bears to hunt at night, but he probably couldn't pass up the opportunity for a tasty horseflesh meal. Grizzlies were known to prey upon the wild horse bands, culling the old and weak when the opportunity arose but especially savoring the tender flavor of helpless newborn foals.

Dropping behind a boulder, Hunter got closer but then lost him in the shadows, unable to spot him outside the firelight. The moon had already set, leaving scant light from the twinkling stars in the partially overcast sky. He tested the wind and searched the eastern horizon, noting a hint of rain on the light breeze with still an hour to go before dawn.

Elise suddenly awoke, instantly knowing that danger was near. She saw Hunter's empty bedroll and unsheathed her dagger, listening to the fear of the horses. Slipping out of her bedding, she felt for her spear in the dim light of the fire's glowing embers. Scanning the surrounding rocks and bush, she sensed that Hunter was out there somewhere close by and something else—bear, cat, or canine—something big, prowling about, closing in on its prey. She stabbed the ends of several long sticks into the coals and climbed atop a boulder, readying her spear.

With a terrifying growl, the huge bear suddenly charged out of the blackness, scattering the horses in every direction. Hunter waited for a clear shot, but the bear was in the midst of the panicked animals in an instant. He ran forward into the fracas, yelling to draw the beast's attention and it spun towards him, swiping with its massive claws. Out of the shadows, Elise jumped down from her rock with several blazing brands in her hand, lunging at the giant with her spear. Startled by the flames, he turned away from Hunter, spinning around towards the torchbearer and stood up. Hunter called out and Elise tossed him a torch, which he caught and immediately hurled directly into the bear's huge face. Just as suddenly as it had appeared, the great beast was gone, driven off by the fire, retreating back into the safety of the darkness and the night was once again quiet.

Elise moved to the horses to soothe and calm them. Incredibly, none were injured though all were trembling from adrenaline and the proximity of the near tragedy. Hunter stoked the fire into a roaring inferno and with backs against stone, the wide-awake pair quietly welcomed the dawn.

CHAPTER TEN

INVISIBLE BENEFACTORS

AN HOUR BEFORE noon Hunter quietly signaled a halt, slipping from his saddle and pulling the crossbow from his shoulder in one fluid motion. Poised beside a fallen tree, he focused his energies and inhaled slowly through his nostrils, seeking clues on the wind. Cocking his head to one side, he listened for anything out of the ordinary. Slowly shifting his weight to his back foot, he suddenly pivoted, sweeping the surrounding forest for a sign. Nothing… but something—human or otherwise—was definitely out there watching. He could feel its presence, and Elise had noticed it as well. Judging from the skittishness of the horses, they too sensed something unusual making them nervous and sketchy. Exactly who or what it was, Hunter could not say.

Standing quietly between their mounts, Elise drew them close, gently stroking their thick winter coats and whispering soft encouragement. Her soothing voice and gentle manner settled them down, calming their wide-eyed stares and flaring nostrils. She turned to look at Hunter who remained silent and motionless as stone. Like him, she was aware of the unmistakable presence of someone or something watching and following them, and was as perplexed by the coinciding lack of sign as he. The laws of nature argued that, if some creature or being was out there, it should leave behind some physical evidence of its passing: marks or tracks—or *something.* If close by, it should be able to be seen or heard. Anything else simply didn't make sense, unless this something was *supernatural* and beyond her ability to physically perceive.

Of course, she'd heard the rumors since childhood about strange creatures living in the wilds, sometimes referred to as Bigfoot or Sasquatch, non-human hominids roaming the hidden places of the Earth, but there was never any solid scientific evidence to prove or disprove their existence. After the End War, travelers passing through New Eden sometimes spoke in hushed tones around evening fires of hideous mutants somehow surviving in the burned-out cities, disfigured by radiation and bizarre diseases that had altered their DNA. They claimed that the progeny of these war victims were a sort of soulless, half-human creature, genetically flawed and doomed to a miserable sub-human existence among their own unnatural kind, cut off from, and hated by, the survivors of the human race. Father had always rejected these stories as fiction: creepy tales made up to scare the wits out of little kids, but as a child, Elise shuddered at the possibility of such a horrifying reality and tried not to think about it.

Now she wasn't so sure. Here in this dark forest, hemmed in by the trees and with the ominous sky pressing down on her, anything seemed possible. She paused in mid-thought and looked up in surprise, snowflakes! She squinted as the first real flurries of the approaching winter trickled down through the pine boughs and landed on her upturned face. With the snow came an increased urgency to get back to New Eden as soon as possible, and their slow-moving passage through this overgrown forest didn't exactly seem like the best route to be taking, but it was too late to turn back now.

Hours earlier, the new day had dawned dark with storm clouds filling the western horizon and a hint of snow in the air. Not long after breaking camp, they came upon a rushing stream edged with thin ice that disappeared into a thick forest of tall pine, dotted with clumps of bare, white-barked aspen and an occasional willow and grandfather oak.

Hunter decided to follow the watercourse; so they entered the wood, but not long afterward, a sense of dread descended like a shroud. As they forged ahead, the day turned somber and their mood subdued. It was as if they'd walked into an old abandoned house and an unseen someone had suddenly slammed the door shut behind them. Dark trees blotted out the gray sky above and the spongy forest floor, carpeted with decades of decomposing leaves and pine needles, muffled their passage. Even the air inside the woods was thick and still and filled with the pungent odor of rotting wood and fungi. As the afternoon progressed, the sky became even more overcast and shadows deepened within the glade.

Several miles later, Hunter led them forward ever more cautiously. The stillness was suffocating and, without the sun, there was no accurate way to know the time of day or direction of travel. Since entering the thick wood, his compass had been rendered useless by some unknown force or cause. The needle just drifted freely back and forth around the dial as though there was some anomaly here in the magnetic field.

He began to be bombarded by strange thoughts, sensations, and emotions. Even the horses were acting strangely. He felt like someone was watching them, but whom? They must be close but, so far, somehow managed to remain silent and out of sight. Hunter was troubled by this new mystery and could not fathom who or what this person or creature might be. Oddly enough, he didn't feel personally threatened but was aware of a definite presence, and felt certain that whoever or whatever was there wanted him to know that it was watching.

* * *

THE OLD ONES moved throughout the forest with little regard for physics. Their ways were not human ways and, therefore, need not obey the "natural" laws as understood by Man. Even Mankind's best and brightest theoretical physicists had agreed that other dimensions and parallel universes were possible, but only the true shamans ever really understood these matters in a useful, practical way.

Rarely did they interfere in the lives of mortals on the three-dimensional plane but, on special occasions, exceptions did occur, especially when there was a definitive sign and they could apply their healing powers to someone without being too heavily defiled by the physical interaction. This was the case with the dying man they found shot, who was now mostly recovered up at the cabin. It was always good when one could help save a life, human or otherwise, but this charitable chapter was rapidly coming to an end. The Old Ones placed the talisman into the human dimension and vanished.

Immediately, Hunter and Elise felt the strange presence diminish like a weight lifted from their shoulders. Even the sun beyond the clouds seemed brighter, and the travelers' hearts were lightened for no apparent reason. A slight movement through the trees caught Hunter's eye, and his gaze was drawn toward a dark spot on the ground a dozen yards away. Oddly, he hadn't noticed anything there a moment ago and went forward carefully to investigate. Reaching down, he picked up the thick beaded belt and examined it closely. It was made of moose hide embroidered with fine Native beadwork in a geometric pattern of turquoise, red, orange, and dark blue. The buckle was carved bison horn. It was oddly warm to the touch, a physical improbability here in the thirty-something degree air. He walked back to the horses to show Elise.

Taking the object in her hand, she felt her heart skip a beat and smiled. It was William's favorite belt! The one he always wore, made for him years ago by a tiny, ancient Native woman named "Monevata" or, in English, *Young Bird*—a Cheyenne medicine woman they'd grown up with, who was loved by all who knew her. Young Bird was probably in her late eighties when she arrived at New Eden and lived out her remaining years there, teaching anyone who was interested all about the medicinal properties of herbs and how to use them to treat and cure various illnesses and conditions.

The intricate design on the belt matched the beadwork on the medicine bag that William had carried around his neck beneath his shirt since he was eighteen, the very same bag that Elise had cut from the bandit leader's throat that day back on the prairie! She explained all of this to Hunter, who was determined to discover who'd placed the belt here directly in their path. He scoured the woods again with his eyes, half expecting to see someone appear out there beneath the trees.

The snowfall grew heavier, and Hunter realized that, beyond the wood, it must be nearly blizzard conditions by now. As the air temperature dropped below freezing, the flakes began to stick and, in a few hours, at increasingly lower temperatures, travel would become tricky. They must press on to New Eden with renewed vigor, but first the mystery of the belt must be solved. With the mournful mood lifted, Hunter led them forward, following a faint trail heading up a slight incline through thinning trees.

* * *

WILLIAM SHIVERED ON the porch as the gathering storm clouds blocked the sun and any promised warmth it might have otherwise provided. A steady north wind hinting of snow only increased his agitation at being trapped in this godforsaken place, a prisoner to his slow-mending injury, slowly driven mad by his inability to take action. He pushed aside his anxiety for wife and child and focused on the facts.

New Eden's fortifications were strong and designed to last a thousand years. He knew that Father would never allow their beloved community to fall to the enemy so easily. Their greatest weakness, though, was a lack of formal training to deal with an organized, determined assault. New Eden had no will for war, neither a desire to learn its ways. Father needed Macintosh to provide the skills necessary to defeat the looming threat from New Hope. With his failure to locate the man and convince him to return to New Eden, William was no longer certain of the future. Much could change in a short time and how long had he now been away?

He calculated the date as best he could and figured it must be almost September by now, but knew that was just a rough estimate at best, having lost track of time when delirious with fever. His thoughts gravitated again towards Sarah and little Jamie. Who would protect them and provide for them if the unthinkable were to happen back home?

While he tried to practice patience, the troubled man wrestled with his demons and his mood grew dark as the mid-afternoon sky. He took some comfort from the fact that he *was* recovering, albeit slowly, and, in another week or so, should be able to travel with some care. With that thought in place, the flakes began to fall, softly at first, but gradually increasing until the trees beyond the clearing were nearly obscured. He considered the snow a sure sign that winter would indeed come early this year as was rumored by many of the weather-wise settlers at New Eden.

The sudden snap of a broken stick out beneath the pines yanked him back into the present, and he instinctively reached for his rifle. He'd noticed some large grizzly tracks the day before and was certain he did not want to end up the hungry bear's final meal before winter hibernation. As he lifted the weapon to his shoulder, a familiar figure appeared in the distance as if in a dream, floating out of the darkened forest through a curtain of swirling white flakes.

The oval face framed by dark brown curls with green twinkling eyes and unmistakable smile betrayed his sister to him, as Elise rushed forward calling out his name. At the last second, he warned her of his injury and, just in time, she stopped and frowned, looking down at his wounded leg with deep concern. He quickly assured her that it was mending just fine, and she grabbed him round the neck and smothered herself in his chest, an errant tear splashing onto his coat from her suddenly welling eyes. An overjoyed William crushed her to him and then held his sister at arm's length, smiling broadly, still in shock at the good fortune of their reunion. His vastly relieved mind raced to discover how Elise could have possibly found him here in the midst of this vast, uncharted wilderness.

In a flurry of sound and emotion, she outlined her flight from New Eden and the journey north. She assured him that Sarah, Jamie and Anna were safe, and explained Hunter's presence, their rescue at his hands, and their present plan of action. Turning around as she spoke his name, Elise realized that her quiet traveling companion had remained back in the shadows beneath the trees with the horses.

Standing in the half-dark, Hunter was reluctant to walk out into the open clearing, brother or no brother. He was still very much concerned about who could be watching from seclusion and wasn't yet convinced that everything here was as safe as it appeared. Someone intentionally placed William's belt directly in their path, luring them here, and, noting the condition of William's leg, it was obviously someone they hadn't yet met. Sensing Hunter's mood, Elise returned to the wood and engaged her companion to come meet her brother.

"He's alone here and hasn't seen anyone for at least eight weeks." She explained what William told her about never seeing his benefactors. "I know it sounds very strange, but apparently they are only active while he sleeps."

Combining this information with the bizarre sensations experienced earlier, Hunter began to understand things a bit more clearly. He scanned the surrounding forest and peered through the thickening snowflakes to the cabin, a stern expression on his angular face. With crossbow at the ready, he followed Elise out into the clearing, still uneasy and expecting trouble.

William watched Elise lead Hunter and the horses out across the open space. The temperature dropped again and the ground was beginning to freeze. The snow was sticking now, and the wind swirled it about the feet and legs of the animals, forming miniature drifts against piles of pine needles and fallen cones.

He noted that Hunter was not as tall as he'd expected. From Father's description of the man and the manner in which the elder Planchet lauded Hunter's accomplishments, Macintosh was etched into his mind as a virtual giant. In truth, he was William's size, about six feet, and broad through the chest and shoulders with a fluid saunter that gave William the sense that the woodsman remained relaxed, yet on his guard.

Elise introduced the two well-matched men and stood back as they clasped hands in formal greeting. Their eyes met in measured gaze as each silently appraised the other.

William perceived the raw power of the stranger and was impressed by his composure and grace. He smiled and thanked Hunter for rescuing his family.

Hunter shook William's proffered hand while maintaining eye contact. Keeping thoughts and feelings well hidden, he remained attuned to the surrounding environment, listening for sounds from the forest and aware of every snowflake and gust of wind through the boughs. He immediately recognized the familial resemblance between brother and sister and could see Colonel Planchet's likeness and strength of character in his first-born son.

At Elise's suggestion, they headed inside, out of the worsening weather, which was becoming more intolerable by the minute. William directed Hunter towards a small stable at the rear of the building, and he moved off with the horses to attend to their needs, while Elise escorted William inside and busied herself about the cabin, stoking the dying fire and heating water for tea.

Hunter checked over the horses, relieving them of saddles and packs, and rubbed them down with handfuls of dry grass. He made sure they had a fresh supply of hay and water before rejoining the siblings who were catching up on all that transpired since last seeing each other.

As Hunter entered the room, Elise rose to help him with their things, but he waved her off, making a couple of quick trips back outside to carry in bedrolls and other necessities. Stowing several items in the kitchen area, he joined William and Elise at the inviting fire.

Settled comfortably on fur-covered benches with the gusting wind howling beneath the eves of the snug cabin, Hunter and Elise listened with rapt attention as William recounted his ill-fated journey north, recalling what he could of the ambush, his injuries, and waking up in this place alone.

"I still can't believe you found me here! Surrounded by hundreds of miles of trackless wilderness and you just happen to choose to follow the creek up into these particular woods?"

William's quick eyes searched Hunter's face for an explanation, but Elise's quiet companion remained typically silent, weighing each new piece of data and fitting it all together to form a more complete understanding of the unfolding situation he'd been called upon to resolve.

From William's recounting of the ambush, Hunter felt that there was a very low probability that anyone else had survived. William, of course, was living proof that there was always an exception to every rule, but he, too, held very little hope that any of his friends had made it out alive.

When her brother's story had been told, Elise filled him in on everything she could from the time he left New Eden to the present. At the appropriate point in her narrative, she produced his medicine bag cut from the dead bandit leader's neck and William's face lit up, amazed and relieved to place it back beneath his shirt where it had rested for so many years. Likewise, when she offered his belt, he gladly received it, yet remained mystified, unable to conjure up an acceptably logical explanation regarding his own situation here.

Many questions and answers back and forth filled in missing pieces of the puzzle, and afterwards the three arrived at a consensus: William would remain here and continue to gain his strength before heading out to Hunter's valley to join Sarah, Jamie, and Anna to winter with them there. Hunter and Elise would leave him one of their horses, and, with William's strong encouragement to embark immediately, press on towards New Eden with all haste. With more time lost than he had figured, William was even more concerned about family and friends back home.

When Elise handed him a steaming plate, William attacked his venison steak as if he hadn't eaten in years. Apparently, his mysterious hosts weren't big hunters, as he'd survived for months on a tasteless gruel made of herbs, roots and berries, but never any meat. After the robust meal, the trio continued their discussion late into the night with William adding to Hunter's map of New Eden, further outlining its tunnels, walls and defenses in charcoal on a deerskin pulled from one of the packs. Afterwards, Hunter reciprocated, providing William with a meticulously detailed map back to his family.

Before turning in, Hunter stepped outside one last time to see about the horses and check the weather. The animals seemed pleased to be inside the cozy shed and out of the wind and snow. He spread more dry grass and refilled their water trough before shutting them in for the night. As he worked, he mulled over the events of the day leading up to finding William here alone, yet, according to William, not without help. It was unusual to hear someone describe having been cared for by unseen benefactors, an implausible possibility, yet believable now since both he and Elise had sensed the presence of something or someone physically undetectable. William's beaded belt, seeming to appear out of nowhere, only added to the conundrum that flew in the face of common sense and logic.

While he considered himself a realist, Hunter remained open to the possibility that beings or entities could possibly exist in an adjacent, yet imperceptible dimension. Native peoples of the Americas all held similar beliefs, passing down stories and folk tales about mythical beings, half-animal-half spirit, who appeared to them in dreams and visions with the power to turn drought to a downpour, or determine the outcome of a battle or buffalo hunt. Indigenous cultures throughout the world fostered such beliefs and even the celebrated *orthodox* religions professed to trust in some great invisible Spirit-Being endowed with the ability to directly participate in believers' lives, forgiving their trespasses and even saving them from eternal pain and death.

Recalling some of the more bizarre experiences he'd lived through during his tumultuous journey around the sun, who was he to say that such things didn't exist? In the final analysis, Hunter recognized that he could not fully explain such paranormal phenomena and filed away the evidence of William's supernatural hosts in the back of his pragmatic mind to concentrate on matters closer at hand and considerably more tangible and predictable.

Outside, the flurries had stopped and the moon shone brightly on the newly fallen snow, transforming the landscape into a frozen wonderland sprinkled with sparkling diamonds against a bluish-white backdrop. The night was still and cold, and his breath became steam clouds rolling out into the frozen air. He stared up at the stars, taking in the beauty of the moment and pondering the possibilities the immediate future might bring.

William's assessment of the conflict between New Eden and New Hope gave him increased cause for concern, especially the disturbing information he shared while Elise was out of the room. Hunter fitted this new data into his overall stratagem and wondered if the information he possessed was even still relevant. Such situations were extremely fluid, and the most current data Hunter possessed was now nearly four months old.

According to William's best estimate, New Eden was still a good three to four week's ride, and that was a fair weather guesstimate. This time of year, the sky could turn ugly in a matter of minutes and an early winter blizzard could double or even triple the projected travel time.

He returned to the darkened cabin where his bedroll was spread out and all but one candle extinguished. Turning in, he relaxed into the thick furs, suddenly aware of the stifling confines of the small bungalow. Just four weeks living outside and already he was uncomfortable within these breathless walls. The low roof seemed to press down, blocking the endless parade of stars in the frozen night sky outside. The fire in the small cast iron stove glowed orange, and he could hear the steady breathing of William in the bunk and Elise on the floor beside her brother, whom she obviously adored.

Beneath the looming events at New Eden, an entirely separate set of problems wove itself in and out of Hunter's awareness. Over the past several weeks, without consciously realizing it, he had bonded with Elise in a way he'd never before experienced. They seemed to blend seamlessly into each other's lives, neither one disturbing the other's space or integrity.

In all his travels and experiences, he had never met a woman even vaguely similar to her. In spite of his decades-old policy never to allow anyone to penetrate his emotional defenses, Hunter recognized somewhere, in the depths of his soul, that he was beginning to care entirely too much for this extraordinary woman, and his psyche wrestled vigorously with this newfound sense of connection.

CHAPTER ELEVEN

BESIEGED

ADAM PLANCHET STOOD alone atop New Eden's western parapet, staring off into the distant mist-shrouded mountains to the north. He wore heavy winter sheepskins leather side out and was wrapped in a buffalo-robe parka, essential protection against the Arctic squall blasting down out of the frozen Canadian Rockies. His bearded face was frosted with ice, masking a strong jaw set hard against the cold.

Above him in the gray expanse, scalloped clouds threatened to unleash more white misery upon the world. Over the past twenty-four hours, the unseasonable storm had paralyzed the region with four feet of snow, as New Eden struggled in the midst of a two-month siege orchestrated by adversaries from New Hope. Though he could not see them now they were out there, camped just beyond his outer wall. In their sixteen-year history, including the dark times immediately following the End War, this was decidedly New

Eden's most challenging moment. The old warrior reflected grimly on the irony of it all.

At fifty-seven, he was still broad across the shoulders and chest with a trim waist and well-muscled limbs. Piercing hazel eyes were set in a rugged lived-in face graced with the classic Native features of high cheekbones, full lips, and Roman nose. Short-cropped, once-black hair, liberally flecked with gray, formed a widow's peak atop his forehead. A sudden, severe gust threatened to rip the Cossack-style hat from his brow, but the grizzled ex-Army Ranger just leaned further into the wind, undaunted by the storm.

Adam Planchet was a survivor. Tough, intelligent, driven—a mixture of French-Seneca ancestry who saw the writing on the wall early on and took appropriate measures to ensure the safety and security of his family and friends. After a highly-decorated military career, he and his wife, Arianne, headed west with their children to carve out a life for themselves far removed from the Twenty-First Century monoculture.

The Planchets envisioned a self-sufficient lifestyle as part of a vibrant community of like-minded individuals living and working together for the common good, growing food in a sustainable fashion and producing their energy and fuel from renewable resources. In the foothills of the Rockies in northwestern Colorado they found several hundred secluded acres west of the Continental Divide. It was a natural wonderland surrounded by tall snow-capped mountains reaching high into the strikingly blue Colorado sky—a pristine land with a hardy climate, abundant water, timber, and wildlife. He purchased the property and set to work constructing his fortress. At least that's what the neighboring ranchers called it. Planchet christened his creation *New Eden,* and two years later his masterpiece was complete just as the U.S. electrical grid shut down forever in the nation's final blackout.

Planchet's utopia was designed as three concentric circles moving out from an axis. At the hub was a central complex of adjoining structures built atop an old abandoned silver mine, ingeniously connected by a network of tunnels that he enlarged and expanded using drills, dynamite, and blasting caps. When completed, the impressive rock-faced buildings blended aesthetically into the broad granite hilltop. From a strategic point of view, all of New Eden's walls and structures were purposefully overbuilt. Rebar-reinforced concrete walls, two-feet thick, were faced with eight to twelve inches of local stone. All of the buildings boasted these same exterior walls over internal timber-frames using twenty-four-inch thick timbers, all designed to last at least a thousand years. Heavy blast doors with steel-mesh reinforced plexiglass windows fitted with two-inch thick, steel-plated shutters guaranteed a suitable level of safety from external attack. Steel-reinforced roofs, covered in heavy copper sheathing, completed the relative structural invulnerability.

The design encompassed what Planchet fondly referred to as his "Three Lines of Defense." The first was the natural barrier of the mountains and the steep river gorge itself. The enclosed valley of New Eden was ringed by tall, snow-capped mountains. At its center was a broad granite hilltop with the silver mine beneath. Atop the hill, the *Great Hall* was encircled by a twelve-foot tall concrete barrier faced with rock known as the *parapet wall*. Below the parapet wall was the interconnected *community housing* complex encircling the hill. Below the housing complex were sheds, shops, stables, barns, orchards, and fields divided by a rushing creek running the valley's length that emptied into a deep gorge at the lower east end. A massive wooden railroad bridge, built a hundred years earlier to haul ore from the silver mine, spanned the gorge and was the only practical entry into the valley.

Before reaching the fortified railroad bridge, a twelve-foot-high outer barrier known as the *perimeter wall* enclosed the several hundred acres immediately surrounding the complex. Four reinforced gates, flanked by guardhouses to the north, south, east, and west, were the only breaks in this outer barrier. Within this rectangular-shaped perimeter wall, four towers, similar in design to old forest service fire lookout towers, made of massive timbers with a weatherproof cabin on top, rose fifty feet into the sky from the four corners of the land, giving lookouts a commanding view of their section of valley. In the event this perimeter wall was breached, the people could fall back to the third and final line of defense, the parapet wall immediately surrounding the Great Hall which was topped by its own impressive lookout tower.

The fertile river valley surrounding the complex was divided into orchards, vineyards, fish ponds, lush gardens and cultivated fields planted with every imaginable type of nut, fruit, berry, vegetable, grain and legume sustainable by the local climate. Along the south-facing slope, long, insulated greenhouses, framed in aluminum and overlaid with reinforced glass, contained a nursery for young plants and trees, as well as winter gardens of green leafy crops. Employing the creative use of geothermal energy, one greenhouse section contained a hot house where citrus trees, avocado, kiwi fruit, and other sub-tropical plants thrived. All areas of the valley were accessible via an interconnected system of cart roads and footpaths.

Water for household use and irrigation for farming and watering livestock came from the year-round stream running through the midst of the valley supplemented by half-a-dozen strategically located deep-rock wells and numerous springs and creeks. Electricity was generated by hydroelectric turbines, windmills, and solar panels that stored excess energy in underground banks of renewable batteries. Geothermal heating and cooling was accomplished by harnessing the temperature differential within the Earth itself.

With this infrastructure in place, Planchet established livestock operations to provide an ongoing abundant supply of fiber and leather for clothing, dairy products, meat, farm labor, and transportation. Carefully managed flocks and herds included Icelandic sheep and cashmere goats for meat, milk and fiber; there were French alpine dairy goats, llamas, Scottish highland cattle, donkeys, and a quarter horse-draft horse cross-breeding program producing well proportioned animals suitable for riding or pulling wagons and farm implements. In addition to the livestock, the community raised poultry, including chickens, turkeys, ducks, geese, and guineas, and stocked their two twenty-acre lakes with bass, brim, catfish, and trout.

Planchet looked out over his creation, pleased with what he saw. He had designed New Eden to be a refuge and it was. Given a determined defense force, it would never fall to an external aggressor. With its storerooms full and people strong and willing, he felt confident that they could make it through the coming winter. Drawing a deep breath, he recalled another extremely challenging time, way back at the beginning...

* * *

WHEN THE APOCALYPSE arrived unannounced, major population centers across the globe were targeted by nukes or chemical and biological weapons, but places off the beaten path like New Eden remained relatively unscathed, though abruptly cut off from the rest of the world. Without access to police, fire, or medical services, or fuel, energy, mass media, transportation, banking, commerce, phone service, the Internet, or GPS, they found themselves entirely on their own with no idea how bad it was "out there."

When all communications with the outside world ceased, Planchet sent out scouts to find out what had happened. A team drove forty-five miles west to the nearest town and radioed back, describing complete anarchy with zero police presence. Among the panic-stricken townsfolk, mob violence prevailed. Stores and banks were looted and battered corpses lay sprawled in the streets. Planchet ordered the team's immediate return, and the stunned community locked down its gates, its disbelieving members remaining inside the perimeter wall monitoring silent radios and awaiting some official word from Homeland Security, the Marines, or the Red Cross—a word that would never come.

In the chaotic days that followed, a few desperate stragglers trickled out to the remote refuge requesting asylum, bearing tidings of brutality and utter social devolution. Armed gangs had formed and homes were broken into. Roving lynch mobs murdered innocent people. Women and girls were not safe. Things happened too horrific to describe. There were even rumors of cannibalism as limited food supplies ran out and the population began to starve. Almost a week after the End War, a dozen malnourished refugees arrived from the east saying they'd met some horribly burned people on the highway to Denver, who claimed that the city had been nuked. They swore seeing a blinding flash and mushroom cloud some forty to fifty miles away.

Soon the sky above New Eden turned a dingy grayish-brown filled with gritty particles that made it difficult to breathe. High winds whipped through the valley, bringing more filthy air with a reek of sulfur and rotting flesh. People and animals got sick. Trees dropped their leaves. Over the next few weeks, the sun's strength steadily ebbed as the dust and ash from the mammoth fires and explosions around the globe rose into the stratosphere, trapping the warmth of the sun and lowering temperatures across the planet.

The people of New Eden did what they could to salvage their livestock and crops as temperatures steadily dropped. In keeping with their self-reliant philosophy and lifestyle, the community had plenty of food, clothing, medical, and other survival supplies stockpiled in underground storage facilities, but nothing could have prepared them for the hardships ahead as the northern hemisphere was plunged into a two-year nuclear winter. Weather patterns became severely disrupted. Prevailing winds and ocean currents stalled or changed direction. Drought and famine engulfed most of the world as billions perished from starvation, disease, and exposure to the elements, a time that would later become known as the *Great Purging*.

When the climate eventually warmed again, the sky gradually returned to blue and the brutal hibernation endured by New Eden's people mercifully ended. Roughly half of their members had survived, including Planchet's entire family. The majority of those who died succumbed to a deadly flu-like virus that swept through the community more than once, sucking the life from the very young, the weak, and the elderly. Tragically, the long nuclear winter drove several community members to the point of ending their own lives rather than face the possibility of an endlessly dark and dismal existence void of sunshine and hope.

Thanks to the strict rationing of food stores, Planchet's people hadn't starved, and, when the first spring-like weather in more than two years auspiciously arrived, everyone got busy planting crops from stockpiled seeds and building new lives from the ashes of the old. As the months passed, air quality improved and the community once again thrived despite postwar scarcities and hardships. Somehow through it all, Planchet managed to keep the dream alive, governing New Eden wisely and well with the support and encouragement of his lovely Arianne, but that was many years ago now.

Pressing mitten-clad palms against cold, stone defenses, he closed his eyes, bending forward at the waist and exhaled, slowly expelling every last particle of air from his lungs. Gracefully straightening back up, he offered a silent prayer of thanks for the many blessings he'd received during his lifetime. He conjured up an image of Arianne, foremost of those blessings, appearing as she had when he first laid eyes on her, and he smiled, grateful for the wonderful years they shared and the children they brought into the world. These days she was never far from his thoughts, even so long after that tragic morning when Fate suddenly snatched her from him with no time for either to say goodbye. Planchet let her go and stretched again, fighting back a pending yawn until finally surrendering to it and emitting great billows of steam from his wide-opened mouth. He wasn't sleeping much these days. No one was.

Shifting his weight to ease the stiffness in his legs, he focused his thoughts again on the fate of his eldest son, William, wondering whether he would ever see him again. His return was long overdue, which meant that he was either dead, injured, or being held against his will somewhere off to the north. He squinted into the distance, as if by so doing he could pierce the thick clouds covering the tall peaks to the northeast. His attention shifted to his precious daughters, Anna and Elise, and to Sarah, William's wife, and Jamie, their child and his first and only grandson, all of whom were out there somewhere as well, sent on a desperate quest to locate and persuade the one man Planchet was counting on to help defeat his enemies. He closed his eyes again and sent out positive thoughts for a successful mission and safe return.

"Here you are Father, I've brought you something warm to help keep away the cold." Opening his eyes, he beheld the enchanting form of his youngest daughter, fourteen-year-old Amy, as close to his heart as any of his natural-born children, though she was not his by blood, but by adoption. She came to Adam and Arianne Planchet in the midst of a terrible blizzard on Christmas Eve nearly twelve years ago. Arianne immediately fell in love with the child, and it wasn't long before Planchet, too, was bewitched by her captivating smile, stunning blue eyes, and thick shock of curly, dark-red hair.

She was nicknamed *Stormy* by the older children, and the moniker stuck, not only because of the weather system that brought her into their lives, but because of her legendary temper that reared its terrible head whenever the child felt she was being treated unfairly or placed at a disadvantage.

Over the years, she grew into a precocious, strong-willed young person, choosing never to back down from a challenge, nor turn away from a path once chosen. Amy was a complicated soul. Some said she was manipulative, presenting one face to her family, while revealing a more cryptic and less generous side to her peers when adults weren't around. She appeared sweet and vulnerable to her parents, though others viewed this as a cleverly designed performance usefully employed to get her own way.

It wasn't so hard to understand, after what she'd been through at such a young age. Her biological parents were massacred along with the rest of their party when she was only two. In the confusion and fire following the attack, the child was overlooked, and after the marauders left, she was alone, wandering for several days and nights among the bodies and wreckage, hungry and afraid. What she witnessed during the attack and afterwards as she rummaged for food, one can only guess. Needless to say, the reality of life, death, and survival in a brutal world was driven home to the young child at an early age. When a trapper and his wife finally found her days later, she was undemonstrative and mute. She responded to their voices and interacted with them on a basic level, but the beautiful smile that had warmed the hearts of her parents remained hidden.

By the time Amy arrived at New Eden three months later, she'd begun to emerge from her shell. Arianne's love washed over her emotional wounds, filling the void left by the death of her mother. Yet, in spite of her outward appearance as a normal, happy child, no one could penetrate her inner defenses. As the years passed, young Amy, like the other children at New Eden, immersed herself in the community life around her, but deep inside she was always alone. To her, there was a vast difference between the reality of her inner self and the person she portrayed to the world. It was as if she were acting on a stage, unbeknownst to the other players, who only experienced her character, not her person. This could be troubling to those closest to her, as her response to any given situation was based solely on her calculated analysis of the expectation of the other and of her determination to ever gain the advantage.

It was not easy being different. In a close-knit family like the Planchets, the connection between individuals was extremely intimate, requiring that one demonstrate an authenticity that was difficult to fake. Amy innately realized that being well thought of by the adults was vital to her survival. Her peers, however, fell into the category of competition, and she always somehow felt like she was vying for attention, or jockeying for position, and always sought to win, *no matter what.*

But as far as Adam Planchet was concerned, his Amy could do no wrong, and, if he was aware of any such character flaws in his precious youngest daughter, he chose to turn a blind eye to them altogether. To him, she would always be the symbol of Arianne's nurturing, compassionate nature, and he would never accept that their youngest was anything less than perfect in every way. Probably because Amy was his youngest child, Planchet took heroic measures to shield her from the unpleasant realities of life, probably more so than the rest of his children. This was not a conscious behavior, and he was not aware of the effect it had on the others. He welcomed her hug and smiled, taking a sip of the sweet, steaming tea and watched her go, confidently negotiating the slippery stone steps on her way back down across the snow-covered footpath to the Great Hall. *At least* she *was still safe,* he thought, *but for how much longer?*

CHAPTER TWELVE

NEW HOPE

AN HOUR AFTER sunset on a hilltop overlooking New Hope's unsightly sprawl, clandestine bootlegger and gang boss Frank McAllister met with relative newcomer and notorious street tough Big Bull Mitchell. The younger Mitchell had requested the meet, and the two faced off across a tiny fire, cloaked in their respective thoughts.

Surrounding them in a loose semi-circle, their personal bodyguards looked on nervously, awaiting word from their bosses, just itching for a scrap. Each was armed with some sort of crudely made weapon—a deadly blade, rough club, or length of rusty chain. The meeting rules were clear: no long-range weapons allowed. Bows, slings, and spears were checked at the base of the hill, guarded by a contingency of toughs from each mob.

"You've got balls Mitchell, I'll give you that," Frank McAllister turned his head and spat into the fire at their feet, "So what exactly do you want?"

Mitchell remained silent and dumped something heavy onto the grass from a burlap sack. In the flickering light, the severed head of Julio Gonzales, McAllister's former rival with a tough gang of his own, rolled downhill a couple of feet and rested on its right ear. The dead staring eyes were crusted with blood, broken teeth clenched, bruised lips drawn back in a frozen grimace of pain.

McAllister carefully masked his surprise. Better watch out for this one, *he warned himself;* Gonzales was a crafty, ruthless adversary, and Mitchell's victory over him was not to be taken lightly. *He glanced casually at Mitchell's sneering mug with a questioning look.*

"I'm taking everything he had," Mitchell hissed, eyes narrowing to mere slits in his scar-etched face, "and 25% of yours."

* * *

TWO DOZEN MILES south of New Eden, in a wide river valley beyond the next set of hills, the densely-populated settlement of New Hope stretched out across the bottomland along both sides of a narrow, fast-flowing river. The hodgepodge collection of sheds, shacks, and common houses boasted a rut-filled main street two miles long with a spider web of offshoots and alleys winding this way and that, connecting its various points of interest and enterprise. These included a saloon and a bawdy house, along with the standard shops and stables, tents and temporary encampments of the newly arrived.

The boomtown had been founded two years earlier by hardworking folks of good intent, many of whom had traveled hundreds of miles from all points of the compass to join the legendary community at New Eden. Unfortunately, Planchet's utopia was no longer accepting new members and they were politely but firmly turned away. However logical his rationale for not violating the laws of sustainability, it didn't quite seem fair to those on the outside of those tall barrier walls. New Eden had plenty, more than enough, but the unsympathetic Planchet wouldn't budge.

In their disappointment and bitterness, New Hope's founders declared that *their* community would be one of *inclusion*, welcoming anyone and everyone who showed up wishing to participate. Where New Eden was a *benevolent monarchy* ruled by Adam Planchet and his family, New Hope would be a *true democracy*, designed, organized, and managed of the people, by the people, and for the people!

In the shantytown outside New Eden's main gates, Donovan Weeks, a wandering preacher (and used car salesman before the End War) came up with the idea for the new settlement and coined the name *New Hope*. Using his considerable powers of persuasion honed through years of practice in his chosen professions, he stirred up some strong interest among those trying to figure out what to do next, now that New Eden had turned out to be just another dead end. He convinced several stout-hearted family men to join with him and his wife, Dahlia, to get things going in the neighboring valley. Together they organized New Hope's first official town council and passed around a roster listing the names of those interested in putting a new town together.

To some camped outside New Eden's walls, the plan sounded like a great opportunity to get in on the ground floor of something big. To others, it seemed like a lot of hard work for nothing, and they weren't about to leave the relative safety of New Eden's shadow to venture across the mountains with a bunch of dreamers who may or may not build anything. Talk was cheap and they'd heard it all before. At least here they could beg for handouts and receive scraps from New Eden's table. Some fools had even convinced themselves that maybe, if they remained long enough, Planchet would take pity on them and they would somehow gain access to the community after all.

A few dozen folks bought into Donovan's rhetoric and joined up. As the weeks progressed, tents, sheds, and small buildings began to spring up, dotting the landscape with a medley of interesting and unusual structures. More people heard about it and became curious, and others, also turned away by Planchet, came to see what the fuss was all about. Folks from the surrounding territories began to hear rumors about a brand new startup called New Hope, and many showed up itching for a fresh start someplace new.

People got busy bartering whatever they had to offer. Woodsmen went into the hills with mules and dragged logs back for building materials. Somebody set up a saw mill they'd salvaged from a distant ghost town and started cutting logs into lumber for buildings and barns. Carpenters made tables and chairs, doors and cabinets. Others fished and traded what they caught. Hunters brought in meat and gatherers foraged for wild foods as gardens went in tended by deprivation-hardened people who started to feel like they just might be part of something special. A tannery/harness shop went up and crops were planted along the rich bottomland.

Before long, the founders' dream began to take shape, and, through the hard work and efforts of a growing, dedicated populace, a real town rose out of the mud, spreading along the hillsides where before only western wheatgrass grew and pronghorn antelope raced the wind across the hills. Even folks from New Eden came by to see this new community and were impressed with the progress they'd made in such a short time. Some returned with gifts of seeds and cuttings for crops, or young livestock for starter flocks and herds.

With summer fast approaching, Donovan and his *People's Council* made a formal visit to New Eden, requesting an audience with Planchet. After listening to their proposal, he agreed to help them with whatever they needed to become self-sufficient as soon as possible. They promised to repay his generosity ten-fold, but Planchet told them that his charity was just that, free without strings attached. A few days later, wagons arrived from New Eden bringing tools and supplies and all of the support their neighbors there could muster. Volunteers devoted weeks constructing fences, barns, community gardens, and planting orchards and berries, tilling the bottomland surrounding the town, and planting fields with corn, beans, tomatoes, peppers, and every good thing that New Eden enjoyed.

Donovan and the council were grateful for all that was done on their behalf and praised the Planchets and the good people of New Eden for their generosity. Out of her abundance, New Eden shared with her sister city across the mountain, and New Hope looked forward to a bright future filled with goodness. That first autumn, the harvest was plentiful and the people of New Hope stayed busy preserving food and stacking firewood for the coming winter. When early snows and freezing temperatures made long distance travel impossible, the constant stream of newcomers temporarily ground to a halt. During the long, cold winter the settlement of more than two thousand souls lived comfortably until spring on the gifts from New Eden and what they'd managed to put aside from their own harvest and hunting and trapping operations.

When the mountain passes cleared in the spring and snowmelt filled the rivers, the first major west coast caravan arrived bringing much desired tools, building materials, cookware, and a myriad of miscellaneous household items scavenged from the derelict towns of the west. The steady stream of newcomers returned as word spread up and down the coast about New Hope, where everyone was welcome. It wasn't long before its first baby was born and a small cemetery sprang up on a nearby hill for those who had finished their days.

As exciting as the genesis was, not everyone showing up at New Hope was sincere and helpful. Lazy malcontents drifted into town, bringing their dirty laundry and stacks of skeletons in closets. Things began to turn up missing. People got hurt. Vodka was introduced from a still hidden up in the hills, and easy women offered personal services in exchange for a hot meal, drink, or shiny trinket.

The vast majority of *Hopers,* as they liked to call themselves, were hard working people who went about their business preferring to ignore the growing problems. Others, afraid of what might happen if things continued to get worse, complained to the council, demanding that something be done to maintain order. Donovan was uncomfortable with the situation but unsure of what to do about it. The founding philosophy of New Hope was a town without harsh controls or anyone lording it over the others. The People's Council called a meeting but ruled that, while laziness and non-participation were selfish and irresponsible, they were not crimes. So they, too, looked the other way and didn't deal with the problem. The real issue was New Hope's lack of an agreed upon set of rules or laws. In their desire to establish a *free* society, they rejected the *rule of law* model, insisting that individuals of conscience would simply *do the right thing on their own* and that no law enforcement or justice system was necessary to enforce ethical conduct—fatally optimistic to say the least.

While most arrivals did their part and worked hard to build something lasting, the community attracted its fair share of parasites once word got out about the boomtown where nothing was required of them. The lazy consumed whatever they could pilfer, steal or beg, while the hardworking folks produced all they could and tried saving back for a rainy day. With a growing minority of undisciplined and disorganized newcomers, New Hope's resources became strained and began to suffer. As some had anticipated, violence broke out amongst the populace. Thefts and aggravated assaults increased, and even assaults on women and murder took place on dark nights in the less frequented places on the outskirts of town.

Again the good citizens pressured the beleaguered People's Council for a solution, but there was really nothing they could do short of creating an organized police force.

As chairman, Donovan persuaded them to act, and they halfheartedly appointed one good man to the post of Sheriff, who was discovered the next morning face down in the street with an ice pick through his heart. Realizing that the situation was only going to get worse, Donovan finally understood why Planchet's model had worked all these years. A true democracy was impossible unless everyone involved was willing to take an active, responsible role. A workable society required the full participation of its members, and, without laws and some way to enforce an agreed upon code of conduct, there would only ever be chaos and anarchy.

The burgeoning population of New Hope, numbering well over three thousand with more arriving daily, clamored for the basic necessities of life—food, clothing, shelter, and the protection of their basic human rights from the criminal elements of society. By late summer, Donovan and the council, without the means to enforce rulings to save the settlement, were virtually powerless. Street violence escalated, and each night brought new terrors. Innocent people suffered vicious attacks by the growing street gangs that began to exert control over the community. About this time, the nightly exodus began.

Had Donovan and the others been students of history, they would have understood how lawless societies were fertile breeding grounds where aggressive individuals could rise to power through the use of cunning and force. By promising relief from lawlessness, a dominant individual could become a law unto him or herself, convincing the good citizens that a strong, unflinching leader was necessary to maintain order and keep them safe. How much better to dwell under the secure restraints of a wise ruler than to suffer at the hands of thugs? By gaining the trust of a beset population, a self-appointed *savior* could appear on the scene and take control of the reigns of power. If ever a town was ripe for such a dictator, New Hope was a classic case in point.

* * *

WHEN FRANK MCALLISTER arrived in the late spring of New Hope's second year, he immediately liked what he saw—a fresh town with lots of people coming and going. *Easy for a man to step in and make a name for himself in a place like this,* he thought, e*specially a man with ambition.* He smiled, pleased with himself to have come so far, so fast.

As soon as he hit town, he sized up the competition. Word on the street was that a guy named Gonzales was running things; he had most of the teens and younger kids frightened and eating out of the palm of his hand. They scavenged useful items they found lying around unattended, strictly small time stuff. He said he'd give them *privileges* and had a couple of seasoned prostitutes in a back room who would do whatever he told them to do. Gonzales was a petty crook, lacking vision and ambition, two things McAllister had been blessed with an abundance of.

McAllister's first order of business was to round up a few strays—loners needing some direction in their lives. He considered it prudent to have other people do his dirty work; it was better that way in case anything went wrong and they were never very hard to find. The outsiders, the homely, the unloved, the drifters, the hopeless, these were his army awaiting his orders. All he had to do was round them up and give them a purpose. Besides, he had a big secret, something hidden back up in the hills. Soon it was going to make him rich and powerful beyond his wildest dreams! New Hope, you see, was a dry town, not one drop of liquor to wet your whistle. He would be changing all that. It was just luck really, just pure luck the way it all happened.

CHAPTER THIRTEEN

YAAKOV

FIFTY-THREE-YEAR-old Russian immigrant, Yaakov Milosevic and his twin sons, Dmitri and Sergei, sat atop three heavily loaded wagons pushing east across the northern Sierra Nevada into what used to be the great state of Nevada, headed for old Colorado. Each wagon was handcrafted from stout oak planks, reinforced with thick iron ribs and pulled by four strong mules, evidence of their hefty cargo. Beneath the warm afternoon sun, the willing beasts sweated and strained against their harnesses as they crested the ridge on old I-80 East.

Yaakov called a halt, and his boys filled water buckets to give their good-natured draft animals a well-deserved drink. He surveyed the wide expanse below with binoculars, following the river as it meandered through green fields several miles away. Here and there were the usual elk and deer moving among the thickets, with a scattering of antelope and bison grazing the more open patches. The sun stood sentinel over a milky blue sky flecked with high, wispy clouds herded towards the distant horizon by warm, dry winds out of the west.

The Milosevics were Old World ironworkers, craftsmen passing down their skills from generation-to-generation. Yaakov was built like a wolfhound with thick gray hair framing a weathered face hosting sharp blue eyes under bushy brows. A magnificent salt and pepper beard flowed down over his broad chest. The thick arms of a blacksmith were balanced by his tree trunk legs. The sons were younger versions of their father, with faces holding fewer wrinkles and sporting silky black beards and longer hair.

Yaakov Milosevic was a man with a plan. He and his sons were going to join the renowned community of New Eden in old northwestern Colorado, the land of milk and honey. In his wagon beneath the bellows and blacksmithing tools was a large copper still hidden beneath false floorboards, the kind you made vodka with, along with thirty small kegs containing his most recent batch ready to trade.

He was happy to be leaving old California far behind. *Too many people and too much violence,* he told himself again, recalling the hard times starting over in half a dozen different towns. *Always the same trouble*, he shook his head, thoroughly disgusted with human nature. *Always, somebody thinking they could muscle-in on our business. But not this time!* He smiled, dipping a blue enameled ladle into an oak water barrel and drinking until the cool liquid ran down his bearded chin.

Behind him in the covered wagon, a dozen large wooden barrels stuffed with sawdust held potatoes for their next batch of vodka and a sack of seed potatoes that would produce the batch after that. All he and his sons needed was a place to settle, a patch of field to put in their crops and a shed to house their still. Of course, they would set up the blacksmith shop as well. Forge and bellows, hammers and pincers, everything was ready. *But the real trade,* he squinted, squinching his eyes down tight and making the landscape dance like a mirage, *the real trade was in spirits!*

He proudly watched Dmitri and Sergei replace the empty water buckets and step up into their driver's seats. They were good men and pleased to be going east as well. Both were seeking new wives as their last ones were lost to pirates who swept in from the coast in the dead of night and snatched them from their beds. The boys were away on business, and, by the time the townsfolk went after them, the raiders were back aboard their ships and sailing off into the distance. He'd heard that New Eden was supposed to be some kind of paradise, one of the last truly civilized places left on Earth and they were tired of starting over. He shifted his gaze to their outrider, a man hired for his wilderness experience and accuracy with a firearm.

* * *

FRANK MCALLISTER HITCHED a ride with the Milosevics out of the border region at the final jump off point before the crossing on what used to be the I-80 freeway near Lake Tahoe, California. He sweet-talked his way into getting hired on as an extra gun for Milosevic and his sons, since the crossing was known to be hazardous, with bandits ready to bushwhack any party they perceived to be vulnerable. Yaakov offered him all the food he could eat and issued him a horse and black power rifle with powder horn, ball, and shot for the crossing, promising a bonus when they arrived safely. Either way, McAllister could keep the horse and gun as compensation, which was more than fine with him.

One day, when asked to help unload a wagon that had broken an axle, he discovered the true nature of Milosevic's business and put a plan in motion that would make him rich and powerful beyond reckoning. With the intrigue in place, he worked hard doing whatever he was told along the way, biding his time, waiting for just the right moment. The closer they got to New Eden, the itchier he became to make his move. *Not yet,* he told himself each evening as they made camp and bedded down the mules, *not yet, but soon.* He kept his excitement to himself. The Milosevics were no pushovers. They were big, tough Russians. His work would have to be performed quietly, one-by-one, lest the commotion wake the others and foil his plans. He smiled to himself rolling over in his bedroll. With all that liquor, he was going to be a goddamned sultan!

* * *

AT THE BOTTOM of a steep ravine, several miles from the outskirts of New Hope, a solitary driver guided his narrow wagon along the rutted track beside a tiny creek, loaded rifle laid handily across his lap. His horse was skittish, ears twitching this way and that, never sure when the man would strike her again with his ubiquitous switch. Her sensitive mouth and tongue were sore from his rough-handed habit of jerking on the reins, pinching and bruising her with the snaffle bit, when all he had to do was gently touch the reins to one side of her neck or the other and she would gladly change direction. Her former master would never have treated her so poorly, but he didn't drive her anymore.

Breaking through a stand of alders, the forest opened up into a small clearing revealing a crude shack hidden way down in back. The driver noted the lack of smoke from the stovepipe through the roof and cursed, jerking hard on the reins to stop.

The mare snorted in protest, stamping her feet, and the man immediately laid into her tender ears with his long, flexible switch. To avoid the whistling sting, she arched her neck, holding her nose as close to the ground as possible. He cursed again and jerked the reins harder, pulling to the right until she spun around and around the clearing in a tight circle as he unmercifully flailed her about the head and face. Not until the poor horse gave in and stood still, trembling under the lash, did he finally stop hitting her. He climbed down, cursing her again and punched her bruised and bleeding nose with his gloved fist before tying her off to a sapling near the shanty's porch.

Unlocking the padlock, Frank McAllister pulled open the front door and looked around the dim, disheveled room. In the center stood a large copper still, the boiler cold and fire beneath out. He yelled at the old man asleep on the floor, cursing him for letting the fire die yet again. Yaakov Milosevic opened his eyes and squinted up at his tormentor silhouetted against the bright doorway. McAllister tossed him a bundle of food scraps, and Yaakov scrambled after them, the heavy iron chain shackled to his ankle rattling as he shuffled across the floor.

Stacked against one wall, a dozen small wooden casks were all that remained of the original vodka smuggled across the desert in the Milosevic wagons. McAllister had spent the balance financing his growing influence in the swelling community of New Hope. With it, he paid his gang and his prostitutes, and traded and bribed his way to power. Without it, he was just another cutthroat grifter, blown along by the winds of opportunity. And this, he smiled, was one opportunity he was determined to exploit to the fullest. In a dry territory, he owned the only working still! He alone had what the people wanted, but he needed more! Those barrels of potatoes were making him rich! The problem was Yaakov. The stubborn Russian wasn't cooperating. McAllister had no idea how to actually make the stuff himself but Milosevic was undoubtably a still-master—possessing so fine an example—and now, after many frustrating and unnecessary delays, his new batch of liquid gold was finally ready for market.

While a gaunt Yaakov wolfed down the meat scraps, McAllister sweated, unloading firewood and empty casks. He hated anything to do with manual labor but couldn't trust anyone to help him with his secret. If someone were to discover the location of the still, he would, no doubt, be a dead man. The rumor circulating in town (originated by McAllister, himself) was that a ruthless gang of Russians, hidden away somewhere in the hills, were producing the stuff, and McAllister was their partner with exclusive rights to supply New Hope with their product. Messing with McAllister was messing with the Russians, a mistake that would undoubtably be fatal. Two men even turned up dead a while back, and rumor had it they'd tried to bushwhack McAllister; so the Russians slit their throats! McAllister smiled at the thought that even in death Sergei and Dmitri had served him well.

As Yaakov stoked the fire beneath the cooker, McAllister spent an hour refilling empties with the newest batch and loading most of them into the wagon. Finishing, he cursed the heat, casually disguising his treasure beneath an old tattered quilt. He would deliver half this load to a hidden storage room in town and distribute the rest through the brothel and saloon, both of which he now controlled. Returning to the shack with his switch to encourage Yaakov to be more attentive to the fire in the future, he stooped down in the doorway to first dress the thin stick with horse manure from his boot.

Inside the dismal shack, Yaakov Milosevic made last minute preparations for his final act of courage. For weeks he'd slaved here, hungry, alone, his mind working overtime to conceive a plan to destroy the sadistic monster who kept him locked up in this godforsaken nightmare. Everything he'd worked for his whole life was gone. His family murdered, his dreams dashed to bits by this demon who tormented him night and day, forcing him to produce the vodka which he knew was only consolidating McAllister's empire with each new cask. Finally, as this fresh batch came to fruition, the plan had fallen into place. When McAllister approached the porch with his switch, Yaakov turned and tipped a concealed bucket onto the floor, spreading the high alcohol content mixture across the room to the casks lining the far wall. Grabbing a burning brand from the fire, he smiled, tossing it onto the puddle and stood back as it caught, the blue flames racing across the floor to the opposite wall.

Looking to the doorway, his smile died as he watched McAllister hesitate on the threshold, scraping something off his boot with a stick. Whoosh! The first cask caught and the blue flames spread rapidly to the next and beyond. McAllister looked up at the curious sound and in the split second before the blast, turned and dove headfirst off the porch into the brush.

The deafening explosion blew the shed roof high into the air and the splintered walls out into the trees, sending burning wreckage flying a hundred feet and catching the woods on fire! Miraculously, McAllister was protected from the flames by a flying piece of sheet metal tacked to the shed wall that landed on him with flaming boards attached to the top.

With the crackling fire spreading rapidly, he scrambled, coughing, to the wagon, whipped the terrified animal with the reigns and raced away before the inferno could take hold of the last of his precious vodka. Out of range of the intense heat he stopped and brushed burning material from the wagon and the horse's back where she'd suffered large third degree burns. Astonished at his amazing escape, a singed and blackened McAllister energetically coaxed the shocked and injured animal back to town with a freshly cut switch, where, after cleaning himself up and securing his precious cargo, he rewarded her loyal service by trading her to the butcher for a side of pork and a pair of tender young hens. *Ahhh*, he reflected, *life was good!*

* * *

FRANK MCALLISTER SLITHERED his way into power, not through good deeds well publicized, nor the rescue of damsels in distress, but with the help of the Russian's vodka. As New Hope groaned under its rapid expansion, McAllister had the one thing no one else had and most everyone else wanted—a good stiff drink! With it, he controlled the streets, owned the whores and grifters, and opened a saloon and a bawdy house right on Main Street. Before long, most everyone was a customer, and he commanded a powerful organization to do his bidding.

From among the idle youth hanging out on the streets inventing mischief, McAllister picked out a couple of older toughs to be his lieutenants and got them to recruit others into the gang. He offered them spirits and extra food and side benefits, meaning they could get away with just about anything as long as they took their orders from him and brought in the *goods*.

The *goods* were anything of value. This included food, clothing, tools, eye glasses, medicines—all necessities, and anything considered a luxury was fair game. His popularity among the young and disillusioned was furthered by propagating the myth that it was "all their parents' fault" that everything was so messed up. If the younger generation was going to have a worthwhile future in this broken world they'd inherited, they would have to take matters into their own hands.

His only competition was Big Bull Mitchell, a down and dirty street fighter who settled everything with his fists or a handy knife blade. If Mitchell wanted something from someone, he simply took it and dared anyone to stop him. Those foolish enough to try were brutally beaten or killed. Cowards clung to Mitchell's coattails like burrs on a stocking. After removing the small-time Gonzales, Mitchell had set up headquarters on the outskirts of town and sent for whatever he wanted from whoever had it. It wasn't long before dozens of ne'er-do-wells surrounded him like a slinking pack of hyenas, slavishly doing his bidding and fighting over the scraps from his table.

By the time their second autumn arrived, the hardworking founders of New Hope, and those trying to build something great, had become disillusioned. Witnessing the growing lawlessness, many lost faith in Donovan's fading dream and quietly packed their things, leaving for the coast in the dead of night. This nighttime exodus became a bitter source of irritation to both McAllister and Mitchell, who noticed that many of the shopkeepers and business owners—families with the most to offer—were leaving and taking their belongings (and teenage daughters) with them. Even Donovan finally called it quits and disappeared for parts unknown.

With the town's population shrinking along with the last of his precious vodka, McAllister abolished the ineffectual town council, proclaimed himself Sheriff and declared martial law. With the town going bust, he realized that ruling New Hope was way too small a dream. There was no future in squeezing a poor, worn out people, and the coming winter was beginning to look desolate. Back at the end of July, after several vicious raids by Mitchell into New Eden's territory left three of their people dead, Planchet had withdrawn his support from New Hope and cut off communications.

Running out of local options, McAllister cast his gaze across the hills to New Eden in what he considered to be a moment of pure inspiration, fixing his eye on a much more succulent prize to plunder. Now *that* would be a choice location in which to rule and reign—a completely self-sufficient oasis in the post-war world! However, whichever way you sliced it, going up against Planchet was almost unthinkable. He was a former military man and his family well-loved and respected. New Eden itself was a fortress surrounded by tall walls with massive gates and its people were well-equipped to fend off an attack. Whoever went to war against Adam Planchet would have to be ruthless—a dangerous man skilled in combat and unafraid of death. In light of the potential hazards, there was no need to risk his own neck, McAllister thought wryly, smiling smugly at his own cleverness. It just so happened that he knew the perfect man for the job!

When the two gangsters met for a second time, McAllister's proposition stroked Mitchell's inflated ego. By combining gangs and resources, they could effectively lay siege to New Eden, and, upon certain victory, would share equally in the prize. And best of all, *Field Marshall* Mitchell could raise an army and personally lead them into battle, while *General* McAllister coordinated logistics from the rear, not as glorious a posting as Mitchell's, but nonetheless necessary (and safe). Afterwards, they would divide up the spoils and live like kings with their pick of New Eden's gracious accommodations and resources.

Bull Mitchell agreed to the plan as long as he was free to conscript an army and mete out discipline to the troops as he saw fit. McAllister had no problem with that. He knew full well that his ambitious rival would eventually have to be neutralized, but taking into account the man's reputation as a cold-blooded killer, he would bide his time and choose the exact moment of his death *after* New Eden was theirs.

McAllister smiled—nothing like a good war to keep things interesting! Seated in his office on the second story of the saloon, he pondered some interesting intelligence he'd received earlier in the day from one of his lieutenants who got it from someone with close friends inside New Eden. Word was Planchet had sent his son, William, north for reinforcements at the end of July, but he hadn't been heard from since. This was good news. Perhaps poor old William wouldn't be coming back. According to the source, Planchet more recently sent another group of riders north, this time led by his daughter, Elise, along with several other members of his immediate family. Now that would be some pretty powerful leverage over Planchet if they were somehow intercepted.

Apparently, they were going after some ex-Army commando living up in the wilderness of northern Wyoming, who'd served with Planchet back in the African Campaigns—interesting. He would tell Mitchell to be on the lookout for their return. It would be extremely helpful if they could take a Planchet daughter hostage. Besides, they certainly didn't need any out of town mercenary coming down and meddling in local affairs, and, if Adam Planchet was going to this much trouble to enlist the man's help, they'd better be ready for him.

* * *

NEW EDEN'S WINTER arrived early, as the surrounding oaks, maples, and aspens dropped their remaining leaves and stood stark and bare against the frosty sky. Gone were the smiles and laughter of the people. Gone were the hopes and plans for a peaceful coexistence with the settlement at New Hope. It had become obvious to everyone that the struggling souls there would never make it through a second winter on their meager provisions. With New Hope's patchwork infrastructure held together by a diligent minority, the town simply couldn't support the multitudes who'd migrated there, and each day the living conditions had deteriorated further as fear and desperation increased.

Donovan realized his mistake too late. When the anarchy finally thrust up its ugly head, the disillusioned leader of New Hope's People's Council decided that it was time to flee to New Eden to warn Planchet. He figured that he and his family would be allowed to stay if he revealed McAllister's strategy to them. He'd arrived five days ago. What Donovan shared with them was incomprehensible. New Hope's food supplies had nearly run out. A drifter named McAllister had appointed himself Sheriff, boasting a gang of two hundred toughs to maintain order. All semblance of decency had evaporated. People were forbidden to leave and were being conscripted into some kind of militia run by a vicious street thug named Mitchell. Many attempted to escape, but, with the brutal militia in control, everything was clamped down tight.

* * *

THE SIEGE OF New Eden began without warning. Under cover of darkness a few hundred armed men from McAllister's and Mitchell's combined militia made a show of invading Planchet's lands. The half-hearted attack was a probe to test New Eden's lines and identify the weakest link in its defenses. After this initial strategy proved unfruitful, they became more aggressive. Attacking at night, they succeeded in killing several guards, wounding some others and driving off a portion of the sheep and cattle.

Morale among the settlers at New Eden plummeted as violence engulfed their once peaceful valley, threatening to destroy everything they'd worked so hard for. The mood throughout the community was somber as grieving family members and friends buried their dead and manned the defenses around the clock.

CHAPTER FOURTEEN

MANY SECRETS

JUST BEFORE MIDNIGHT, Amy Planchet slipped out of her room on the third floor of the Great Hall, quietly closing the door behind her. She stood perfectly still, hugging the wall, afraid to breathe, eyes searching the dimly lit corridor in the direction of her father's chambers. It was late and the passageway was empty. She cocked her head and listened, ready to duck back into her room if need be, but all was quiet. Dressed in layers with dark hooded over-cloak and soft boots, she made her way quietly to the back staircase. Wide wooden steps led down past the second floor to the main level. Above the second floor landing, she hesitated in the shadows just outside the throw of light from the wall-mounted oil lamp. Clothed as she was, she couldn't afford to be discovered, especially not tonight. No one moved along the hallway at this hour, and she continued to the main floor below.

The stairs ended in the vast communal kitchen fitted with stainless steel sinks, tile floors and countertops, and lots of cupboards and workspace. All was dark and quiet. She could see the sliver of a new moon peeking through the high bank of windows designed to let in plenty of sunlight during the day. Tonight they were dark sockets framing tiny pinpoints twinkling in the blackness above. She moved down a shadowed hall lined with half a dozen storerooms on either side. She felt her way to the end and stopped before a locked door. Producing a key from her pocket, she inserted it into the lock and turned until she felt a release before twisting the brass knob. The door swung in and she quickly entered the room, immediately re-locking it. She sighed, greatly relieved to have made it this far unseen.

From beneath her cloak she produced an oil lamp, which, when lit, revealed a windowless room lined with floor to ceiling shelves containing row upon row of canned food in glass jars. Moving to the far corner, she reached up with her fingers and pulled a thin hidden latch until she heard a click. Placing the lamp on the floor, she put her shoulder against the heavy shelf and pushed. It swung away easily in spite of its weight, revealing a secret tunnel beyond and cold stone stairs leading down into the pitch black dark. Stepping through the opening, she secured the false shelf behind her, and, with the lamp held aloft, began the steep descent to her rendezvous.

* * *

AMY FIRST VISITED New Hope back in the summer, traveling across the mountain with a group of young volunteers to help build fences and plant a huge kitchen garden. She was stunned at the number of settlers already living there, and more seemed to be arriving constantly, trickling in one or two at a time with an occasional caravan hosting several families in wagons. Witnessing such transience was unnerving; New Eden had always been such a closed, stable enclave.

She was unaccustomed to meeting new people, and at first, felt pressed upon, but soon became enthralled by the idea that here she was an unknown. There was a certain freedom to reinvent oneself in a place where no one knew the intimate details of your life's history. As she grew more familiar with this new sensation, it became exciting to blend in, anonymously observing as the bustling town of more than two thousand souls expanded and took shape.

On her third visit she met Daniel. He was a new arrival, just turned seventeen, tall and slender with dark brown curls and twinkling eyes. The attraction was immediate and intense. She returned as often as she could after that. Once or twice a week she would arrive and break away from her group as soon as possible. There was always adult supervision to get around, usually one or two chaperones looking after the rest, but, as a Planchet, she was afforded a longer leash than the others and always managed to finagle her way out of the task at hand to wander off and seek him out. Once she found Daniel, they would head into the woods or ride up in the hills where they could be alone.

They talked about everything and enjoyed simply being in each other's company. He was from the Pacific coast and had grown up with his uncle Jeb, traveling up and down between what used to be Canada and Mexico ever since he could remember. He spoke of wild towns and dangerous times, of fighting off gangs of bandits, and of pirates in sailing ships raiding up and down the coast, stealing food and kidnapping women they'd take back to their offshore hideouts to keep as slaves! Daniel's people made their living scavenging from abandoned cities overgrown with stunted trees and rodents the size of small dogs. Whatever booty they found they'd barter to the gypsy traders whose caravans came through periodically on their way to the next village or settlement.

Amy was captivated by his stories. Her life, in comparison, was dull—at least since coming to New Eden, and that's all she could really remember. Like her, Daniel had no recollection of his biological mother or father, having been raised by his uncle Jeb since before he could talk. Jeb risked everything to cross the desert with his family to join New Eden. He said that New Eden was famous on the coast where people always talked about what a paradise it was. Amy was disappointed and angry that Father had turned Daniel's family away.

Soon the two adopted orphans fell into a comfortable cadence of their own, holding hands as they walked and shared their thoughts and dreams. One afternoon, during their time together, Daniel suddenly turned and kissed her on the mouth. It was warm and wet and probably the most magical experience of Amy's young life! Her heart was beating so hard that she thought it would jump from her chest. At fourteen, her physiology was awakening as she rapidly underwent that wondrous and confusing transformation from tom-girlishness to young womanhood. Her crush on Daniel was the first time she'd fallen for anyone, the first time she was even interested. Back home, as a royal member of the Planchet dynasty, she held herself aloof, never letting down her guard. Her peers believed she was selfish and spoiled, but here was someone with whom she could be her *other self* and make a clean break from old patterns and ways of being.

Before long, the goodness at New Hope began to unravel, and its relationship with New Eden became severely strained. Some very bad apples drifted into town and awful things started happening. People started getting hurt and worse, and it was no longer safe to travel back and forth.

From some of the disturbing news Daniel shared, Amy became concerned for his safety. She wanted to protect him somehow, to be with him, and wished he could come stay at New Eden, but it was impossible. Thus far, she had managed to keep their relationship secret and there was no way to approach Father about it—especially now that he was preoccupied with the growing threat from New Hope. He had wanted to send her north with Elise, but Amy begged him to let her stay and keep him company. She implored him, swearing that she didn't feel safe away from him and, of course, Planchet granted her wish, unable to deny his youngest daughter any happiness.

When all visits between the two settlements formally ceased, Amy was determined to figure out a way to maintain her relationship with Daniel. She fantasized about the two of them running away together and living in one of the settlements he spoke about out on the coast. Even getting messages back and forth became problematic. After three weeks of silence, she finally received word that he would wait for her outside the perimeter wall every night after midnight in a nearby glade they both knew about. Her spirits soared but crashed immediately afterward when she realized that, under the present circumstances, meeting him was impossible. The gates were locked and closely guarded, especially after dark. The newly organized defense force was on the lookout for anything unusual night and day. With New Eden officially locked down and Daniel waiting in the woods, Amy became desperate.

Just when she was about to give up hope of ever seeing him again, the solution came in a flash of pure genius: she could use *the tunnel!* There were many tunnels connecting sites and buildings on the land and commonly used on a daily basis, but this one was different. Amy recalled a time when she was younger, only ten or eleven, when Father took the entire family on a dark journey through a secret passageway to a hidden cave outside the perimeter wall! He said that only the immediate family knew about it and it was only to be used in times of dire emergency. Well, she reasoned, this was her emergency and, though she hadn't been back to that tunnel since, she remembered that the entrance was somewhere just off the back of the kitchen at the end of a door-lined hall.

When she finally met Daniel two nights later, they embraced and held each other for the longest time. She was trembling, half from fear of discovery and the joy of being together. She sat behind him on his horse, and they rode off into the hills where they talked about a future far away where they would always be together. After that first secret meeting, Amy snuck out every night she could to be with him. She always made it back by dawn, and no one the wiser, but the late nights began to take their toll, both mentally and physically. She started sleeping in until noon, causing Father to worry and inquire about her health. She explained that she was having trouble sleeping and wasn't feeling up to par. Planchet was concerned but had his hands full dealing with the siege and didn't investigate further, an oversight he would live to regret.

* * *

THE COUPLE KISSED their goodbyes and Amy disappeared in the direction of the ravine. Daniel waited until he could no longer see her and turned his horse towards home. He was thankful for the fresh snowfall that would soon wipe out all evidence of his mount's hoof prints. The half moon offered some visual assistance along the trail, but the shadows were very dark and Daniel felt a shiver run down his spine as if he were being watched. Nudging his horse's flanks, the gelding perked up, glad to finally be on his way back to the relative warmth of the stables.

In the shadows near a snow covered tree, a cloaked man made sure Daniel was away before walking his horse out to Amy's trail. He followed her footsteps between two evergreens and came to the entrance to the cave. Lighting a lantern, he stooped and stepped inside. It opened up into a small chamber, and he could make out the petite boot prints leading back thirty feet to a rock face where a barely perceptible line in the stone traced the opening of a doorway that was secured from within. Checking the area more thoroughly, the man returned to his horse, extinguished the lantern and rode off. He smirked, feeling very important and could only imagine the reward he would receive once he reported this to the Boss! *I'll probably be promoted!* he thought giddily, *and then I'll have privileges!* He referred of course to the prostitutes who now worked for McAllister. He didn't notice the cold wind buffet him as he rode on with a big smile. He dug his heels in, and the horse bolted forward. "C'mon you old nag!" he barked, slapping her with the reigns. He was in a hurry to get back!

* * *

THE FOLLOWING EVENING, as Daniel saddled his horse for the ride over to New Eden to see Amy, he thought he heard something unusual and froze, squinting into the darkness beyond the corral. *Is someone there?* he questioned silently. He waited, counting the seconds while barely breathing but heard and saw nothing. *Getting jumpy, I guess.* He shook it off and mounted up, heading for his rendezvous. Everyday, it was becoming more difficult to sneak out of New Hope. The town's new militia was on the lookout for individuals or families attempting to leave. If they caught you, it was a beating and maybe worse. All males old enough to fight were being pressed into service. Apparently, McAllister expected every able-bodied citizen to contribute to the siege of New Eden.

I never signed on for this crap, he fumed, trying to figure a way out of the worsening situation. His uncle Jeb recently confided that he now regretted ever leaving old California and wished to go back. Daniel agreed about the leaving, but if he hadn't come here, he never would have met his Amy. He was convinced that they were meant to be together, and he was determined to make that happen. He'd be damned if he was going to let anyone, self-appointed dictator or not, screw up his life! A sharp gust ambushed him and tried to rip his hat from his head. Daniel just hunkered down and rode on with a renewed purpose, oblivious of the distant shapes keeping pace with him on his back trail.

* * *

DOWN, DOWN, DOWN she went, carefully following the wide rock steps, lamplight flickering off gleaming walls, winding through tunnels of stone and earthworks fortified with heavy timbers. Holding an oil lantern, Amy made her way gingerly across a stone bridge spanning a gurgling subterranean stream. From the hidden door in the kitchen storeroom, the secret passageway led straight through the heart of New Eden's fertile valley, twisting and turning for nearly half a mile before passing beneath the perimeter wall and ending in a small cave near the bottom of an overgrown ravine.

Before emerging from the thick bushes surrounding the cave entrance, she paused to extinguish the lamp. Above her, in the winter sky, a three-quarter moon illuminated the path through the trees. Up ahead, a mounted rider with a spare horse waited in the shadow of a bare, sprawling oak. Rounding a bend in the trail, Amy sounded her best nighthawk impression. When Daniel failed to answer, she hesitated and repeated the call. She could distinguish a horse and rider on the hill ahead and was certain she should be able to hear his reply from here. Suddenly, there was movement from all sides as the night came alive around her. Cloaked shapes detached from the trees, blocking her advance and cutting off her escape!

* * *

BULL MITCHELL LED the midnight charge from the tunnel, sweeping quickly through the Great Hall, club in one hand, killing knife in the other. When they reached the third level, Adam Planchet was dozing in his study, a book of poetry in his hand. Bull Mitchell burst into the room with a dozen of his men, and Planchet instinctively reached beneath his chair to pull a .45 from a hidden holster, firing rapidly into the mob, killing three and wounding four others before being overwhelmed and wrestled to the floor. During the melee, he suffered a savage puncture wound to the chest. Pinned face down against the desktop, he bled profusely, drenching his books and papers with the crimson flow.

When Frank McAllister strode triumphantly into the room a minute later, he saw the blood and became enraged, demanding to know who was responsible when his specific orders were to take Planchet *alive and unharmed!* When no one spoke up, he glanced at Mitchell and knew from his smug expression that the psycho-killer had done it, but there was nothing McAllister could do about it now. Mitchell's reward was coming—all in due time. As the killer left the room to continue the assault on the rest of New Eden, Planchet was carried to a leather sofa where his wound was inspected and the worst realized.

Lying on his back, paralyzed from Mitchell's blade that had severed his spinal cord, Adam Planchet knew that it was over. He could feel himself fading as the room became dim, and McAllister's words wouldn't register in his brain. He pondered his life and wondered what death was going to be like. He didn't fear it. Arianne had gone on before and was waiting for him there; he was sure. He only regretted not being able to better protect his family and wished they were here with him now.

Looking down at the defeated Planchet, McAllister gloated in victory and leaned over the dying man to clarify just how it was that he was able to take his stronghold so easily. He explained that his precious little Amy was the reason he was dying and told him not to worry because McAllister had plans for his youngest daughter. Mercifully, Planchet wasn't able to hear any of the twisted details pouring from McAllister's lips. He was already gone.

* * *

DOWN THE HILL in New Eden's community housing complex, the sleeping inhabitants were quickly overwhelmed by the surprise attack from within and, before anyone could mount a counter attack, it was over. The lucky ones managed to flee under cover of darkness, escaping into the frigid night over the walls. Those who resisted paid dearly.

In his family's unit on the second floor, Cal Sanders woke suddenly out of a deep sleep. He lay still in the dark listening to the steady breathing of his wife, Suzanne, and quietly got up to check on the kids. Their nine-year-old twin girls, Ayla and Arin, were down the hall in their room, and their teenaged son, Zeke, was up in the loft. The apartment was quiet, but Cal thought he heard some unusual noises outside. Something didn't *seem* right about it, and he pulled back the curtains to peer out the window and gasped! Multiple dark shapes moved around the perimeter of the building and he heard stealthy footsteps and men's low voices down below! The sounds and shadows drew closer, and suddenly he heard a crash as a door caved in and muffled screams and yells drifted in and out of the commotion coming from the building next door!

As quietly as possible, he gathered up his family and they pulled on clothes, boots, and parkas and moved down the back stairway headed for the basement tunnel level. Cal and Zeke carried the twins, and Suzanne brought bread, a lantern, and their pistol. They barely made it to the basement tunnel entrance as doors leading to the upstairs housing units were kicked in and the sounds of battle spread throughout the complex all around them.

Once in the tunnel, they made their way steadily downhill towards the workshop area, arriving with hearts pounding, terrified of being discovered. Cautiously climbing the stairs to the first-floor of the darkened workshop, they looked through the windows up the hill and witnessed total pandemonium taking place. What appeared to be an army of hostile men with torches stood over small groupings of scantily-dressed settlers cowering in the snow. Over the din of gunfire and screaming, children cried out in fear as others begged for mercy.

Cal instantly realized that New Eden had somehow been overrun by New Hope's militia, and all that mattered now was that he get his family to safety. In the early light of the coming dawn they slipped out the side door of the workshop and across the adjacent field to the base of the twelve-foot perimeter wall. Standing on a small wooden bench, Cal interlaced the fingers of both hands and bent down as Zeke stepped into them, wearing a rope they'd grabbed from the shop tied around his waist. Rising up, Cal tossed Zeke to the top of the wall where he grabbed on and pulled himself up to straddle it. Suzanne was next, one hand steadied against the wall, feet in Cal's hands, and he lifted her up until Zeke caught hold of his mother's outstretched hands and lifted her up. From there Zeke doubled the rope around his mother's waist, and, with Cal counterbalancing both of them with the taut rope tied around his own waist, lowered her to the ground on the outside. One-by-one the twins were hoisted up and over the wall and down to their mother safely on the outside. As Cal prepared to scale the wall himself, half a dozen men on horseback came charging down the hill and raced across the field towards him, firing weapons and commanding him to surrender. "Go now, Zeke, and guide them to Southland's ranch; I'll meet up with you there when I can! NOW GO!" He yelled at his hesitant son, seeing the fear in his boy's eyes, but finally Zeke turned and jumped to join the others.

As Cal tore the rope from his waist, Zeke pulled it up and over just as the throng converged on his father. They leapt from their mounts, beating him down with clubs and cruel lengths of cable or chain. Afterwards, they made a feeble attempt to scale the wall, but, without rope or ladder, soon gave up. Having spent the last five hours out in the frigid arctic wind waiting for the gates to be opened from within, they quickly forgot trying to pursue the escapees and galloped back up to the housing area to claim their fair share of the spoils.

* * *

WHEN THE MILITIA broke down her door, Sasha Stolze was naked in bed with her mate, both of them sound asleep after a sensual evening of lovemaking. When Henry jumped up to see about the commotion, he was shotgunned nearly in half before her eyes. With her mind reeling from shock, she watched events unfold in slow motion, as if she were outside her own body. She saw herself scramble to her work table and grasp the nine inch, razor-sharp blade she used for cutting out patterns from deerskins. As the first man reached her, she plunged it into his neck with incredible force, and he screamed, clutching his torn throat as streams of crimson blood shot far across the room, spray painting the ceiling and walls in red death. Everyone froze as the crazed woman wailed in a high-pitched tirade and slashed at them, slicing two arms and a face with the deadly knife as they stood transfixed by her spectacle. Finally, a man picked up a nearby chair and smashed it over her head, and she went down as the mob swarmed her, dragging her half unconscious form to the still warm bed to wreak their terrible vengeance upon her.

CHAPTER FIFTEEN

HOMECOMING

AT FOUR HOURS past sunset, Hunter and Elise rode on by starlight. They were close now, too close to stop and rest, their destination near enough to press on through the few remaining miles. Not far ahead, on the eastern approach road, was the old railroad bridge leading to Elise's valley and New Eden's east gate. In the cold November night, crystalline particles of powdery snow swirled about the legs of their beleaguered mounts as they traced a faint trail beside a frozen stream. With the enemy so close, they moved forward slowly, weapons ready, keeping to the shadows of the snow-covered junipers bordering the creek. Any moment they expected a deadly ambush, but so far all was quiet—unnaturally so.

Stretched out behind them were hundreds of miles of rugged wilderness filled with endless ridges, sweeping valleys and plateaus, steep, forested mountains, unbridled rivers, violent storms, and many unexpected dangers as they traveled ever south southeast towards their journey's end.

Despite the biting wind, Hunter rode with the long flaps of his thick sheepskin cap rolled up, preferring to suffer cold ears than miss an audible clue that could save them from walking headlong into disaster. He halted his mare beside a snow-draped tree and swept the surrounding terrain with steel eyes. He listened intently beyond the sound of the wind through the boughs and the faint gurgle of water rushing beneath the nearby scalloped ice.

At the pause, Elise slipped from her saddle and moved to attend to the comfort of the three remaining weatherworn animals in her charge. Approaching the nearest, she cupped her hands around its face and blew warm, soothing air onto its nose and mouth to melt the icicles dangling from its chin. Speaking soft words of encouragement, she withdrew a slice of frozen apple from deep within her coat and offered the welcomed treat before moving on to her next tired, but spirited, equine friend.

As she calmed them with her quiet voice, Elise fought to gain control of her own pendulous emotions, wavering between hope and a gnawing fear of what she might discover in the morning's uncompromising light. She knew that, within a few short hours, her speculation and anticipation would dissolve in the reality of what had actually happened at New Eden since she'd fled in the dark of night more than four and a half months earlier. Returning to her saddle, she did her best to dispel the worry from her mind, but the foreboding would not completely fade.

Their journey from Hunter's cave had been marked by signs and the certain involvement of an unseen hand. Immediately after finding William alive and miraculously on the mend, they struck out for New Eden with a renewed sense of urgency, driving onward through the remaining butte country of southern Wyoming and into the rugged lands of northwestern Colorado. It was there, within a week's ride of New Eden's outer borders, that disaster had struck—an epic blizzard with sub-zero temperatures forced them to scramble for cover and fight to stay alive. When the skies finally cleared, they discovered that one of their pack animals had drowned after stumbling blindly into a steep creek bed during the whiteout.

Dividing their supplies among the four remaining animals, they found it slow going through deep drifts under increased burdens. For the better part of a week, immediately following the storm, Hunter led the way on foot, using his staff and a pair of sturdy snowshoes to break trail for the others. Elise donned a pair of them as well, leading the horses through on foot more often than not. Each mile was hard won, and the work long and strenuous, but the troupe pressed on at a grueling pace, it being imperative that they reach New Eden as soon as possible.

A few days later, as the skies finally cleared and the sun brought back hope, a bitter cold snap blanketed the region in a frigid shroud. With temperatures dropping into the minus forties and the wind chill factor even lower, they all suffered greatly, waiting it out through two bitter-cold weeks of high winds, when numbness and frostbite crept into hands and feet, and hypothermia threatened to chill them to their very cores.

In an effort to save the horses, they covered them in sheepskins, their legs wrapped in furs. Elise kept their spirits up, always beside them, encouraging the animals with soothing words to give them hope. When they could finally continue, she monitored them closely, making sure none broke a sweat, as frozen perspiration would quickly condemn them to a desolate grave beneath the pale, indifferent veil of ice and snow.

Frigid days and nights blended into one continuous stream of misery as each new dawn brought increased challenges to their survival. When November arrived, a second great blizzard swept in suddenly, hammering the heroic party into submission as they made a desperate stand in a shallow rock overhang ringed by cedars. During the height of the storm, it was so incredibly cold that their beleaguered fire would barely radiate any heat at all, and Hunter worked valiantly through the night to save his company from certain extinction.

The following day, with skies again clear, he led them out across the frozen surface of a broad river covered in three-foot scalloped snowdrifts, pockmarked with slippery bare spots where the buffeting wind had swept the ice clean. Nearing the far shore, Hunter dismounted to adjust a frozen stirrup while Elise continued on, taking the lead. As her horse stepped forward, she felt his feet begin to slip and she shifted her weight to compensate, but the young gelding lost his footing, back legs splayed, and he came down hard on his rump, crashing through a section of thin ice made weak by a half-submerged tree hidden just beneath the surface!

Hunter sensed the commotion and looked up just in time to witness the fall. He grabbed his braided lariat and, with two quick turns around the saddle horn, ran towards Elise who was endeavoring to stay aboard her foundering horse and hold her head above the frigid waters.

He called to her as the struggling animal lost its battle against the strong current and disappeared beneath the ice. Hunter's lasso splashed over Elise's head as she went down with arms outstretched, the current tugging on her water-logged sheepskins. As the river enveloped her head, she managed to slip the noose under her armpits and hold on, spinning as the frigid water sent her mind and body into shock.

Hunter braced his legs and hauled on the line, holding it taut against the sloping edge of the ice. He pulled with all his might and managed to reel in a foot at a time. It seemed like forever before Elise's head and shoulders broke the plane of the water and he was shocked to see her limp body dangling at the end of the rope! Leaning down, he grabbed her sodden figure and, with a mighty effort, dragged her onto the snow and away from the opening. He instantly checked for a pulse and found none! Her face was blue and she was not breathing.

He immediately began to breathe for her, getting a few breaths into her before switching to chest compressions. He worked fast, switching back and forth between breaths and compressions until she began to cough and choke. Rolling her onto her side, he allowed the water to drain from her lungs, and, as the pink slowly seeped back into her cheeks, her eyes fluttered, and relief washed over him. Checking again, he found a weak pulse and felt her shallow breath on his cheek but could see that she wasn't fully conscious.

Must get her out of the wind and raise her core temperature! She was suffering from hypothermia and was in imminent danger of losing her life. Quickly pulling Elise out of her wet clothes, he wrapped her up in his parka and placed her over his horse, securing her there with his lariat before leading the animals the rest of the way across the river and into the shelter of the trees along the opposite bank. Approaching the shore, he spotted an overhang where the current had undermined a high bank causing several evergreens to topple over, offering a shelter of sorts.

He huddled the animals in close and laid Elise down out of the wind, again checking her pulse and breathing. She was barely holding on. He worked feverishly to get a fire going as snow began to fall. Adding dry tinder to the tiny flame, a grave Hunter raced against time to save her life.

Elise was trapped in a terrible nightmare, lost in a blizzard and freezing to death. She was bare, and the cold was overwhelming. In all her winters, she'd never experienced such a numbing storm as this. She shuddered as a severe gust snatched her up, swirling her away into the sky. She could feel herself freeze, eyes glaze over with ice, suspended in the terrible cold, sailing through the snow-filled atmosphere, twirling around and around like a leaf blown about on the wind.

Buried beneath layers of warm sheepskins and soft furs, Elise moaned and shivered violently, teeth chattering uncontrollably in the blustery night. Her core temperature dipped dangerously low, and her mind slipped into a near-comatose state. When she wouldn't regain consciousness, Hunter did what was necessary to save her life. Removing his clothing, he slipped in beside her, skin-to-skin beneath the furs. Warming her, he willed her to live, vigorously rubbing her chilled appendages with his hands until the warmth and color returned, and then spooned her smaller body with his own. In her dream state, Elise was vaguely aware of a warm, glowing presence enveloping her, keeping her from slipping down into the abyss.

Hunter shared his life-giving heat with Elise throughout the long night, refusing to allow her to succumb, persisting until morning finally dawned and she lay still, warm, and alive. She awoke twenty-four hours later, weak from hunger, but, over the next few days, recovered without permanent damage beyond the vague memory of a dark visitation in the frigid night by the Reaper who was again thwarted by one stronger and more skilled than he.

While Elise regained her strength, Hunter cared for their steadfast animals who had also suffered greatly from the cold. He was able to keep them alive and dry, and, when the weather finally broke, all were eager to return to the trail and finish the few remaining miles of their journey.

* * *

ON NEW EDEN'S eastern border, Hunter and Elise carefully picked their way across the starlit, snow-blanketed meadow, coming to a halt at the edge of a hard-packed road running alongside a frozen stream. Hunter referred to William's map in his head and consulted briefly with Elise before turning right onto the eastern approach road. The night was dark and very cold, with the rising moon not yet visible in the clear, star-filled sky above. The travel-hardened companions walked shoulder-to-shoulder, mounts to the outside, lone pack horse to the rear, so that, at first glance, anyone observing their passage would be less likely to perceive a human presence.

Approaching a small wood, Hunter sensed something out of the ordinary and touched Elise lightly on the arm signaling a halt. Without warning, a great snowy owl swooped out of the blackness just ahead, a struggling hare gripped tightly in its talons. Passing within inches of their position, the terrified prey splattered the snow-covered road with dark drops of warm, red blood before vanishing unwillingly into the night!

Processing what she had just witnessed, Elise was reminded of the frailty of existence, again pondering the inescapable natural process in which all living beings were involved from birth to certain future death. Age-old questions stirred up a philosophical turmoil that had plagued her since childhood: *Why must some creatures die that others might live? And where was the justice in all of this chaos?* She logically recognized the need to feed but had always wished somehow for a gentler solution.

The wind picked up, and a pale three-quarter moon peered warily above the jagged skyline to the east. In the increased light, Hunter knelt on one knee on the road, carefully scanning the surrounding terrain through the scope of his bow. Up ahead, he spotted an old farmhouse, its yard choked with evergreens, half-seen, half-deduced from the deep shadows cast there by the moon.

From the darkness close by, an owl called out, answered by its mate somewhere further ahead. Hunter recognized the pretense at once: someone *posing* as an owl was signaling a comrade. He made an adjustment toward the sound and took careful aim near the base of a small tree. Instantly, Elise was at his side, silent as a shadow, gently but firmly pressing down on his elbow. With a questioning glance, he eased off the trigger and watched as she cupped ungloved hands to her mouth and called out in her own version of the night hunter's haunting "*Whoo—Whooo.*" A swift response echoed from across the darkened field.

Beneath the pastel moon, Hunter witnessed the excitement build on Elise's oval face as she carefully repeated her call, adding a low trill at the end. The unexpected response came immediately in the form of a high-pitched yipping of a lone coyote, soon to be joined by several others scattered throughout the icy foothills. With heart pounding, Elise began rapidly striking flint and steel, and Hunter watched as responding sparks flashed from several nearby locations. Rising from the frozen roadway, an elated Elise, with green eyes sparkling, beamed a huge smile at Hunter and handed him her reigns before joyfully dashing off towards the house.

CHAPTER SIXTEEN

WITHOUT HONOR

THE WINTER CHILL permeated New Eden's Great Hall, seeping through its thick, stone-faced walls despite their robust construction. The once bright and busy meeting place where community members would gather to relax and spend their downtime playing games, enjoying music, or visiting with friends, now lay dark and empty, a silent monument to the present miserable state of affairs. Throughout the sprawling, three-story structure, the cold was all-pervading. With four months of serious winter still ahead, the firewood supplies had already dwindled dangerously low, and most of the building was without power or water. To make matters worse, Planchet's sophisticated geothermal energy system that provided steam heat for the radiators had been sabotaged, and the daytime indoor temperatures barely rose above forty degrees Fahrenheit, dipping perilously lower at night.

In the ten days since the takeover, chaos had reigned supreme over New Eden. McAllister and Mitchell wasted no time in commencing their battle for ultimate control. Though agreeing to work together during the siege, they were still bitter rivals at heart, with each man's eyes fixed upon the empty throne so tragically relinquished by Adam Planchet. Immediately following the overthrow, discipline collapsed as rival gang members and militia conscripts pillaged storerooms and fought over the choicest living quarters, providing an opportunity for most of New Eden's residents to escape during the mass confusion. When the victorious celebrants discovered the barrels in the wine cellar, all hell broke loose among them as drunken brawls and killings quickly spread throughout the complex.

As the violence escalated, McAllister found his forces quickly outnumbered, and he retreated to the Great Hall with fifty of his loyal followers, barricading themselves inside the building. Sequestered there within Planchet's final line of defense, they successfully fought off several half-hearted assaults from Mitchell's forces, who, after a few casualties, decided that it was better to move back down the hill below the parapet wall to the community housing complex where there was still plenty of food, drink, and creature comforts left behind by the fleeing residents.

While McAllister commanded the hilltop and the Great Hall, Mitchell's much larger force controlled everything below the parapet wall, including the housing area, barns, stables, sheds, shops, greenhouses, and outbuildings. Everything located between the two barrier walls, or over ninety-five percent of New Eden, was now under Bull Mitchell's direct control, condemning McAllister and his faithful to virtual imprisonment within the confines of the Great Hall.

Many from New Hope, who were either conscripted into the militia or had joined the siege with high hopes of plundering the bounty at New Eden, now realized that this was most likely not going to play out to their advantage. In two's and three's, they began quietly slipping away in the dead of night with what little supplies they could manage. With his rag-tag army shrinking, Mitchell put out word that anyone caught deserting would be hung or worse. As the days passed, a growing number of bodies appeared swinging from frozen tree limbs on the end of a noose.

Immediately following the assault, starving refugees from the now-defunct community at New Hope had poured through the gates and ravaged the barns and storerooms. Savage fighting broke out over precious food stores and other valuable supplies before Mitchell heard of it and arrived with a cadre of bodyguards to personally put down the revolt, killing several looters and mercilessly driving the remaining pitiful creatures back out into the heartless cold.

After the overthrow, New Eden's day-to-day operations ground to a halt until Mitchell rounded up a couple of dozen survivors, forcing them to do the cooking and cleaning, chop wood, feed the livestock, and attend the greenhouses. Nearly two hundred community members had managed to escape by fleeing into the surrounding hills and forests. Others died defending their homes and lay stacked in an unheated shed like so many sticks of firewood alongside their dead militia counterparts. The remnants trapped within New Eden's walls were forced to fully cooperate with their brutal conquerors or face the excruciating consequences.

* * *

HIGH ABOVE THE silent Great Hall, Frank McAllister commandeered the Planchet family living quarters for himself, surrounded in adjacent rooms by a handful of loyalists who still believed they would eventually beat out Mitchell and win the day. McAllister was inclined to a more realistic view of current events. He knew that his dream of governing New Eden was over, successfully thwarted by Big Bull Mitchell who would never allow him or his men to leave New Eden alive. His one trump card, according to his twisted logic, was little Amy Planchet, who had been confined to her room since the takeover where she refused to talk, eat, or cooperate in any way.

He sat at the large mahogany desk in the book-lined study, reading Adam Planchet's most recent journal entry. Dressed in fine buckskins, fleece-lined moccasins, and wrapped in a long, rabbit-fur coat to ward off the cold, the wannabe commander of New Eden paused, lifting a green ceramic mug to his lips for a soothing drink of hot herbal tea sweetened with honey. Looking around the room at all of the books, it was comforting to know that, for the time being anyway, they were his to read, burn, or do with as he wished.

He barked an order to the guards stationed just outside his door, and a minute later they entered with a shackled girl between them, hands bound behind her back, red hair disheveled, dark shadows under strikingly blue eyes, her proud face glowering at him in utter disdain. The defiant fourteen-year-old bore scant resemblance to the happy, care-free Amy Planchet of the former New Eden. He dismissed the guards and stood up, walking around the desk to draw close to the silent girl who shrank from his presence. He reached out and placed his hand on her slightly bruised shoulder and she violently shook him off.

"Touch me again and you're dead!" Her eyes bore into him like branding irons.

McAllister smiled and chuckled, "Big words for such a little girl, don't you agree?"

"You won't be laughing when Hunter gets here!" She hissed the words, eyes glaring at him, nostrils flaring in anger.

McAllister slapped her hard across the face and grabbed her roughly by the arms. He'd heard it all before. *Hunter this, Hunter that!* He struggled to hold her, leaning in for a kiss, but she spat in his eye and tried to knee him in the groin! Flashing a strained smile, he wrestled her over to the leather couch and pushed her down onto her belly. Holding her there with a knee in the small of her back, he leaned over, whispering into her ear, "Where's your big hero now, little *traitor*, little *father betrayer?"*

She screamed a string of unintelligible obscenities, but he just laughed, mocking her. With her mind and soul in turmoil, Amy resisted but was again easily overpowered. As she writhed defiantly beneath him on the couch, McAllister turned smiling and reached for his well-used switch.

Two hours later he sat alone at Planchet's desk mulling things over, unsure of what to do next. If he stayed here, trapped inside the Great Hall, the food and other supplies would eventually run out, and fighting would break out among his men. Hell, they might even mutiny and try to ransom him off to Mitchell, or when all else failed, turn to cannibalism!

And what if this Hunter person actually does show up to take New Eden back, what then? All he'd heard so far was how tough the man was, a mighty warrior, professional, unbeatable. It didn't matter now. *Let him come. Mitchell will fight Hunter, and Mitchell will die! Or maybe they'll both die! Yes, that would be better!* His face flashed a maniacal smile, and he chortled to himself at the thought of both of them dead and out of the way!

As the dreary days passed, McAllister's squirming brain tried in vain to imagine a way out of his present conundrum. Leaving was impossible. Mitchell had them surrounded. Even the tunnels were guarded. He needed leverage, some type of advantage! He'd spent the last of the vodka bribing people to take part in the siege, so it was gone. Everything he'd established at New Hope had turned to crap and now this! His grand scheme to rule New Eden shot down by Bull Mitchell, a street thug he'd hoped would be killed or at least injured in the takeover, but no! The bastard came through unscathed and even more empowered by the easy victory over Planchet! McAllister looked around at the fine woodwork and leather furniture. He'd hoped to reign here for a very long time. It was much better here than he had imagined. Now he would probably die here trapped in this stinking room!

* * *

ON THE NIGHT of Planchet's murder, a group of thirty-seven community members, men, women, and children, retreated to the Great Hall in the confusion following the overthrow and barricaded themselves high in the west wing behind strong oak doors with iron hinges. Their hiding place was discovered two days later as McAllister's men rummaged through the building looking for supplies. McAllister ordered the doors brought down, but after four hours of battering and hammering away, he realized it was a futile task; they were ridiculously overbuilt like everything else Planchet had made. Unsure of what was hidden behind them, McAllister posted guards and turned his attention to his more immediate problems.

Safe behind the strong locked doors, Jake Stein, Sam Curry, and a dozen other men and women immediately took it upon themselves to organize a resistance movement from inside New Eden's borders! Trapped behind enemy lines and cut off from their fellow prisoners down below in Mitchell's camp, they needed intel and a way to navigate without being discovered. From their windows on the third floor atop the hill, they could see out over most of New Eden and posted lookouts there to report on all enemy and other activity. A meeting was called and duties assigned to everyone in the west wing, down to the youngsters who could help look after the three toddlers.

Sam Curry understood New Eden's physical design better than anyone. He'd known Adam Planchet the longest, joining the community at its very inception. As well as being their blacksmith, he was New Eden's physical plant engineer and knew the ducts, access shafts, ventilation systems, tunnels, and passageways like the back of his hand. His twin seventeen-year-old sons, Donnie and Sam, Jr. were probably as well acquainted with the place as he was, having spent many hundreds of hours with him as he worked on New Eden's various systems throughout the years. Sam, Jr.

was present and accounted for, but Donnie had fled to the outside with the rest of the community and was out there somewhere, probably trying to figure out how to rescue or get word to them.

Jake Stein had been a writer before the End War and was an avid lifelong reader. He understood how things worked and what to do in all kinds of situations because he'd read so many stories and books. Solutions to things just came naturally to him.

The resistance leaders met and talked over their situation and decided that those who successfully fled to the outside would definitely organize a counter attack. What they needed more than anything right now was intelligence about the position and strength of the enemy and knowledge of where their own people were being held. If the west wing group could gather that data and get it to the outside, the chances of any counter attack being successful were much higher. Leadership called a general meeting to discuss their strategy.

"We can use the ventilation ducts to move around the building." Sam Curry looked at the crowd seated around the big room before the large fireplace. "We need some smallish, slender spies who can be very quiet to move around the building and observe enemy activity throughout the Great Hall."

"I'll do it!" A skinny twelve-year-old boy name Noah volunteered.

"Me too!" The short-for-her-age fourteen-year-old, Quince quipped, pulling her long hair back into a ponytail.

All told, seven young people, some as young as nine, agreed to play hide and seek in the ductwork throughout the building, gathering data through the registers and reporting on enemy movements, their sleeping locations, organizational headquarters, guard posts, and schedules. They would also listen in on conversations to find out as much as possible about the enemy's plans.

"We're also going to need someone to go outside the building and get word to those prisoners we see doing the chores down at the barns and outbuildings on the lower portion of the land." Jake Stein waited, looking for volunteers.

Sam, Jr. and a boy named Zed agreed to slip out the window after dark and shimmy down a drainpipe to the ground. From there, they would make their way over the parapet wall and down to the barns to wait until dawn when the prisoners arrived to care for the livestock.

"Excellent, now let's get busy and discover everything we can about the enemy and our friends down below!"

* * *

ON THE SIXTH day after the fall of New Eden, Robert Planchet received unexpected good news. Eight people who managed to evade capture by hiding out in the tunnels beneath the complex escaped to safe houses in the outlying territory, recounting chilling tales of violence and division among their enemies. Sam Curry, Jr. and Zed had succeeded in sneaking out a window on the third floor of the west wing and hid out in fields and barns speaking with prisoners and observing Mitchell's camp for two days through binoculars. They'd made their way across the railroad bridge at night to deliver a thorough report of their findings.

Robert was encouraged by these reports and especially excited about the apparent lack of night guards on the perimeter wall. The lookout towers were still manned during the day, but, during the frigid nights, with no way to see anything down below in the dark, those posted there mostly just tried to stay warm and out of the wind.

With the return of Elise with Hunter, a plan to retake New Eden was rapidly devised, and Donnie and Sam, Jr. volunteered to return over the wall to get word to those on the inside to be ready to do their part when the time came. In the dead of night, they slipped back over the perimeter wall next to the orchards and split up, one heading toward the west wing and the other to the big hay barn.

* * *

FRANK MCALLISTER WOKE to a knock on his door. It was late, and he was not happy being roused out of bed at such an hour.

"What is it?" he barked, opening the door and squinting from the lamplight held by his top lieutenant.

"Sorry to disturb you, General, but one of the men has something to tell you that I think you'll want to hear." He smiled a crooked smile, showing broken teeth and a few gaps where teeth should have been. The man was ushered in, and McAllister pressed him to speak.

"What's so important?"

"Sir, I was passing beneath a ceiling register on level two of the west wing a few minutes ago and heard voices." He stopped, looking uncomfortable.

McAllister looked at him skeptically, "And...."

"And there weren't nobody around."

He started to get angry, certain that this buffoon was probably drunk or just imagining things.

"They was talking about us." He stopped again, looking sheepish.

"So, what were these voices saying about us?"

The fellow relaxed a bit and started in from memory, "There are a total of forty eight enemy billeted here in the Great Hall. The leader, named McAllister, is using the Planchet family chambers for his headquarters and is holding Amy prisoner in her room..."

"Stop!" McAllister was suddenly very interested. "You will take me to this register at once!"

"Yes sir."

When McAllister got there, he found a ladder propped against the wall, and he climbed up close to the register while the upstairs meeting was still in progress. As soon as he recognized the nature of the presentation, he dismissed his men out of earshot and sat spellbound, listening to the details of Robert Planchet's plan to retake New Eden, assisted by none other than the mysterious Hunter who had recently arrived from the north with Elise Planchet! The speaker went on to discuss the timetable and exact sequence of events scheduled to take place in the early morning hours just two days away! He sat mesmerized until the meeting dispersed.

Before leaving the site, he ordered his men off the second floor and away from that register. He alone must have the secret knowledge of what was about to happen! As he strode back to his chambers, McAllister's head spun with the implications of what he'd heard. Somehow, there were people living behind those locked doors in the west wing watching his every move. They might even be watching him right now! They seemed to know everything, but how? It was impossible. He glanced around, imagining some hidden camera system or peepholes but found nothing unusual.

The following evening, McAllister prepared his escape in secret, certain of his fate if he failed to avoid the coming storm. He could feel it brewing just outside the walls. His foiled victory over Planchet, the taking of New Eden only to end up a prisoner in his own castle—all of it meaningless now that Elise Planchet had returned with Hunter. He again thanked his luck for the news about the counter attack, giving him an opportunity to get out of this situation alive and in one piece! It was another undeniable sign that he was truly destined for greatness! Why else would he still be alive? Besides, he still had a plan, a good workable one. He stood gloating over Planchet's desk strewn with blueprints. *He'd escape New Eden the same way he came in, through the tunnels!*

Beneath the hill where he sat plotting was a sophisticated labyrinth connecting the Great Hall with the community housing area and the shops, sheds, barns, stables, and greenhouses throughout the complex. The "secret" family passageway used by Amy to rendezvous with Daniel was only a small part of the old mining system excavated over a hundred years earlier. When Planchet bought the property and laid out his utopia, he designed an ingenious way to move from place to place on the land by expanding the tunnel system, using it to house his geothermal heating system and the steam pipes and electrical lines to interconnect the widespread buildings.

When retreating to the Great Hall, McAllister sealed off the entrance to Amy's secret passageway, lest Mitchell use it to regain the stronghold. The tunnel system entrance used by New Eden's residents in the day-to-day operation of the community had also been secured. It was this second tunnel entrance that he would risk to make his escape. With Mitchell's forces busy defending the pre-dawn attack, McAllister could make his way to the stables and in the confusion of battle, strike out across the bridge before anyone was the wiser. With less than twelve hours before Hunter's counter attack was scheduled to take place, McAllister made final preparations so that, when the assault finally came, he would be ready.

* * *

BIG BULL MITCHELL tightened the noose, making sure the knot moved smoothly along the frozen rope. The third deserter in two days looked down at his blue, swollen feet, his boots already removed and reissued to one of the troops. He knew better than to speak. He'd seen more than a dozen men hanged by Mitchell and the less attention he paid you the better off you'd be.

Moving to the next condemned prisoner, Mitchell recognized the spy they'd caught up in the big hay barn the night before. His battered face was a mess. *His own mother probably wouldn't recognize him. But he sure sang pretty! Lots of good information came outta his mouth before it was all over.* Mitchell slipped the noose around the boyish neck and backed away.

He turned around and addressed his troops, all two hundred and fifty-three of them. They stood at attention in the bitter winter wind, listening to their glorious Field Marshall drone on about duty and honor and dying for the cause. Most could care less about his empty words, his meaningless campaigns, his codes and creeds. They weren't a real army, just a cold and miserable rabble with food rationed to one hot meal a day and no hot water for showers or laundry. Also, there were no privileges like they'd been promised, except for the officers who had the best of everything, including the women!

Finishing his speech, a snare drum rolled and at the wave of Mitchell's hand, a pair of mules were slapped soundly on the rump and bolted forward, hoisting the condemned high into the gray afternoon sky. They wriggled a while like worms on a hook, eyes bulging, soiling themselves, until finally going limp as their oxygen-deprived brains ran out of gas.

Dismissing the formation, Mitchell pondered the intel gained through last night's interrogation of the young spy. Elise Planchet had returned, and with her, the one the coward McAllister had warned him about. "Be on the lookout for the man called *Hunter*," he'd whispered, "Planchet has sent for him. It could only mean trouble."

Bull Mitchell didn't give a shit; he liked trouble. He relished it. He was born to wage war on anyone who got in his way. He'd always been a fighter, ever since he could remember. His father, the drunk piece of dog shit, used to beat the hell out of him for no apparent reason, just to be beating him. Eventually, Little Billy Mitchell grew up into Big Bull Mitchell and solved that problem with his bare hands. He would never forget the intoxicating joy of that moment, squeezing the very life out of that mean son-of-a-bitch while his bloodshot eyes bugged out of his worthless wine-soaked head. Since then, nobody had ever beaten him. *And nobody ever will!* he thought, smugly. Stepping out of the cold, he headed up to the officer's quarters where he planned to call on one of those pretty little Eden wenches who had learned real quick how to show him some respect.

CHAPTER SEVENTEEN

LOST IN THE DARK

HUNTER GLANCED UP from the map-strewn table as Elise slipped through the doorway and out into the icy night, escorted by three of her brother's most trusted companions. She was off to the Lancaster homestead to attend to the sick and wounded there. Hunter would remain behind with Robert, Spencer, and their lieutenants to put finishing touches on the battle plans. At dawn tomorrow, with surprise as their greatest weapon, more than a hundred and twenty determined exiles would strike with swift and deadly force to break the militia's stranglehold and retake New Eden.

Much had transpired since he and Elise had arrived. After an emotional reunion with her younger brother, Robert brought them up to date on all that had happened since Elise and the others went north. The news was worse than Elise expected, though Hunter was not surprised by anything Robert was willing to share. He was certainly less than candid in his sister's presence, holding back most of the grisly details. Hunter read between the lines and didn't need a description. He was intimately acquainted with the darkness of the human heart, having experienced firsthand the depths of personal tragedy and suffering facilitated by war.

Elise was unprepared for the reports of atrocities committed by McAllister, Mitchell, and their thugs. Most disturbing were the dark rumors about her family. Survivors claimed that her father had been badly wounded during the overthrow and was imprisoned somewhere within the Great Hall along with her youngest sister, Amy, who had foolishly provided the key to the militia's victory. Despite these tragedies, most of her friends had managed to escape during the confusion, and scores of refugees, with entire families intact, were safe in homesteads and barns scattered throughout the surrounding hills and valleys.

Robert immediately handed over command of the resistance forces to Hunter, while Elise assumed responsibility for the makeshift hospital, using her renowned skills as a healer to care for the sick and wounded. The news of Elise's return brought hope to New Eden's refugees, and determined volunteers began streaming in to prepare for battle under Hunter's experienced command.

During the week and a half since the takeover, Robert's volunteers had done their best to harass and demoralize the militia posted in guard houses along the compound's re-secured perimeter wall. Stealthy archers succeeded in picking off one or two each night, and several militiamen, with very little fight left in them, had jumped the wall and defected.

During their interrogations, they were more than cooperative, providing vital information about the enemy's forces and plans.

In exchange for their participation in the siege, *Field Marshall* Mitchell had promised to share the spoils of victory with them, pledging abundant food and shelter inside the compound where they would winter in comfort. Everything changed after the takeover. Mitchell's maniacal behavior intensified. Only his original gang members received privileges, and anyone foolish enough to complain was promptly executed for treason! Frozen corpses swung from tree limbs and mutilated bodies were stacked in the woodshed. To discourage mutiny, Mitchell collected all weapons and what little ammo there was, issuing them only to his most loyal followers. He placed the conscripts and recent recruits between his gang and any counter attack that might materialize from the ousted community members, using them as human shields. Charged with guard duty along the perimeter wall, they were billeted in drafty barns and sheds and ordered to fashion staffs for themselves out of saplings from the woods as their only weapons!

* * *

NEARLY TWO HUNDRED refugees gathered in an old barn at a ranch built back in the mid 1870's by a cattleman named Surrey. It was one of several such spreads scattered throughout the territory where those fleeing New Eden found shelter. The people had come to hear Elise and see this Hunter person for themselves, hoping against hope that their prayers had really been answered. Hunter looked upon them with compassion, a ragged congregation, underfed and poorly clothed, but determined to put an end to their brief exile and retake New Eden at any cost.

After a detailed briefing from Robert and Elise, more than a hundred and twenty volunteered on the spot to participate in the assault. These were not trained warriors, just everyday men and women, young and old, who'd lost everything and were willing to risk injury or worse to retake their homes. Hunter saw the desperation in their eyes and sensed their anger and frustration. Many had loved ones still trapped inside the walls, held against their will by ruthless men devoid of conscience.

Without sufficient food or supplies, it was unlikely that many of the newly exiled community members would make it through the long, cold winter months ahead, and they all knew it. This assault would be their last chance, one final defining moment to take back their lives or die trying. After much discussion, they divided the volunteers into three teams. One was to be led by Robert, another by Spencer, and the third by Hunter and Elise. They appointed platoon and squad leaders to create an efficient chain of command.

With charts and maps of New Eden spread out on tables, the teams went over their targeted objectives, discussing various contingencies and probabilities. Foremost in their minds was the safety of their own people inside the compound. Close to a hundred defenseless men, women, and children were unaccounted for and presumed held against their will or hidden somewhere inside the buildings, and the rescuers would be operating in near dark conditions. Hunter voiced his concern about 'friendly' casualties. Having tasted the madness of battle, he knew from experience that, once the assault began, the chances of events unfolding as planned were slim. Anything could and would happen, and he needed everyone to understand how confusing the situation might become.

* * *

DURING THE FORTY-EIGHT hours since his arrival, Hunter had worked closely with Robert Planchet, Spencer Wells, and their cadre of friends in designing an overall strategy to retake New Eden. While team leaders pored over maps and charts, Hunter listened as Robert and Spencer went over drawings of New Eden's layout with him. He was especially interested in details of the interiors of the structures and the tunnel system. The intelligence from inside the compound revealed that the militia commanded by Bull Mitchell was billeted in the two-story housing structures ringing the hill just below the parapet wall with the rest of the rabble in outbuildings throughout the valley, while McAllister and his bunch were locked up inside the Great Hall atop the hill.

Hunter was concerned about the size and strength of the garrison within the walls. A force totaling more than three hundred controlled the high ground, and, although they were reportedly fighting among themselves, their leadership would not likely give up their spoils without a serious fight. His initial objective would be to surprise, damage, and disorient them to such an extent as to take the will to fight out of them. To that end, the highly resourceful Hunter had managed to bring a few helpful items with him from Wyoming that he'd been saving back for just such an occasion.

With the others looking on, he produced three hard cases from a duffle bag among his mustang's baggage. Placing them side-by-side on the table, he opened the first lid to reveal a forty millimeter grenade launcher with a dozen flares and tear gas rounds. The second case held a silenced .308 sniper rifle with night vision scope and a hundred rounds of ammo. The final case contained six claymore mines and several blocks of C4 high explosive with detonators! A second large duffle on the floor contained two-dozen gas masks in individual carrying cases. The high explosives, tear gas rounds, and rifle were definitely capable of accomplishing his initial objective, if deployed effectively.

Those watching glanced at each other in amazement, too stunned for words. They'd never seen such a lethal collection of weaponry, and Hunter gave a brief lecture on the safe use of the highly dangerous ordnance. New Eden's entire arsenal consisted mostly of a collection of old hunting rifles and a handful of shotguns and pistols with very limited ammo to go around. Tomorrow at dawn most of their force would be fighting with bows and arrows, spears, axes, or pitchforks!

As there would likely be lookouts in the towers and guards in the gatehouses with unknown numbers of roving patrols, speed of attack and stealth under cover of darkness would give them the tactical advantage. Once inside the perimeter wall, their first objective was the towers. Any lookouts or sharpshooters there must be quickly neutralized before speeding on to the militia housing to quickly destroy as many of the fighters as possible.

Hunter and Elise would lead their team in beneath the Great Hall through the old mining tunnel network. There, they would split up, with Hunter climbing the rooftop tower and Elise's people sweeping the building to rescue Adam and Amy Planchet and release the holdouts barricaded on the third floor of the west wing. Everyone would be on the lookout for the warring gang leaders. They knew that Frank McAllister had taken up residence in the Planchet's family quarters in the Great Hall, but Bull Mitchell's specific whereabouts was unknown. The psycho killer could be anywhere and, of all their enemies within New Eden's walls, Bull Mitchell was Hunter's primary concern. Robert and the others had provided detailed physical descriptions of both men, and Hunter was sure to recognize them if and when their paths should cross.

Diversionary explosions at the southern and western gates would be followed by powerful blasts to the north and east. Spencer's group would pour through the north breech while Robert's group and a dozen others on horseback would attack from the east and head for the housing complex.

After many hours of analysis and discussion, their plans were finalized. The assault would begin in the dark predawn hours. After Robert and the others left to make last-minute preparations, Hunter waited a few minutes in the darkened room before going to make a few of his own. His thoughts turned to Elise, wondering how well she was holding up under her tough facade. A master at masking her feelings, he knew she was deeply concerned about her father and Amy. Losing either of them would be like severing a part of her very soul.

* * *

HUNTER PLACED THE final explosive charge at the hinge side of the massive wooden west gate and withdrew to join Elise in the culvert beside the approach road. He re-checked the connections and went over the details one last time with the detonator operator, making sure she was clear on exactly what to do. She was one of two operators geared to set off decoy explosions intended to confuse the enemy, giving the assault teams more time to race to their objectives.

An hour before sunrise, all was quiet along the perimeter wall. Not surprisingly, no one appeared to be stationed in the gatehouses as it was extremely cold—well below zero with a biting wind that burned right through to the skin.

From what he was able to discern through his night scope, any lookouts posted in the unprotected towers were staying well out of the bitter wind and were either sleeping or bundled up and trying to. That would change when the gates were blown. Robert and Spencer were standing by with their teams to the north and east, awaiting the signal to blow their respective gates and rush uphill to the housing structures just below the parapet wall.

A gray-haired ex-marine named Bo was entrusted with the flare and tear gas launcher and would move into the compound with Robert's team. Once enemy housing units were identified, he would lob tear gas into the structures and the assault teams, wearing gas masks, would rush in and clear the buildings. He would have to move quickly to provide support for Spencer's team as well. Two young men in their late teens carrying axes were assigned to him as bodyguards.

Hunter and Elise led their group through the underground passageway running beneath New Eden to the lower level of the Great Hall. "Meet me at the stables at dawn," Elise spoke softly, her face shrouded in the shadowed hood of her thick, fur-lined parka. Hunter nodded and was gone, heading for the third floor roof access ladder. Elise and her assault team would remain below in the tunnel until the first explosions.

Fighting knife in hand, crossbow and rifle slung over his back, Hunter easily jimmied the lock and entered the storeroom, slipping out into the hallway to the kitchen. He paused, suspicious, listening with senses stretched. All was quiet in the Great Hall, and he was wary of the lack of sentries. The tunnel entrance itself was a mystery, which appeared to have been recently fortified, but now was curiously free of barricades. *But by whom and why?*

Crossing to the foot of the staircase, he slipped cautiously up the shadowed landings to the top floor, half expecting an ambush. At the end of the darkened third-floor hallway he located the wrought iron ladder leading to the roof. Up the rungs in a flash, he slowly pushed open the hatch and raised his head into the crisp night air. In the center of the roof, dead ahead, the timber-framed tower rose sixty feet into the starlit sky. A torch flickered through the windows in the small lookout shed perched on top, and he heard voices drifting across the roof from above in the dark.

From his vantage point atop the Great Hall, Hunter looked out over all of New Eden and saw torches flickering in the distant towers in the four corners of the valley. He checked his luminous watch dial. Four minutes to go. He crossed to the base of the tower stairs in the deep shadows and began his ascent, wondering how many he'd find up there.

* * *

ACROSS THE VALLEY in the cold dark, Robert's mounted calvary huddled against the eastern wall on either side of the massive wooden gates eagerly awaiting the signal to attack. In the confusion caused by the planned consecutive explosions, their objective was to speed uphill towards the housing area and take out the militia as they streamed from their barracks. Spencer's group would attack on foot from the north gate which was closer to the hill, but with a much steeper approach.

Atop the ladder, Hunter crouched beneath the lookout platform. Like everything else he'd designed, Planchet made the towers difficult to win in an assault. The first eight sections were wide wooden stairs, but a vertical ladder spanned the final twenty feet, opening into the center of the floor above. He tried to ease the trapdoor with his shoulder but found it secured from within. He checked his watch, counting down as the first pair of explosions ripped the silence, their thunderclap concussions echoing off the surrounding walls and mountains.

He heard excited voices in the chamber above and the trap door swung open. A pair of legs appeared through the hole, and Hunter swung around to the opposite side of the ladder, grabbing the surprised man by the shoulder as he passed and hurling him to his death far below. Instantly springing up through the opening, he took the remaining two lookouts by surprise, slashing upward with his blade across the first man's throat and nearly severing his head. Spinning around, he brought his knife down in a violent arc, plunging the blade deep into the second man's chest at the base of his neck and dissecting his heart.

He dumped their bodies out a window over the railing and slid his rifle from his shoulder. Snapping the legs of the bipod into place, he sighted in on the farthest tower and squeezed off three rounds into the distant figure silhouetted in the torchlight. Moving to the next tower, he did likewise, and so on, until all four towers were clear.

As he slid the sling from his elbow, someone suddenly grabbed ahold of his legs and jerked him down through the opening in the floor! The rifle flew from his grasp, sailing out over the railing and clattering onto the rooftop below. Spreading his arms out wide, he grabbed the floor, stopping his fall, and kicked his assailant in the throat with both heels, sending him shrieking after the rifle.

As he made his way down to the roof, the first hint of dawn appeared on the eastern horizon, and he could hear sporadic gunfire and the cries of battle as New Eden's rightful residents moved quickly against their enemies. Swinging his trusty crossbow from his back, Hunter loaded a razor-tipped bolt and headed for the stables to rendezvous with Elise.

* * *

WHEN THE FIRST explosions sounded, Elise's team poured from the tunnel into the kitchen and split into three groups, spreading out through the Great Hall, clearing the rooms as they went. Her group headed for the third floor to clear and secure the Planchet living quarters. Donnie Curry, the blacksmith's son, strode beside her, pitchfork poised in his calloused hands. They moved methodically through the building in two-person teams, checking each room in search of Amy and Adam Planchet.

She was dismayed by the condition of her once tidy home. Where everything had been orderly and spotless, the rooms were now dirty and in disarray. Storerooms had been ransacked and crates and boxes broken open with food and supplies strewn about everywhere. Unwashed cooking and eating utensils filled cluttered tables and filthy sinks. The dried remains of many meals lay buried beneath stacks of dirty dishes on unwashed counter tops and soiled tile floors.

Gaining the third floor hallway, she hurried towards her family's chambers to discover the doors wide open and the place completely trashed. She moved quickly from room-to-room, calling out for Father and Amy, but no one answered. Checking his study, she found his books and papers dumped off the shelves and piled onto the floor. His large desk had been broken into, the locks on the drawers smashed and his personal belongings rifled through. After a quick search of the family quarters and adjacent rooms, neither Amy nor Adam Planchet were located.

Returning to her ransacked living quarters, Elise fought back angry tears at the violation of her once safe world. Suddenly, a young man approached in silence motioning for her to follow. She could tell by the look on his face that something terrible had happened. Her heart raced as he led her down to a cold storage room in the basement, not far from where they'd exited the tunnel, to a small group gathered in silence. Lying on the cold stone floor, wrapped in an old woolen blanket, was her father's dead body. She froze in the doorway. He looked so small lying there, face pale and taut, eyes wide open and staring, lips drawn back in death's cruel mask.

Slipping into shock, the scene before her became blurred, surreal, other-worldly. Her legs failed and she fell to her knees, everything happening in slow motion as pressure in her chest made it difficult to breathe. Someone who reached out to hold her was mouthing comforting words, but she was cut off, unable to connect to what was being said. Her grief was the only thing real—her loss too devastating to accept. She knelt there in silence for several minutes, peering at his face, memories flashing, until her grief gave way to rage, and she bent down, kissed his pallid forehead and led her forces to the rendezvous at the stables.

* * *

AS THE SECOND pair of blasts rocked the compound, Robert's calvary poured through the demolished eastern gate and sped up the curved road towards the community housing complex ringing the hill below the Great Hall and its parapet wall. From the wrecked north gate, Spencer's men moved straight up the hill, taking up positions beside the enemy housing units. They crossed the steep distance in under two minutes, meeting little resistance. With their teams in place surrounding the housing area, ex-marine Bo used the grenade launcher to lob tear gas canisters into the windows, and squads wearing gas masks waited outside the doorways for the exiting militia to cut them down.

* * *

AT THE FAR end of the lower horse stables, Frank McAllister filled a wagon with the booty he'd collected during his ten-day stay at Planchet's crippled utopia. Outside, the battle raged, and he recognized the loud voice of his nemesis booming above the din, yelling orders and cursing his men. He involuntarily shuddered at the sound of it and moved cautiously to a darkened window to peer out just as a bright white flare burst in the night sky above, bathing the surroundings in eerie light and casting strange moving shadows as it drifted downwind on its tiny parachute. He could make out Mitchell's silhouette standing uphill on the cart track, a deadly scythe in his massive hands. *Die, Mitchell, die!* he prayed, still hoping for a miracle in the midst of all this chaos. As the melee grew louder and the fighting closer, McAllister looked around, needing to create a diversion to make good his last-minute escape.

Wrapping a kerosene-soaked rag around the tines of a pitchfork, he struck flint and steel to spark a flame. The makeshift torch quickly caught and he sped to the far end of the long building, torching the straw and hay in a dozen places before hurling the fork up into the second floor hay loft where it swiftly burst into a deadly conflagration. Mesmerized by the greedy flames, he stood back, watching the fire quickly spread throughout the stalls to the timbers and roof.

As the smoke and flames blossomed, scores of terrified horses and mules trapped in their stalls whinnied and screamed while the fire raced throughout the vast stable complex. When New Eden's people heard the cries of the animals, smelled the smoke, and realized what was happening, those nearby broke off their attack and rushed towards the stables to save them. McAllister thrilled to the anguished cries of the innocent and helpless creatures, delighted to be the cause of their terror. It made him feel almost godlike to wield such destructive power!

He could hear would be rescuers yelling over the roar of the flames, calling for a bucket brigade from the nearby stream. *Too late you fools! Nothing can save your precious horses now!* With the fire completely consuming the upper end of the building, no one would interfere with his leaving by the lower stable's back exit. Suddenly he heard a nearby voice calling out to Elise! *Elise Planchet? Here?* He went again to the window and the inferno revealed a man armed with a crossbow yelling and running for the stable entrance as the roof suddenly came down with a terrific crash! The running man screamed her name and tried to approach the burning building but was forced back by the intense heat.

McAllister studied him thoughtfully. *This must be the famous Hunter they'd all heard so much about!* Turning back to load the last of his precious cargo, he caught a glimpse of Bull Mitchell emerging from the shadows swinging his scythe and nearly catching Hunter off guard! By the light of the burning building, the two men battled it out as time stood still. In the half-light, he could see Hunter duck, roll, and spring away at the last second as Mitchell moved in for the kill. Suddenly, the bigger man spun about, hurling the scythe directly at the crossbow rising up in Hunter's arms. Hunter went down and Mitchell was on him in an instant. McAllister felt certain that Hunter was as good as dead when a blade suddenly flashed and Hunter spun round atop the bigger man, blood spraying everywhere! As another flare lit up the sky, McAllister could see that both men were down! Mitchell lay still, as did Hunter! *Yes! They are both dead!*

His prayers had been answered! But no, what's this? Hunter moved slightly and slowly sat up, obviously badly wounded, one arm useless, barely able to stand!

The smoke grew thicker in the wide central walkway of the lower stables and another section of roof fell in with a boom, snapping him back to his present purpose. Turning around with a fixed stare, he picked up one last bundle wrapped in a quilt and tossed it atop the rest of his treasures. Chortling with glee, a crazed Frank McAllister leapt aboard the loaded wagon, vigorously lashing the mules, and sped out the back doors into the wintery dawn, heading for the bridge.

* * *

ROUNDING THE WIDE hill, Hunter saw bright orange flames leaping into the sky through the roof of the stables far below and could hear the high-pitched screaming of the noble animals burning alive in their stalls. He ran downhill in the dark heading for the nearest entrance to the long, two-story structure. Down at the far end of the stables, brave rescuers led terrified horses out of the flames and others threw water on the building in a bucket brigade from the half-frozen stream. In the midst of the fray, Elise poured the frigid water over her head and, with a wet rag held to her mouth, ran into the burning building, which was beginning to come apart and list dangerously to one side. She reappeared half a minute later, leading two panicked horses to safety and passed them off before heading back in for more.

As he arrived on the scene, Hunter watched her reenter the burning stables and called to her over the roar, but she disappeared into the smoke-filled structure. As he sped towards the flaming opening, the roof suddenly buckled and the heavy timbers came down with a tremendous crash, bright flames shooting out in all directions! He screamed out her name and tried to get closer, but the sixteen-hundred degree heat beat him back, making it impossible.

In the shadows beside the shoeing shed, a crouched figure turned from watching the fire to locate the one crying out Elise's name. *There, so that must be Hunter, the one sent for by Planchet, the one I will destroy!* The brutal killer had just witnessed the fire greedily consume Planchet's eldest daughter, and now, he, Bull Mitchell, would crush this outsider from the north and toss him into the flames as well!

Hunter stood as close to the fire as he dared, arms in front of his face to block the heat, staring in shocked disbelief, certain that there was no way Elise could have survived the massive collapse! He moved around to the side to see if he could get closer, when, in a blur of motion barely registering in his peripheral vision, a malevolent Bull Mitchell, murder in his glittering eyes, rushed from behind a haystack and swung a scythe across Hunter's body, just inches from his chest. From instinct alone, Hunter crouched and jumped sideways, rolling into a ball as he hit the ground. Mitchell rushed forward, slashing wildly, but Hunter gathered himself and catapulted away as the deadly blade again sliced through the air close enough to his face to feel the wind from it.

Mitchell was astonished that Hunter somehow evaded his initial strikes, still certain that his next swing would cut his enemy in half. At six-six, two-eighty-five, he was a formidable opponent, a dirty-fighting natural-born killer who'd never lost a battle since beating his drunk father to death with his bare hands at the age of sixteen. Certain of his own invincibility, his conceited brain harbored no doubts about the outcome of this contest.

As Hunter recovered his balance, he brought the crossbow up for a shot, but Mitchell faked a lunge and spun about, sending the scythe cartwheeling like a massive boomerang. The hardwood handle struck Hunter square on the forearm, knocking the crossbow from his grasp as the blade came around to sideswipe him. He collapsed into a ball as his forearm and ribs snapped from the force of the blow and something inside gave way. The giant was on him in an instant, massive hands seeking his neck, but he spun about and rolled over, intentionally offering Mitchell his back.

As the strongman's arms slid down to encircle his chest, Hunter raised his knee up and grabbed the fighting knife strapped to his left ankle. Gripping the haft, he arched up and drove the point into the soft flesh behind Mitchell's beard. Blood squirted from the slit as the blade sliced through his lower palate, impaling his tongue and piercing the roof of his mouth.

Wearing a look of utter disbelief, the possibility of his own defeat incomprehensible, Mitchell released Hunter's chest to instinctively protect his throat, but, with a final violent thrust, Hunter angled the hardened steel point deep into the brawler's skull and pivoted like a Whirling Dervish, cleanly severing the bully's brainstem!

Mitchell's body instantly went limp, and Hunter pushed the corpse off to one side, collapsing as a blinding pain ripped through his mid-torso, forcing him into a fetal position. Grimacing in agony and supporting his fractured right arm, he struggled to his feet and checked the wound in his side. Blood slowly seeped from a three-inch gash where a jagged white rib bone poked out through the skin. Awkwardly cutting the dead man's shirt into strips, he hastily fashioned a sling for his arm and a bandage of sorts. Wrapping his side as tightly as he could bear, he succeeded in temporarily staunching the oozing flow of blood. In his mind's eye, all he could see was roaring flames and the stable collapsing as Elise entered the inferno to rescue one more screaming horse. *There was no way she could have made it out alive.*

A rising rage coursed through Hunter's soul like a cyclone, giving him the strength of ten men and blotting out all pain. He could hear the battle nearby and knew that New Eden's victory was at hand. Suddenly, there was the crack of a whip and a clattering of hooves, and he caught a glimpse of a heavily-laden wagon drawn by four mules leaving by the back gate of the lower stables below. Standing in the driver's seat, bright red hair and beard unmistakable in the early morning light, the infamous Frank McAllister was making his escape!

Hunter knew McAllister would have to go the long way around through the outer fields to arrive at the railroad bridge—the only way in or out of the valley. From studying Robert's maps, he knew a shortcut he could take on foot, used often by couriers, but it was steep and covered in ice and snow. It was his only chance. He'd have to race to get there ahead of the wagon. Stepping over Mitchell's wide-eyed, bloodied corpse, he summoned every last ounce of strength and dashed down the hill towards the bridge.

* * *

IN THE GROWING light of the late November morning, with a wide band of storm clouds low on the horizon masking the rising sun, a badly wounded Hunter emerged from the shadows and stationed himself at the far end of the old wooden bridge. He looked around at the snow-covered timbers. This would be his last stand; a last ditch effort to prevent McAllister's escape. With his strength slowly ebbing away, Hunter was determined to bring this nightmare to an end here and now. He pushed the image of Elise and the burning barn from his mind, certain that he would soon be joining her.

Catching his breath, he leaned on the railing for support and looked over the side at the massive wooden trestles, an engineering wonder when built at the latter part of the 19th Century by the Mountain Pacific Railroad. The complex matrix of heavy timbers rose high above the canyon floor, spanning the three-hundred-yard chasm across the steep river gorge. Hunter could hear the roar far below, like a distant herd of bison thundering across the Great Plains, as millions of gallons of frigid water rushed noisily downhill toward the distant valley and beyond.

Careful to conserve his rapidly waning strength, he eased himself down until he was seated on the snow and ice-covered planks, back braced against the post of the waist high railing. He closed his eyes for a moment and rested there, fighting off the waves of nausea threatening to engulf him and calling upon hidden reserves to remain conscious. Under great duress, the experienced warrior clearly grasped the gravity of his situation.

Not since Africa had he borne so grievous an injury and, without immediate medical attention, he understood with certainty that, as far as this life was concerned, time was rapidly running out. In addition to a fractured forearm, which rendered his right hand practically useless, an excruciating pain radiated from his right side, spreading throughout his chest cavity, intensifying with each ragged breath as he struggled to load the crossbow using only his feet and one good arm. The makeshift bandage wrapped awkwardly around his chest did little to support the broken ribs or reduce the flow of blood oozing from the puncture wound six inches below his armpit.

Beneath him on the glistening snow, a dark, creeping stain slowly spread, transforming the whiteness to sticky red slush. As he fumbled with his weapon, Hunter felt a vibration through the frozen planks and looked to the far end of the bridge where a heavily laden wagon outfitted for winter travel with wide skids instead of wheels came charging into view. Standing upright on the floorboards, reins held tightly in one hand, a cruel whip in the other, Frank McAllister raced the overloaded cargo sled across the frozen span, ruthlessly lashing the mules and running dangerously close to the nearside railing. Iron-shod hooves pounded the bridge as they labored hard not to slip on the ice under the obscene load. Great clouds of steam poured from their flaring nostrils as they charged forward for all they were worth.

Just managing to load his weapon, Hunter struggled to lift the crossbow using only his good arm. Sighting through the scope and steadying the weapon on his knee, he took careful aim at his rapidly approaching enemy and waited for the perfect shot, knowing that, if he missed here, there would be no second chance.

Fifty yards behind McAllister, and unseen by Hunter as he concentrated on his target, a cloaked and hooded figure on horseback raced across the bridge, gaining on the sled with each passing moment. As Hunter focused on McAllister's midsection and prepared to fire, the strength in his hand momentarily faltered and his finger slipped from the trigger!

On board the careening craft, McAllister drove the charging mules like a demon from the Netherworld itself. Intoxicated with hatred, black eyes bright with madness and glee, he gloated at the sight of the great Hunter crumpled before him, heroic blood crimson against the freshly fallen snow. He whipped the team harder, holding the wagon mere inches from the rails, relishing the imminent annihilation of this meddler who had appeared out of the wilds to nullify his brilliant victory and ruin his plans! To run him down like a dog in the street would be sweet revenge indeed! Then, he would return again in the spring with yet another army of dreamers to take back what would undeniably rightfully belong to him as the *husband of the only remaining Planchet heir!*

Out of sight in the back of the speeding wagon sprawled across hastily loaded food stores and other stolen supplies and treasures, a bruised and battered Amy Planchet awoke with a start and immediately realized her situation. Rising slowly to her feet, she steadied herself, peering down into the passing gorge and looking ahead, knowing that this moment was her one and only chance at redemption. With seconds to impact, she crouched low and hurled herself forward, leaping onto the back of the evil tyrant who had used her, destroying everything she'd ever loved.

Caught completely off guard by Amy's furious attack, McAllister struggled to maintain his balance, his large body tipping dangerously toward the gorge. When the fading Hunter finally managed to squeeze the trigger, the shiny steel dart found its mark high on McAllister's left thigh, shattering the bone before ricocheting across to the opposite side of the bridge and embedding itself in the rail.

Clinging hard to McAllister's back, Amy bit savagely into his neck, her fingernails gouging deeply into his eye sockets, repaying her captor for the cruel days and nights of humiliation and abuse she suffered to satisfy his sadistic pleasure. Her violence forced him to drop the whip and reigns, barely allowing time for the galloping mules to sidestep the inert figure lying in their path. As the animals swerved, the sliding wagon jerked toward the center of the bridge in a sudden sideways shift, pitching the now shrieking McAllister, arms flailing with young Amy still clinging to his back, headlong over the railing and down toward the jagged rocks lining the raging torrent below.

Moments later, the cloaked rider reigned in beside Hunter's motionless body and leapt to the ground. Kneeling, she threw back her hood to reveal Elise, who hadn't perished in the fire, but had managed to escape down a ladder to the lower level moments before the flaming roof collapsed! She cradled Hunter's face with her hands, and searched for signs of life in the man she'd grown to admire so completely. At his throat she detected a faint pulse and cried for help as others arrived. Spencer immediately applied pressure to stop the bleeding and worked quickly to minimize shock and stabilize the wounded man's vital signs.

As several men loaded Hunter into the wagon for the ride back to the infirmary, Elise stood at the railing, peering down into the shadowy depths, and reliving the horror of watching her youngest sister disappear over the side, still fighting her tormentor as she plunged to a certain death into the turbulent waters below. In the gloom, her body was nowhere to be seen, probably swallowed up and carried off by the strong current. Turning away, she retrieved Hunter's crossbow where it had fallen in the snowbank and rushed back to her horse to see what she might do for him.

CHAPTER EIGHTEEN

INTO THE GREAT BEYOND

THE COLDEST WINTER in three decades wore out its welcome that year, to later become known as the *Year of the Siege.* It wasn't until the last week of April that spring finally broke through the ice-encased Rockies, bringing its long awaited warmth and color to thawing lakes, mountains, and meadows, and warming the hearts of man and beast. At the first hint of new growth, famished four-legged foragers dove in, devouring every blade of grass and new shoot they could wrap their tongues around.

Within the battle-scarred walls of New Eden, life slowly returned to normal, though, without question, the community would never again really be the same. Each family or individual had lost something precious. If not life, limb, or a loved one, then something intimate within the psyche was fundamentally altered. The myth of security had vanished, replaced by the realization that harmful people can still do destructive things if good people allow it. Along with the return of milder weather came renewed hope for a better future, and everyone worked in unison to rebuild and repair their world.

As the snows melted in the high mountain passes, many of those who fled during the overthrow returned to put their shoulders to the task at hand. One immediate necessity was the clearing away and burning of the accumulated debris and rubble of the siege, scattered outside the walls and particularly surrounding the gated entrances. Jumbled piles of wood and trash, makeshift tents and other such refuse was hastily left behind by scores of retreating militia as they fled into the surrounding hills on foot, driven out by the settlers into the bleak whiteness to die of exposure or starve to death in the bitter subzero temperatures.

The grisly task of gathering and disposing of bodies revealed by the melt went to Robert and the security force. In each case, some attempt at identification was made, although militia members from New Hope were simply given a number and burned outside the walls. Their charred bones were crushed with large rocks into dust and this bone meal was later used to help fertilize the fields. Robert considered it their way of "giving something back."

The bodies of dead New Eden members were entrusted to their families or closest friends to bury or cremate as the deceased might have wished. Once the earth was thawed enough to facilitate digging, the community cemetery, terraced into a nearby hilltop, was expanded to receive more than eighty new graves.

With Adam Planchet gone, his progeny assumed responsibility for leading the restoration efforts. Robert directed the newly commissioned all-volunteer security force that patrolled the surrounding territory and created a buffer zone between New Eden and potential dangers from without. Pairs of scouts on horseback scoured the countryside, on the lookout for remnants of the vanquished militia that never materialized. The deep snow and arctic-like temperatures of the harshest winter on record had apparently done a thorough job of finishing them off.

Major structural rebuilding efforts were delegated to those most skilled and able in that particular specialty, and it was interesting to note that the ratio of males to females remained about equal. Elise managed the hospital with a cadre of fellow caregivers and devoted her time to rehabilitating the sick and injured. Others concentrated on food production, while older children divided their time between caring for the younger ones and tending to the animals.

Although their numbers had been noticeably reduced by the starving militia encamped outside the walls, plenty of foundation stock remained to rebuild the flocks and herds, and abundant lambs, kids, calves, and foals came into the world that year to make their frolicking mark upon it. Fields and gardens were cleaned up and plowed under, beds prepared and planted, orchards pruned, and the warm, gentle rains of springtime watered the fertile ground, promising a bountiful harvest throughout the coming summer and fall. Hunting improved with the weather as large groupings of elk and deer returned to the greening valleys to graze.

One day in mid-April, a dozen stragglers arrived at the gates begging for food. They were mostly starving women and children with a couple of old men from the now abandoned ghost town of New Hope. As they sat devouring their meal like ravenous wolves, they recounted heartrending tales of hardship and brutality endured under the iron fists of McAllister, Mitchell, and their bloody henchmen. Two teenage girls were visibly with child and Elise invited the pitiful souls to remain at New Eden as guests until other arrangements could be made.

Each day as she went about her rounds, Elise saw improvements in her patients. For some, the healing process was quick and they were back up and helping others in just a few weeks. It warmed her heart to see even small degrees of progress made in each case, as wounds healed and broken bones mended over time. Others, not quite so lucky, learned to cope with a newly acquired disability. For these there would be no return to normal. Suffering the loss of an eye or a hand or foot, or having been horribly disfigured by fire or worse could never be undone. Likewise, those that were psychologically damaged—victims of assault, orphans, and others who'd witnessed the death of loved ones or other such horrors—would never be the same. For these survivors, picking up the shattered fragments of their lives was no simple task. Elise did what she could for them all, applying her extensive knowledge of herbal medicines and holistic treatments with remarkable skill and positive results. However, for one of her charges in particular, recovery was painstakingly slow.

In a quiet room a short distance from the sick ward, Hunter lay sleeping, vital signs weak, yet stable. In truth, it was a miracle that he was even alive, given the severity of his injuries. As McAllister met defeat on the wooden trestle bridge, Hunter collapsed into unconsciousness from blood loss and shock, and remained so for six perilous weeks, teetering on the edge of life and death. Jake Stein, the community veterinarian, had immediately performed emergency surgery to repair his punctured lung and a nicked artery in his chest cavity caused by the scythe wound to his side. Once stabilized, all they could do was keep him quiet and comfortable and pray that infection didn't set in. Elise directed Hunter's convalescence, but didn't allow herself to demonstrate favoritism. Besides, she was fully occupied with forty-odd other patients to attend and assigned one of her most experienced nurses to provide his daily routine care.

One cold day in mid-January, Hunter suddenly opened his eyes and asked the young nurse attending him for something to eat. Upon hearing the news, Elise rushed to his room, holding back her emotions, but just barely. When she arrived, the doctor was just leaving, and in hushed tones in the hallway he told her to go easy, as the lucky fellow was still very weak and somewhat disoriented but cognizant of his surroundings and circumstances. He gave her hand a reassuring squeeze. She promised to make it short and stepped through the door.

Hunter was propped up in bed sipping vegetable broth from a spoon held by a middle-aged woman who patiently insisted that he slow down and allow his body to adjust to the more complex form of nourishment. During his coma, the doctor had succeeded in rigging a feeding tube, using a length of tubing salvaged from an old farm machine. This contraption enabled them to keep Hunter's body nourished and hydrated by feeding him thin barley broth, lightly sweetened with honey.

A pale but present Hunter looked up at Elise and managed a weak grin. She beamed back but sensed something odd about his appearance, though she was not able to immediately identify it. Then it struck her. It was his eyes; they seemed much bluer now, when before, they always appeared to be steel gray. How odd, she thought, making a mental note to consult her medical texts as to the significance of this unusual phenomenon. She hung back as he was spoon-fed, relieved beyond words to see him awake. Regardless of his thin, haggard appearance, this was the same man she'd come to know and respect during their intense journey together. With a smile that masked her concern, she teased him saying she knew all along that, like an old bear, hunger would eventually drive him out of hibernation. As the nurse finished tidying up and left, Elise came forward to sit on the edge of his bed. "It is so good to see you, Hunter, we were all very worried..." Tears threatened to well up, but Elise willed them back and was spared the embarrassment.

Hunter just looked across at her, no particular expression on his gaunt face, delving her thoughts and reading her emotions. "It is good to see you as well, Elise." He spoke with effort in a hushed tone. "I am curious to know how you escaped the collapsed barn where I was certain you'd perished in the flames."

She briefly recounted the story of the ladder and flight to the bridge where she described McAllister's defeat and Amy's heroic death in the rocky waters of the hundred-foot gorge.

"Did you recover his body?" He asked quietly, his voice weak and cracking from long disuse. He searched for the answer in her eyes.

"His corpse was never found—but neither was poor Amy's." She turned her face to avoid his x-ray stare. "But no one could have survived such a fall and, besides, the current is so strong there, a person would simply be dashed to pieces and swept far downstream, maybe even all the way to the falls."

Hunter tried to concentrate. His mind wouldn't focus, and he felt a vast weariness overwhelming him. A thousand questions swirled around in his head, but he couldn't seem to connect them to his vocal chords. Elise sensed his confusion and got up to leave. "Sleep now, Hunter, please, you must rest. Later, all of your questions will be answered, and we can begin to help you regain your strength. Suffice it to say that the worst is over, and all is on the mend. You've been through so much, and we are all very grateful for your sacrifice. You saved us, just as Father said you would, for, without your help, we would never have gotten our lives and dignity back." She tenderly touched his hand and was troubled by his rapid pulse and clammy skin. Hunter was already fast asleep as she slipped from his room to find the doctor.

* * *

IN THE TWO months since waking, Hunter's mind and body had rapidly improved, and oftentimes Elise would see him out walking or riding in the hills, helping the scouts bring in game for the table. Good news arrived in May with the safe return of William, Sarah, little Jamie, and Anna, who had wintered safely together at Hunter's cave. As soon as the passes were open, a heavily armed cavalry of twenty volunteers and a string of pack mules went north to collect them, and their return to New Eden was cause for much rejoicing, mixed with sorrow, as the loss of their father and youngest sister weighed heavily on everyone's heart.

Tall, dark-haired William appeared as fit and robust as ever, though he walked with a limp that would mark him for the remainder of his days, a silent testament to his near death experience and mysterious connection to the Old Ones. He'd learned the devastating news about Father and Amy, and details of the siege, fall, and retaking of New Eden from his longtime friend and leader of the expedition, Jess Morley. Using a highly-detailed map drawn by the still recovering Hunter, Morley's troupe navigated the three-hundred-odd miles to the headwaters of the Green River near Gannet Peak to Hunter's valley without incident, taking just twenty-seven days to make the trip.

Sarah had become her old self again, restored in body and soul, and was filled with abundant joy and energy, every ounce of which was required in looking after little Jamie, who'd grown like a weed, was into everything, and like his father, refused to acknowledge physical universe limitations (even when they bruised his nose or skinned his knee).

Anna, who had blossomed in the months since Elise saw her last, was nearly eighteen now and quite the young woman. She brought out gifts of tanned elk and moose hides that they'd all worked on through the long winter months, along with healing plants from Hunter's garden and fresh herbs gathered along the way. Each had grown stronger and more resourceful as a result of experiencing the hardships together, and they were more close-knit as a family than ever before.

The New Eden they returned to was also irrevocably altered. Of the three-hundred-plus inhabitants dwelling there prior to the siege, nearly one third had lost their lives or remained unaccounted for. Another hundred-odd were physically injured, half of them seriously, and a handful were severely withdrawn and would probably never fully recover from the devastating emotional trauma they'd suffered.

As to New Hope, a short year ago there were nearly four thousand souls living there, and today only a few dozen or so remained. Where they'd all gone, no one really knew as there was no organized body keeping track of such things. It was estimated that over half the community had slipped away across the mountains before the onset of winter and another couple of hundred died during the siege or in its aftermath.

The sordid truth was that Frank McAllister and his cutthroats murdered many, while Bull Mitchell executed even more for treason, desertion, or simple disrespect. Some evidence pointed to cannibalism as another possible explanation. Large piles of human bones behind New Hope's community kitchen seemed highly suspicious, but could simply be the place those who starved to death were stacked, in outdoor cold storage, until spring thaw when they could be buried. Physical degradation due to weather and predation by carnivores and insects made it impossible to know for sure. Suspicions were further aggravated when the short-lived community's few survivors were unable to suitably explain their winter-long menu. What really happened there would probably never be revealed or discovered, but for whatever combination of reasons and factors, the busy, bustling settlement of a year ago was now a virtual ghost town.

CHAPTER NINETEEN

CIRCLES IN THE SKY

THE STRIKING DUN mare stood quietly as Hunter tightened her cinch and made last minute adjustments to her saddle and other equipment in final preparation for their long journey north. She was tied off in the wide center aisle of the newly rebuilt horse stable, calmly allowing him to control her with his firm, steady hand. She swished her tail at an annoying fly, content to be going for another ride up into the hills and shifted her weight as he lifted one foot at a time to clean and check her hooves.

Up and down the long corridor, inquisitive heads poked out of shadowed stalls to see what was going on. Hunter smiled at their curiosity, noting each one's unique markings and personality. Looking around at the familiar setting, he realized how he'd always loved barns. The nostalgic smells of fresh hay and straw bedding mixed with horse manure and urine, sweat and harness leather, all blended together, evoked pleasant memories of a more innocent time when the world wasn't quite so cruel, or at least he wasn't then so painfully aware of it being so.

Finished with his preparations, he rewarded the animal's patience with a crisp slice of apple from his pocket and a thorough scratch behind the ears. Standing back, he looked her over and was pleased. The new saddle and bridle, with matching saddlebags handcrafted from the finest black-dyed harness leather and trimmed in silver, fit perfectly, though they were a bit on the fancy side—an unexpected and much appreciated gift from New Eden's Leather guild. Beneath the saddle, a Navajo-style wool saddle blanket in the brilliant colors of the sunset was another gift, this from the Weaver's camp. Sarah had made a beautifully braided leather halter and lead rope, which was stored for later use, but the best gift of all was that of Sagebrush herself.

Of the many fine animals coming out of New Eden's equine breeding program, this well-trained, good-natured four-year-old mare had quickly become his favorite. She was everything one could ask for in a mountain-bred saddle horse: intelligent, sure-footed, and steady on the trail. On one recent hunt into the southern hills, she'd barely flinched when a 900 pound grizzly suddenly charged out of a dense berry thicket near an alpine lake. The trusting mount courageously held her ground as Hunter brought his crossbow up in the nick of time for a near point-blank-range shot, downing the ferocious giant a couple of yards from the mare's trembling, adrenaline-charged legs.

At 15.5 hands, she was raw-boned and well-muscled and could ride all day without tiring—a true Rocky Mountain mustang descended from a majestic dun stallion, a champion of the open range with classic dun markings over a medium gray coat. Like her sire, she bore the thick, black dorsal stripe down the middle of her back, with distinctive black shoulder stripes and a two-toned black mane and tail fringed in light gray. Her face was equally dramatic with dark cheek patches, black eyeliner around large liquid eyes and matching black outlined ears. The characteristic zebra stripes on her lower legs and chest were the final proof of her pureblood lineage, pointing to DNA markers found only in unmixed bloodlines from the earliest Spanish stock released in North America by the conquistadors in the mid 1600's.

With bedroll and poncho lashed securely behind the saddle and the remainder of his gear—trail food, canteens, slicker, parka, hat and such—stowed in saddlebags straddling her rump, Hunter was set to depart. Untying the reins, he led her out into the chilly spring mists of morning. Waiting nearby was one final offering from the grateful citizens of New Eden: a stout twin pair of black Montana mules, the very same pair, in fact, which had nearly trampled him on the bridge! The brawny brothers pawed the ground impatiently, faces burrowed deep into feed bags attached to halters as busy tongues ferreted out the last few sweet oats, all that remained of their tasty morning treat.

Piled high upon their broad backs and securely lashed to sturdy wooden pack frames were carefully balanced loads of gear and supplies, enough to see Hunter and his animals through their upcoming trek: food, camping equipment, a small, skillfully-crafted buffalo hide tipi, and other necessities such as fishing and hunting gear, a locally smithed axe and shovel, and several other useful items as might be needed along the trail. The twin five-year-olds seemed to understand that they were about to embark on a protracted adventure, and Hunter could sense their anticipation in flaring nostrils and the way their ample fuzzy ears pivoted this way and that.

He appreciated these many gifts and accepted the livestock out of necessity, having lost all but three of his own animals during the cold snap and blizzard on the journey south that nearly took all of their lives. The trio of brave horses that survived the winter journey were still not one hundred percent, but would likely recover their full strength in due time under the watchful care of Anna, who had made it her personal crusade to rehabilitate them. Sagebrush and the twins would serve him well, and he was grateful to have them.

Back home in Wyoming, he'd turned out his remaining stock to fend for themselves before heading south to New Eden. With plenty of new grass and rushing creeks filled with spring runoff, the odds of survival were in their favor. Besides, they'd been born on the range, and the adjustment back to their roots would come naturally.

Chances are they would have already been assimilated back into one of the local wild horse bands that roamed the Wind River Range and called that region home. He figured this was especially likely in the case of his two youngest mares who would be keenly interested in the protection that a strong stallion could provide while blessing them with genetically superior foals. He realized that in returning to their wild origins, they might not be inclined to revisit the restrictions of domestication. In his experience, a wild horse had more raw spirit and grit than one born in captivity, but they always required a bit more taming before they could be trained; he almost hated to domesticate them, though, in a practical sense, there was little else in the way of mounted wilderness transportation these days.

Now, on the other hand, these mules here were bred for strength and stability and seemed to take genuine pleasure in transporting their loads in the service of humanity. They were a handsome pair to be sure, strong and willing with steady dispositions and, barring some unfortunate mishap, should provide excellent companionship and service for at least a couple of decades or more. Hunter had heard of mules that were nearly forty years of age, and, although they were generally unable to reproduce (most "male" mules being sterile), he felt confident that these two would be an important part of his life for a long time to come.

The success of New Eden's animal husbandry program was not surprising. The community here had successfully crossed male donkeys with mares nearly since its inception, and these animals were outstanding examples of the quality specimens they were able to consistently produce.

Removing their feedbags and leading the pair from the corral, Hunter checked the morning sky and scanned the horizon, glad that today would finally mark the beginning of his journey home. With the summer solstice fast approaching, it was high time to be getting back to his valley to make the necessary preparations for the inevitable Rocky Mountain winter that would invariably arrive again without mercy.

Though it had now been more than fifteen years since the brutal, two-year nuclear winter following the End War, the weather still remained unpredictable; from year-to-year, climatic fluctuations in temperature, precipitation levels, and season length remained the norm rather than the exception. With the recent arrival of near perfect traveling weather,

Hunter was determined to take full advantage of it to begin his journey under optimal conditions.

His heading home was long overdue. Now that he'd recovered from his injuries and regained most of his strength, his need for space and solitude drove him hard to return to the wilds where he felt whole. Though the community here afforded him as much personal space as was practical, and everyone did their best to respect his privacy, it was impossible to avoid some interaction, some sharing in lives and struggles, worries and dramas, heartaches and joys when living in such close proximity to more than two hundred people. After nearly a decade alone, these past seven months immersed in the lives of so many others was quite enough to last another lifetime.

And while no one stopped and stared, Hunter could feel their eyes upon him as he swung up into the saddle and led the mules forward toward the eastern gate. He understood that many in the community did not want him to leave. During the past weeks and months, some even tried to talk him out of it, attempting to *sell* him on the value of community and healthy social interaction. Both William and Robert did their best in this regard, but Hunter remained neutral and was unaffected by their attempts at social conversion, feeling no obligation to defend his decision, nor argue his position to return to his previous lifestyle.

There was nothing anyone could do or say to convince him to permanently remain in a group setting such as this. Just witness what had become of Planchet's utopia. No way. Where there were people, there would always be upset and social unrest. One person would always want to dominate another, and so there would be wars and slavery and unspeakable atrocities committed, even here in New Eden, by humans attempting to rule over one another.

All that he'd witnessed throughout his life convinced him that the human race was ever-destined to self-destruct. In microcosm, this most recent example was the same madness that caused the End War in which billions lost their lives. Mankind would never rid itself of this antisocial virus because apparently Man *was* the virus! To rule over one's fellows and control others for self-gratification was apparently inherent in the human socio-psychological blueprint, and war and social injustice would never be eradicated as long as the species continued to nurture and embrace this instinct to dominate.

Hunter longed for the purity and solitude of rugged mountains and alpine lakes; his soul ached for the wild places where *Homo sapiens* was but a temporary passerby and where the crimes and chaos of humanity were mostly undetectable and altogether forgotten. It was toward this promised landscape that he now set his mind and will, and there would be no looking back for the self-exiled loner who had dutifully repaid an old debt.

Last evening, while making his rounds and saying his personal goodbyes, he harbored no regrets, certain that his decision was the correct one for him, though there was one person here that he knew he would miss, and there was nothing he could do to change that.

Over the past months, Hunter and Elise had grown together like two trees in a forest, entwined in each other's branches simply because they were planted so close to one another. Their roots shared common soil—both felt the same wind, sun, and rain—and they had sheltered and supported one another through some pretty rough times without ever violating the others' space, sensibilities, or dignity. Even during the blizzard, when for survival's sake he'd lain with her without clothing, skin-to-skin and heart-to-heart, there was never an invasion of privacy or sense of impropriety. He wasn't even sure how much she remembered as they'd never talked about it, but deep inside there was a bond, an unbreakable connection between them that simply could not be denied.

As he rode through the orchards, fruit ripening on the boughs, it seemed such an idyllic place to live. What more could a man ask for, he wondered? And yet, looking out to the horizon, the mountains answered him, calling deeply to his being, evoking the irresistible longing within him to look beyond here and now to discover what lay just beyond the next ridge.

Did he ever get lonely? William once asked when laying out his best argument for staying to become a permanent fixture in New Eden's community life. Loneliness was something that never affected him. In fact, he'd never really felt alone because he was so connected to the universe around him. How could one be lonely when surrounded by mountains and forests, rivers and lakes, filled with multitudes of unique and varied incarnations: birds, squirrels, great herds of mammals numbering in the tens and even hundreds of thousands, large bears that could rip a man's face off with one swipe of their claws? And how about encountering an attacking lioness? Here was two-hundred pounds of feline ferocity, strong enough to take down the largest bull elk and able to haul young deer and antelope up into trees in her jaws to protect her kill from ground-based competitors like coyotes and wolves. And what about wolverines? Lonely? Never. Challenged? Most definitely.

Hunter understood his place in the natural world. His existence ebbed and flowed with its cyclical currents and seasons. His days were defined by the tasks required of him to survive in a raw, unforgiving environment. The tools he fashioned from the oxidizing iron of the past, the clothing he crafted from animal hides and furs, and the entire multitude of miscellaneous items, utensils, furniture, shelter, all that he produced was born of necessity.

His relationship to nature was defined by his need to survive in and coexist with the natural world. Only in the wilderness could a man fully understand this. Only in the wild places could one truly come into his own. To walk upright among all of this marvelous creation was a gift as much as a solemn responsibility, and he felt a genuine sense of stewardship toward the world around him. Even when quenching a life to supply his own, there was a reverence in his heart. He was profoundly grateful to the Earth for its bounty.

Living on his own was simple, linear, and he was never required to think about how his actions might affect another human life. On his own, there was scant opportunity for self-interrogation, the second-guessing of one's intentions. He knew himself well and was comfortable being Hunter.

But last September, all of this balance and harmony suddenly shifted. A new variable, like a pebble in a quiet pool, invaded his consciousness the moment he'd seen the smoke from her fire. After so many years alone, Elise suddenly arrives on the scene and his equilibrium is altered. She was unlike any woman he'd ever known, competent and complimentary. Complete within herself, strong, able, and needing no one. Never before could he just *be* himself around anyone, much less a woman of her ability and intelligence. Now he'd grown accustomed to her presence and was familiar with her ways around camp and on the trail. She was never any trouble, even when her life tried to slip away in the blizzard and he had to work all night to keep her warm and alive; it was no burden.

He wondered what it would be like now to go back to being completely on his own, with no one to look out for or to share meals or moments with. He was no longer so sure of his own future, but knew that he could not ask her to leave this place, her home, where all of her childhood and family memories took place. Her struggles, her hopes and dreams were all here.

She belonged in this place; her people needed her to lead, to heal, to care for livestock and the sick, and she would never choose to leave this place for what, a life of solitude and hardship in the raw wilderness? Doing without friends or family or safety or the many conveniences a community like this could offer a young woman like Elise? What about children and family? Isn't this what most women her age wanted? The two of them had never discussed such matters. There was no reason to do so.

He could never expect anyone, especially her, to have to make that choice. No, it was better for him to go now and better that they'd left it this way. Good that they never crossed over that threshold into (dare he think it?) love. They were friends with a bond born of hardship and sacrifice and would always be so.

He saw how the young, eligible men looked at her. There were several apt suitors just dying to capture her attention, and he knew that as long as he was present, she would never allow herself that luxury. Besides, he was too old for her, she being not yet twenty-six and next winter would mark his thirty-ninth lap around the sun. Did she feel obligated to wait for his permission? He refused to wield that much power over another's life and happiness, and so buried the tender feelings he held for her, keeping their relationship on a safe, manageable level.

Absorbed in these thoughts, Hunter settled in to the comfortable rhythm of his horse's gaited walk, with the heavier clip-clop of mule hooves and the creaking of harness leather for accompaniment. He led them along a path beside the fast flowing stream that wound its way through the bottom of the valley.

Settlers working the fields or tending livestock waved as he passed through rich, irrigated ground planted in hay, oats, corn, and soybeans. Crossing a small, wooden plank bridge, the path bisected a wider, east-west thoroughfare. Guiding Sagebrush to the right, they soon passed beyond the planted fields and started the long, gradual rise to the eastern gate.

At the top, he paused to look back. The cool mid-morning breeze caressed his face, blowing through his now shoulder-length cropped hair. Before turning in for the night, he had cut off his long braid and left it hanging in the stable where Elise was sure to see it. He did so on impulse, not totally certain of his own motives. He only wanted to leave something of himself behind for her to remember him by, and was aware of the Native practice of cutting one's hair as an act of mourning and respect for a friend who had passed on. He reckoned the loss of their relationship was worth at least that much respect, especially now that it would be but a collection of moments, memories of the time they shared. Looking back at the last outpost of civilization he ever planned to gaze upon, Hunter turned his horse and vanished over the ridge.

CHAPTER TWENTY

FIRE, WATER, EARTH, SKY

ACROSS THE WIDE valley, on a grassy knoll dotted with grave markers, Elise knelt, pulling weeds from the flower beds bordering the Planchet family burial plot. Her heart was heavy this morning, and her emotions warred within her. She fought the pain she felt inside, her mind refusing to acknowledge the depths of her heart's anguish. Before dawn she found herself drawn to this place, the one safe spot in all of New Eden where she could really be alone and was free to let down her guard.

Father was buried here beside her mother and, just a few weeks ago, Amy's remains were located about a mile and a half downstream from the trestle bridge, and now she was here as well. They shared a large granite headstone quarried from a nearby cliff face and brought up here in a wagon by William and Robert. Their loved ones' names and birth-death dates were chiseled into the dark stone by members of the mason's guild, leaving plenty of room for those who would join them sooner or later to be buried here in the Planchet's final resting place.

The wind gusted and a dark brown ringlet fell into her eyes. She pushed it away and glanced across the valley to the eastern gate road. She thought she saw a rider and pack animals passing over the top, but, before she could get to her binoculars, whatever had been there was gone. Suddenly she felt washed out, as if a flash flood had ripped through her soul, carrying away the goodness and meaning of it all, leaving behind only stark, boulder-strewn banks stripped of foliage.

Her thoughts drifted back to yesterday evening and her meeting with Hunter. She sat in the large workroom adjacent to the dispensary taking a quick inventory of the medicinal herbs used in teas, poultices, and creams, and noting those she was running low on. She would pass the list to her enthusiastic cadre of apprentices who were charged with the vital task of collecting fresh specimens. Sensing a presence, she glanced up from her work to discover Hunter standing quietly in the doorway, silently watching her with those hauntingly gray eyes now somehow mixed with blue since his injury.

She smiled, blushing, and stood to clear a space for him at the table, but he waved her off and crossed the room without the assistance of his usual crutches or cane. She watched him move, noting the fluid, confident gait, with only a slight hitch remaining in his right side, as if he still favored it, perhaps more out of habit than necessity. She was pleased to see him so fully recovered. His ruddy complexion and understated strength had returned, replacing the ghostly pallor he'd worn during his long convalescence.

Carefully unwrapping a bulky bundle in his hands, Hunter presented Elise with a scaled-down version of his formidable crossbow! She gasped in surprised and beamed at him, not quite knowing what to say. He'd secretly worked on it for the past several weeks, finishing it only this morning. "I thought you might be able to use this when out hunting or fighting off hordes of ruffians." He smiled. She picked it up and held it in her hands, pleased by the perfect weight and balance of it.

"Now I'll have to start practicing right away. Thank you, Hunter, for such a wonderful gift!" She held up the bow and admired its workmanship. Bringing it up to her shoulder to sight down its length, she was surprised at how comfortably it fit. It was an exact three-quarters replica of Hunter's bow, but with iron sights mounted on top instead of a rifle scope. A quiver stuffed with bolts completed the set. Elise suddenly realized how much she missed being around him. Her daily visits to supervise his treatment the months he was bedridden gave her a legitimate reason to spend time with him on a regular basis, and she had grown accustomed to it. Now that he was up and about, there seemed no opportunity. When he was finally able to leave the infirmary, she became absorbed with her many rebuilding and healing duties within the community.

"I wanted you to have it before I returned north." His words took her by surprise. She didn't want to think about Hunter returning to his valley so soon. "Thanks to your expert care, my strength is restored and I am grateful for that and for all that you and your people have done for me."

"It is we who are thankful to you," she replied, "for honoring your oath to my father and saving us from our enemies, a fight that was not yours but which you embraced from a sense of loyalty, and for which you nearly paid with your life. It is we who are forever grateful to you, Hunter, for all that you have done for us here." He looked away, not comfortable receiving the compliment."I know that my father would have been very thankful as well…" her voice wavered, and Elise could not continue her sentence.

Hunter looked upon her with compassion. He wished he could have somehow prevented Adam's death. "He was a brave man of vision and this world will sorely miss his goodness," he spoke with respect. The loss of her father was still much too recent for Elise to see beyond the grief of his passing—she was still dealing with the unjust finality of it.

"You did everything you could…" she offered.

"Everyone did their bit." He changed the subject. "But now, with summer upon us, duties call to me from my valley in the north. There are many preparations I must make for the coming winter." He hesitated slightly, wishing he could fully speak his mind. After an uncomfortable silence, he offered a fleeting smile and a nod, and was gone.

Watching him go, she recalled their journey south and the adventures and challenges they shared along the way, and was saddened now to think that their acquaintance would suddenly end. She'd secretly hoped that he might find some meaning here in the community, some reason to stay on, at least for a time, but she was only fooling herself. The man was a hermit, a loner who only became fully alive in wilderness and solitude. An incredible sadness came over her soul and she broke down suddenly and wept.

* * *

CROSSING THE WIDE trestle bridge, Hunter set his jaw and never looked back. At the White River, he pointed the animals north toward Wyoming and settled them into a comfortable pace while he relaxed and enjoyed his solitude and the perfect traveling weather.

With New Eden receding steadily behind him, he was once again alone and surrounded by the vast, open aliveness of the wilderness. His spirit soared as he drank in his surroundings, like intoxicating liquor or the heady smell of an excited lover and was released. *This* was his home. *Here* he was truly in his element, the one place he felt completely comfortable and in tune with all the cosmos.

* * *

CONCEALED JUST BELOW the ridge of a distant hill, the misshapen figure of a man squinted through binoculars with his one good eye. Having observed Hunter's change of direction, he limped back to his scruffy-looking mule, stuffed the glasses into tattered saddlebags and stood on a small boulder to struggle awkwardly into the worn-out saddle. Beside himself with glee, the unkempt character dressed in ragged clothes, goaded his ill-tempered mount onward with a thin stick, keeping pace with, but well behind and out of sight of, Hunter who was completely unaware of being followed.

Breathing heavily and chortling under his breath, the stranger's disfigured face displayed an obscene crooked smile, revealing four missing front teeth. He couldn't believe his luck! The broken man's heart burned black with hatred as he reached for the cracked hand mirror hanging from a leather thong tied to his belt. He held it close to his face on his good eye side and hated Hunter anew. Peering at his grotesque reflection, even *he* had a hard time remembering what the old Frank McAllister used to look like!

How he'd survived the fall from the bridge could not be explained. He simply remembered twirling through the air and coming down through a thick stand of snow-covered spruce lining the riverbank. Young Amy, still clinging to his back, hit first, taking the brunt of the fall and cushioning McAllister's impact. As they crashed through the trees, the branches knocked them apart and that was the last he ever saw of her. The speed of McAllister's plunge was slowed by the thick boughs, and he miraculously landed in a deep snowdrift at the base of the trees. He wasn't sure how long he lay buried there, but at some point the following day he came to and worked his way out of the drifts, dragging a badly broken leg behind him. Finding two suitable pieces of wood, he strapped them to his leg with his belt to form a crude splint. Searching further, he found a walking stick to help him keep the weight off that leg.

As more snowfall blanketed the area, he slowly made his way downstream to a fork in the river where it joined a medium-sized stream. Recognizing the place, he followed the watercourse upstream and soon arrived at a small cave he'd used as a vodka cache for a few weeks after first arriving in this territory. It appeared that someone had been using the shelter part time as a hunting camp until winter arrived in earnest. They'd even cut and stacked a generous supply of firewood and kindling. He found a couple of warm bedrolls made from old woolen blankets and a stash of pemmican, dried fruits and jerked meat in a large tin. There was also a flint and steel for striking fires, and an axe, some candles, a teapot, and cast iron kettle with plates, mugs, and flatware.

There he remained, warm and dry, as he slowly healed and made it through the long cold winter to spring. When he was strong enough to walk, he snuck in close to the fields one dark night and came back with a mule. He eventually made his way cautiously back to the ruins of New Hope and scavenged enough to put together a camping kit—knife, hatchet, and a few other items he found lying around the ghost town.

Throughout his painful ordeal, all he ever thought of or dreamed about was killing Hunter. He hated that meddler with every fiber of his being and every ounce of strength in his body. He irrationally blamed him for all that was wrong with his life. He completely forgot about how Mitchell had nearly finished him, trapping him inside the Great Hall like an imprisoned rat. He only knew that he was destined to rule New Eden and had been robbed of his rightful throne there, and every waking moment of his life he hated Hunter more.

He hated him for interfering in his plans and destroying everything he'd worked so hard to attain, and for taking away his eye, and turning him into a gimp. This hatred gave him purpose, and that purpose kept him alive. He vowed to himself a thousand times, and to the wind, and the rain, and the sun, and the stars, that he would have his revenge on the meddler. As the weather improved, he took to camping out in the mountains on the outskirts of New Eden.

He pilfered a pair of binoculars from a shepherd's cabin way up in the hills, along with some better fishing gear, and from the dark corner of a closet came a sawed-off, double barreled shotgun with four clean shells that must have been stored and forgotten, or more probably, whoever put them there was long since dead.

When Hunter began taking his daily rides, McAllister was watching. It was too risky to follow him, and McAllister was afraid of being seen or that his tracks might be noticed, but, from a well hidden cave up on the side of a nearby hill, he could watch the comings and goings through the gates and keep an eye on things. Now that Hunter was obviously on the move, outfitted as he was with the loaded pack mules and all, the time for McAllister's revenge was drawing nigh and what a sweet revenge it would be! He chortled and struck the miserable animal beneath him three times with his stick for no apparent reason beyond pure meanness.

* * *

LATER THAT AFTERNOON, Elise returned home feeling strangely disquieted. As she entered the stables to brush and feed her horse, she noticed that Sagebrush's stall was empty and her tack missing, and only then fully realized that Hunter had actually left! She felt an ache in the pit of her stomach as if she'd been kicked. She knew this moment would eventually arrive but hadn't wanted to accept it. Even after Hunter's gift, she hoped he might put off leaving until sometime in the future.

Suddenly, it was real and he was gone! Elise brushed the pretty little bay's coat. She had secretly hoped that he would change his mind and stay on at New Eden to make his home here. Everyone admired and respected him, and there was an ongoing bet among the community members that the two of them would settle down together as soon as he was feeling up to par. Anna used to bug her about it all the time, wanting to know the status of their *relationship*, but Elise just acted annoyed, assuring her little sister that there was nothing going on and that they were just really good friends. She grew accustomed to seeing him about and speaking with him, and just felt good knowing he was here, certain that she could always rely on him, no matter what.

She moved around to the other side of her horse with her thoughts weaving in and out of the past and present, evoking emotions she hadn't known were there. She thought about how she felt nearly losing him on the bridge and thinking she might never have a chance to speak with him again, and how relieved she was when he somehow pulled through the surgery and recovered and was finally doing so well again. Over the past few weeks, she'd spent little time with him due to her busy schedule and the fact that he was very often off riding up in the hills alone or out hunting with the others to bring in game.

Finished with the rubdown, she led her filly into the paddock. Passing Sagebrush's empty stall, she noticed something curious hanging on the near railing. She reached for it, momentarily perplexed to discover the long braid tied with thin strips of rawhide at both ends until recognizing the color and texture and suddenly realizing what it was!

Hunter had cut off his beautiful hair, but why? It once reached to the small of his back and, as she held the length of braid up against her body, she realized that he must have chopped it off at the shoulders! She sought the meaning in it. Was he in mourning? Shearing the hair was a ritual observed at the passing of a fellow tribesman in some native cultures, but if so, for whom, and why leave it here in the stables?

Lifting his braid to her nostrils, she closed her eyes and inhaled, drinking in Hunter's scent. A shiver raced down her spine as tangled thoughts and emotions mugged her senses, filling her soul with him. She was swept away by the force of her feelings. In a collage of color and light, of sounds and smells, her time with him flashed through her mind, and she finally understood and admitted to herself that she loved him! She pictured him, strong and handsome, tough yet true, with his beautiful blue-gray eyes, high cheekbones and full lips…

All of a sudden she began to shake and new tears welled up in light of this unmistakable truth—but now he was gone—leaving without even offering her a final opportunity to reveal her true feelings to him! She was both confused and surprised at the depth of her upset. After all, she always knew that he would not stay on here forever; how could she even expect that of him? He was a loner and uncomfortable around people, but never so with her. There had always been a truce between them, a peace that allowed them to share the same space without feeling like they were intruding or being intruded upon.

The fact is she would have gone north with him if he'd only asked, but he hadn't and that was that, and now he was gone and the ache in her heart was unbearable. She cast her eyes wildly about the barn as if she might catch one final glimpse of the only man she'd ever known to whom she could fully give herself without compromise. Feeling cheated and more lost than ever, she clutched his braid to her breast and collapsed into a sobbing heap against the corral fence, slowly sliding to the straw-scattered floor where she wept.

Hours later, she quietly made her way back to the Great Hall, barely noticing the passersby out for an evening stroll. Emotionally spent, she managed to make it to her room and collapse on the bed, her soul and body numb, shrouded in heartache and the cruelness of her fate.

* * *

THE FOLLOWING MORNING, Elise was roused from a fitful sleep by a loud pounding on her bedroom door. She frowned and called out, "Who is it?"

Anna turned the knob and peeked in. Seeing Elise still in bed, she crossed to the window and threw open the curtains to let the bright morning sunlight into the room. Elise squinted and buried her face in her pillow as Anna approached, talking a mile a minute about how Hunter had gone north and why was Elise still here?

"Look at me Elise," said Anna."What are you doing lying around in bed with the morning already half gone and so many miles to go to catch up with him?"

Elise sat upright in bed and stared at her sister. "What in the world are you talking about?"

"I'm talking about Hunter, the man you are in *love* with, who is heading back to his wilderness *without you.* Why aren't you with him? Everyone knows you two belong together." She cocked her head and gave Elise an exaggerated look of incredulity. The truth in Anna's words fell hard on Elise's heart like a storm wave crashing against the shore, dissolving the wall between what she really wanted and what she felt was her duty here at New Eden.

"Everyone knows how much you've sacrificed, and we appreciate all that you've done for the family and the entire community, but now it's time for *your* dreams to come true!"

"But he never asked me to go with him." She tried to argue, unsuccessfully.

"How could he, Elise? He knows how your life revolves around your service to New Eden. He would never want to deprive you of your family and friends here, can't you see that?"

Elise recalled little things he'd said, that at the time she didn't really understand, but none of that mattered now. She only knew that she wanted to be with him and believed that he felt the same about her. She'd known it deep down for a long time but was afraid to admit it to herself, afraid that somehow she would lose this man who came into her life and changed everything for the better.

Anna stood and headed for the door saying, "So get yourself up now and get dressed and ready for your journey; you've got a day's catching up to do, and William and Robert are downstairs with your favorite horse saddled and ready to go." Elise just stared at her sister in amazement and smiled. The little girl she took under her wing when their mother died was all grown up now and giving her orders! She threw back the bed covers and went to her closet to pack.

An hour later, a stunned Elise walked out onto the sunny front porch to find a large crowd of well-wishers gathered there. What appeared to be half of New Eden stood cheering as she descended the steps to her waiting horse and pack animals. Robert and William loaded her final belongings onto the mules as her lifelong friends hugged and kissed her goodbye. Everyone was teary-eyed, but happy, having apparently known for weeks the inevitability of her union with Hunter.

She shared tearful goodbyes with Anna and Sarah, who thanked her again for all she had done during their journey north last year. Little Jamie gave his Aunt Leesy one last big hug and kiss, and she turned to go. Climbing into the saddle, she looked out over the crowd and smiled, finally at peace with her decision and eager to embark on her newest adventure.

With a final wave goodbye, she rode off, flanked by her brothers and a dozen of Robert's best men who would accompany her north until she caught up with Hunter, which should happen sometime within the next day or so. Half an hour later, with the distant crowd dispersed, Elise paused at the top of the road for one final look back at her beloved New Eden before turning and passing out of sight over the ridge.

CHAPTER TWENTY ONE

VOICES FROM THE PAST

THE PREVIOUS AFTERNOON, with ominous storm clouds darkening the horizon, Hunter had abandoned the White River valley, guiding his mare and pack animals into a heavily forested ravine beside a cascading creek. A half mile upstream, the watercourse split, and he chose the left fork into the western hills. After a long, steep ascent he spotted what he was looking for halfway up a boulder-strewn cliff: an ancient limestone footpath leading to a wide rock ledge that formed a shallow cave. William had told him of this place, which was sometimes used for overnight shelter during forays into the surrounding territory.

Dismounting Sagebrush in the gathering dusk, he collected two bundles of firewood along the noisy creek's bank and lashed them atop the pack mules. The good natured beasts didn't seem to notice the additional weight as they casually browsed among the lush sedge and sweet grasses lining the trail. Leading his charges forward on foot, he managed to scramble up to the shelter's broad entrance and bring them under the protection of the ledge just as a blinding flash of lightning struck nearby, its loud thunderclap heralding an imminent assault by the threatening squall.

Offloading the animals' gear, Hunter spent a few minutes brushing them down and checking them over. Not long afterwards, a rapid-fire sequence of lightning bolts rippled across the sky, causing strobe effects and deafening thunder that rolled down through the gorge and echoed out into the distant hills. Moments later, a violent storm front ripped through the wash, as the heavens opened and a torrential downpour, whipped by gusting winds, fell from the sky in ragged sheets, blotting out the world beyond the protection of the rock overhang.

Safe within their weatherproof shelter, Sagebrush and the twins enjoyed a modest treat of sweet oats, as Hunter nurtured a comforting fire ringed with stones. The warm blaze crackled brightly, holding at bay the damp darkness trying to seep in around the edges from the cloud-soaked night. At one end of the rock enclosure, enough kindling and firewood to last for several days was stacked neatly against the wall. Using his own gathered sticks, Hunter replenished the fuel he used, ensuring that the next traveler seeking refuge here would not be caught out empty-handed.

Grateful to have escaped the drenching downpour, he was energized by the storm and knelt on a comfortable bed of furs adding medium-sized sticks to the campfire as he listened to the thunderous sound of the rain. Overhead, the twelve-foot ceiling was smudged with centuries of black soot, bearing witness to the countless pilgrims who'd sheltered here, from time immemorial.

Most interesting were the prehistoric petroglyphs and pictographs adorning the rear rock face, high on the wall and well-preserved from the elements. There was a fascinating collection of parallel lines and geometric shapes, intermingled with human and animal likenesses, as well as the more mystical half-human, half-animal figures, posted here perhaps as a sign or warning. Whether omens left behind during ritual hunts and vision quests, or the casual doodles of a prehistoric Picasso, the images were stunning examples of the earliest form of recorded human art—evocative, mysterious, and transcendent offerings by forgotten artists from a distant epoch.

By wavy firelight, Hunter could make out dozens of distinct characters etched in or painted on the ten yard long rock panel. Here were shaggy-headed bison and charging elk with exaggerated antlers, among strange looking bird-beings and bipeds with lion heads holding spears that appeared to transform into snakes. There were strange floating stick-beings with large oval heads and almond eyes, with what appeared to be rays of light radiating from behind their heads.

Hunter marveled at these samples of primordial human art. He knew that the meaning of such images was shrouded in mystery, and Anthropology's experts had differed widely in their interpretation. Some had argued that they were simple depictions of everyday hunter-gatherer life, while others suggested they were graphic articulations of hallucinogenic visions experienced during shamanic trances. Either way, the images spoke to him of both the continuity and the impermanence of human culture and community.

He wondered about the individual artists and pondered the significance of their work. Whenever encountering such rock art throughout his travels, Hunter felt a strange sense of familiarity and an inexplicable connection to the life of the artist, as if by merely viewing these symbolic depictions, he was drawn back into the shrouded mists of Mankind's mysterious origins.

He could easily imagine small family bands of nomads from the north, dressed in animal skins and furs, hunting and foraging throughout this territory some twelve to fifteen thousand years earlier. At the same time, ferocious, but thankfully now extinct, American lions, saber-toothed cats, short-faced bears and dire wolves roamed these hills and valleys, undoubtedly preying on our human forebears, as well as on the indigenous horse, camel, dwarf pronghorn, ancient bison, woolly mammoth, mastodon, and giant ground sloth populations that once flourished here.

For these earliest nomadic tribes, a shelter such as this would have made an excellent strategic choice, as it was situated well above the flood plain, yet close to fresh runoff from snowmelt in the heights above. The steep frontal approach from either above or below would likely discourage potential attackers, and with a stacked rock wall erected along the opening, this position would have been fairly easy to defend by even one or two well-armed and determined occupants. He could only imagine the life and death dramas that had taken place herein over the past millennia.

Thousands of years ago the mysterious artists and nomads had vanished into the mists beyond reckoning, and it was now Hunter and his animals who occupied this place, a solitary figure passing through this land on his way north, back to the familiarity of his hidden valley high in the Wind River Range of the Wyoming Rockies. Headed *home*, where he'd staked a claim and established a life in self-imposed exile, cut off from the scattered remnants of the human race. *Home, was that what it was,* he wondered? *Was it really his home or merely a place to act out his lone existence, each day blending imperceptibly into the next?*

Staring into the dancing flames, his thoughts were drawn once more to New Eden and to Elise Planchet, the only woman he'd ever known with whom he shared a deep, personal connection. She was one of those rare souls who understood the value of silence and the need for space, and who could bear witness to intense moments without compulsively imposing her will upon them. Nor did she acquiesce or compromise her own reality in any situation, under any circumstances.

She occupied her chosen space without defilement or drama and consciously brought grace and beauty to each moment of her existence, a true blessing to those fortunate enough to be able to claim her as their friend. In this regard, he considered her to be unique in the world, a self-contained woman needing nothing and no one to complete her as a human being. To Hunter, she was the perfect companion, and he was certain that if he lived for a hundred years, he would never find another treasure like her.

Unfortunately, regardless of how he felt about her, Elise was married to her people, to family and community, and he could never expect, nor would he dare ask her to give up those relationships and her comfortable, well-respected station in life to share a hard road with a cave dweller who was more at home harvesting game in the vast panorama of the uncharted wilderness than sitting astride a plodding plow-horse, dutifully sowing and reaping his portion from the well-tilled community soil.

Resigned to the inevitability of his solitary fate, an uncharacteristically melancholy Hunter made a final check on the animals to find that they were already dozing off, comfortably settled in among the flickering shadows at the far end of the cave. Moving back to the fire, he added a couple of stout logs and banked up coals against a thick oak chunk with his staff. Pausing at the edge of the shelter mere inches from the screen of runoff pouring down from the cliff face above, Hunter stared out into the sodden blackness, unable to see or hear anything beyond the deafening roar of the deluge. Hoping for a break in tomorrow's weather, he crawled into his bedroll with a heavy heart and was quickly (and mercifully) lulled to sleep by the rhythmic drumming of the rain.

* * *

THE FOLLOWING MORNING the day dawned gray and dismal, echoing Hunter's glum mood. The steady downpour had continued its aerial bombardment throughout the night and in the gully below, the swollen stream had climbed the steep walls of the ravine, washing out the trail and imposing a disappointing delay upon his journey. He opened one of several large, lightweight bundles wrapped in hide, and apportioned out a ration of hay for the animals before digging out some potatoes, bacon, and eggs for himself, compliments of New Eden's larder. He set about making breakfast, as the rain slacked up a bit and the sky grew lighter in the east.

* * *

A MILE DOWNSTREAM, a soaking wet Frank McAllister waited out the storm in abject misery, huddled in a clump of trees on the side of a hill, a quarter mile above the confluence of the swollen creek and the fast flowing White River. Over his clothes he wore a small deerskin cloak wrapped about his head and shoulders, designed to lessen the effects of the rain, though it didn't seem to be of much use at the moment. A sleepless night out in the open had taken its toll on the crippled, one-eyed former Godfather of New Hope and Usurper of New Eden, who tried to catch a few winks beneath a dense clump of cedars, just back from the edge of the steep bank with the raging torrent roaring past beneath his feet.

Just behind him up the hill, his hungry mule was tethered to the trunk of a slender alder, where it had nibbled everything within reach down to the mud and was trying to gain access to a particularly tasty-looking clump of grass located just twelve inches beyond its outstretched tongue. Straining against the reigns to gain the few extra inches necessary to accomplish his goal, he clenched the bit in his teeth to keep it from cutting his tender mouth and leaned forward with his muscular back and legs. Without warning, the young sapling snapped clean off a foot above the ground and the twelve-hundred-pound draft animal lurched forward, sliding uncontrollably down the steep, muddy hillside towards the water.

* * *

THE BRIGHT MORNING sun was already halfway to its zenith when Elise and her phalanx of riders finally cleared the eastern gate and headed across the bridge and down towards the White River valley where they planned to pick up Hunter's trail. From the top of the hill looking north, the sky ahead was a brilliant blue until just along the horizon, where a low, gray cloud bank retreated before a steady breeze that herded the rain clouds north towards the Canadian border. Overnight the weather at New Eden had been dry and windy, but Elise had heard distant thunder and could tell that it had rained on the trail ahead.

She conferred with Robert, and he agreed that Hunter probably hadn't made it very far before being forced to seek shelter from the violent thunderstorm so common this time of year in the mountains. Elise figured that if the sky was looking bad yesterday afternoon, Hunter's logical choice would have been to try to make it to Painted Cave where he could wait out the storm in relative comfort. Maybe, if she hurried, she could catch up to him before he reentered the valley to continue his journey north. She calculated that they were still about twenty miles south of the creek, which, due to the presence of the loaded pack animals, was a moderate three or four hour ride.

Following Hunter's day-old trail through the lush valley was easy. This time of year the ground was still fairly soft; his horse and loaded mules left readily distinguishable hoof prints as they passed through the rich grassy bottomland adjoining the river. Game was abundant in the beech and alder thickets framing the wide watercourse, and Robert decided that, if they caught up to Hunter before nightfall, he and the rest of the escort would overnight at the cave and do some harvesting on the trip back to New Eden in the morning.

Deer and elk sign were plentiful and returning with fresh meat would be much appreciated by the folks back home.

Robert rode quietly beside Elise, wondering what life would be like in New Eden without his older sister there to contribute her special knowledge, skills, and talents towards solving the myriad community challenges and issues that inevitably arose during any given season. While he, William, Sarah, and Anna were well-versed in how the community was designed to operate, things had abruptly changed with the passing of their father, and the Planchet heirs were truly on their own for the first time. In the past, regardless of the gravity or urgency of the situation, Adam Planchet invariably devised a ready solution, immediately knowing the exact actions needed to solve any given problem.

Now that William had assumed the primary leadership role in the broad administration of New Eden, he demonstrated more of a tendency to make important decisions after first consulting with his siblings. For Robert, making the transition from informed spectator to active participant and taking on such father-like responsibilities was a bit daunting, and his sister's valuable input and unique viewpoint would be sorely missed.

He understood that Elise was following her heart, and, according to the childhood teachings of their parents, that was not only *not* selfish, but was as valid a reason as any to guide one's decisions in life. Some would even go so far as to say that *not* being true to one's self and following one's heart was a guaranteed recipe for a miserable, failed existence. Besides, he reasoned, Elise more than deserved to be happy and fulfilled, especially since she had given up so much personal time and freedom over the years to tend to

Father and the younger children after their mother passed away. Even knowing that Elise was leaving for all the right reasons didn't minimize the loss they would all feel with her gone.

* * *

WHEN THE MULE'S tether suddenly broke, Frank McAllister had no time to react. The big, raw-boned draft animal came sliding down the hill like a freight train and crashed directly into him, knocking his wind out and pitching him forward, head over heels, into the rushing waters below. Following him off the slippery bank, the mule came up swimming, which was more than could be said for McAllister.

Tumbled along in the rushing current and dashed against rocks and half-submerged logs, his lungs and brain cried out for oxygen. When he was finally able to surface and catch his breath, the undercurrent sucked him down again, where he swallowed some water and began to choke and spasm uncontrollably. Pinned against a large rock, he managed to hoist himself up long enough to gulp a breath of precious air, but a second later, as the floundering mule swept past, its churning hooves and pummeling knees struck McAllister in the side, driving him underwater and knocking him senseless.

Far downstream, his battered corpse eventually spilled out into the muddy White River where it tumbled, rolled, and slowly vanished beneath the murky surface. Moments later, a soggy mule followed, swimming powerfully for the shallows where it scrambled up the bank and began devouring the lush grass at the river's edge.

* * *

THE HOURS PASSED quickly for Elise, who rode beside the swollen river with a renewed sense of freedom and adventure. A part of her was saddened about leaving the familiarity of her precious New Eden, but she understood that it was time to move on. Reflecting on the turbulent events of the past year, she recognized that, being forced to journey north to locate Hunter, she'd been thrust into a greater destiny. And in spite of the tragedy of the siege and its aftermath, her life was now enriched.

Trusting her intuition, she knew she belonged with him. Whatever the future might hold, it would be best spent with the only man, beyond her immediate family, that she'd ever truly admired. Since their first encounter, he'd won her heart in a thousand different ways—in his knowledge and respect for the natural world in which he lived, for his strength of character demonstrated time and again, for the importance he placed on being true to one's word, and in his willingness to sacrifice himself in a just and worthy cause.

The crossbow on her back and quiver at her side were constant reminders of his first bold missile speeding across her camp to slay the bandit chieftain poised to kill her. That selfless rescue alone was enough to make him a legend among any tribe of people in any time or place. There was never a question in Hunter's mind about keeping his word to a comrade given so long ago. There was simply no compromise in him, no rationalization of his world or its events that took place behind that handsome face. She admired his integrity, for he called it as he saw it and there was no back off or hesitation in his being or doing what he believed to be right.

* * *

THREE MILES SOUTH of the trailhead leading to the cave, two outriders spotted something unusual floating in the water at the river's edge and rode over to investigate. Drawing near, they realized that it was a half-submerged human body and signaled for the others to join them. The muddy corpse had drifted downstream, becoming entangled in the branches of an ancient fallen cottonwood.

Alarmed at first to think that it could somehow be Hunter, Elise was quickly relieved to discover otherwise. After hauling the body ashore, they determined from the amount of water in the lungs, that drowning was the probable cause of death, although from the number of bruises and lacerations, the man appeared to have been beaten so badly that he'd lost an eye and all his front teeth. Whoever he was, he hadn't been dead very long, probably not more than a day or so from the lack of bloat and *rigor mortis*. There was no accurate way to determine how long he'd been caught in the swift current before hanging up here on the tree; he could have come from fifty miles upstream for all they knew.

No one in Elise's escort recognized Frank McAllister's badly swollen face as they laid him in an unmarked, shallow grave beside the river, his battered corpse covered with sand and entombed beneath heavy rocks to discourage scavengers. In the end, karma had once again prevailed, as the cruel, sadistic, once proud conqueror of New Hope and New Eden was denied his revenge on Hunter, bested, as it were, by a mule.

* * *

THROUGHOUT THE MORNING, Hunter watched and waited impatiently, as the flooded stream slowly receded back down the sides of the ravine. He busied himself by re-inventorying his gear, sharpening his skinning knife, and making some minor adjustments to the mule packs. Around midday, he decided to take a chance and began breaking camp to return to the river and his journey north. By the time he finished packing the mules and saddling Sagebrush, the limestone path was again visible and he was able to carefully lead the animals diagonally back down the steep, ancient trail.

Slipping through bordering evergreens, the skies cleared, and the warming sun caused wispy columns of steam to rise up from the sodden earth. With temperatures edging into the seventies, it felt good to be on the move. Hunter settled in to the comfortable rhythm of his horse's smooth gait beneath him. He glanced back at the mules who seemed content to be on the trail again as well and heading someplace new.

The gorge was alive with birds, squirrels, and an occasional startled deer, which bounded off down the path ahead of them. Around one bend in the stream, they surprised a young grizzly that took off running across the rushing channel, spraying water everywhere as he scrambled up the far embankment and into the trees above. He moved with surprising speed and agility for an animal of his size, and Hunter was glad they hadn't met a mother with cubs in the narrow confines of this space.

A quarter mile from the river, Hunter spotted something half hidden in some rocks and grass up on the hillside. He loaded his crossbow and dismounted, quietly approaching the remains of what appeared to be a recent, very rudimentary camp. Partially hidden beneath a fallen log, he discovered a dilapidated saddle with a few dismal items in the saddle-bags, along with a ragged blanket and some bent cooking and eating utensils.

Hunter checked the vicinity for sign, but the rain and flood had pretty much wiped the area clean. Looking higher, he could see where a small tree had snapped off near the ground, the surrounding grasses nibbled down to roots. From there, he traced where something large had slid down the hill and over the steep bank into the water below.

Unsettled by his discovery, he scoured the area again, finding nothing more. Back in the saddle, he rode with his weapon ready. He had a strange sense about the camp, that someone may have been following him, waiting for the storm to let up before closing in. Inside he became very still. *Friend or foe,* he wondered? His restless eyes searched the surrounding hillsides, analyzing every tree, rock, bush, and shadow.

Half an hour later, he cautiously emerged from the ravine, leading the pack animals out into the broad river valley. Warm sun graced the meadow, and a light breeze chased wisps of scattered clouds across the blue expanse above. Overhead, a red-tailed hawk soared across the river to join its mate in their treetop nest near the water's edge.

Turning north toward Wyoming, he thought he heard a faint, familiar voice way off in the distance. Looking back, he was surprised to see a lone rider galloping toward him at breakneck speed, dark hair flying in the wind and calling out his name. Wheeling his horse about, Hunter's face broke into a broad smile as Elise rapidly closed the gap.

END OF BOOK ONE

THE ADVENTURE CONTINUES IN BOOK TWO:

THE GATHERING

The much anticipated second installment in the AFTER THE FALL adventure series follows Hunter and Elise as they travel to the Pacific Northwest to join Anna and her partner, Skye, a Native American shaman from old B.C., Canada. Soon after their arrival, Elise, Anna, and Skye's twin sisters vanish, kidnapped by slavers and bound for the auction block at THE GATHERING—a vast, regional marketplace on the coast where anything is available for the right price. When Elise manages to escape, she sets off a desperate race against time as Hunter and Skye move swiftly to track down the slavers and rescue the captives before they disappear forever into the murky underworld of the post-war slave trade.

Dripping with adventure and tempered with intrigue, this epic good-against-evil nail biter skillfully twists and turns as master storyteller JOHN PHILLIP BACKUS weaves another rich narrative tapestry, peopled with cutthroat pirates, powerful warlords, religious fanatics and secret societies, each with designs of their own in a future world that becomes more probable with every passing tick of the clock. Journey with our heroes as they apply their wits, courage, and martial skills to decipher the slavers' cryptic trail and unravel the mystery to its surprise conclusion. Along their challenge-strewn way, diverse groups converge and secret alliances unite in a complex matrix where people are not always who they seem and, ultimately, all roads lead back to THE GATHERING. You are invited to enjoy the following excerpt...

1
THE CALLING

Everyone has a path that is uniquely their own—as individual as a snowflake—each person unlike any other. To find one's unique way in the world, that is the secret, that is the key—to discover one's calling. To know, beyond the shadow of a doubt, exactly why you came into this world...

WHEN THE FIRST West Coast caravan arrived in New Eden after spring thaw, Anna Planchet was ready. She'd been feeling strange—slightly agitated or off balance and dissatisfied with her life somehow—her perfect life, in this perfect place, in this wide, imperfect world. Her restlessness had been brewing all winter. No matter what she did, it was not enough. Whatever this longing was, this *angst,* she had no clue, but something was stirring, impatiently trying to emerge from within her soul and she just had to let it out. It didn't matter to Anna what it was, just as long as she could be delivered of it and return again to her peace.

The instant she saw him she knew. He was beautiful. His thick black hair, plaited in twin braids down to his mid-chest, was adorned with feathers and wrapped in ermine skins. His clothing was tailored and fringed—deerskin leggings with moose hide moccasins and long deerskin over-shirt belted at the waist with a finely-woven sash. He was of Native blood from the Pacific Northwest, a bit older than she, perhaps twenty-five. Strong, lean and muscular with straight white teeth and an easy smile revealing slight dimples in his beardless cheeks. His skin was the color of copper with a sheen as smooth as silk, and the most remarkable eyes she had ever seen, eyes as blue as the ocean, as blue as the deepest blue sky, with little gold specks in them reflecting the sun, and twinkling like tiny sparklers in the dark embrace of his long, black eyelashes.

She hung about his wagon pretending to shop. He was a woodcarver by trade and crafted the most incredible masks and totems, flutes and pipes—all from western red cedar—which she inhaled like perfume when she picked up his offerings to examine them more closely. She ended up choosing an ingeniously carved box with mother-of-pearl inlaid lid, copper hinges, and colorful designs etched into the top and around the edges.

When she asked how much, he just looked at her, smiling, those amazing eyes gazing deeply into hers. She felt a tremble within and was transfixed there in his presence and waited, unable to move from that spot. Finally, he spoke and placed the box gently back into her hands, "It is yours, sister of the sun," he smiled assuredly, bewitched by her strawberry blonde locks and hazel eyes, "I made it for *you*."

Anna never questioned it—and from that moment forward never wanted to leave his side. Now, one month later, the couple was headed northwest, angling toward the coast and then north up into old British Columbia, Canada to join his people there. Anna was learning him, understanding him more clearly each day. Their nights were filled with loving and he gave her ecstasy and release beyond her wildest imaginings. Her yearning within was gone and her peace had returned in full measure. Within her womb a tiny life now grew, multiplying its cells moment-by-moment. She felt anointed and blessed, and wondered what a child, created from their pairing, would be like.

Skye Ravencloud was a man of many talents, many gifts. Life was his opportunity and his challenge, and he lived it with purpose, reverence, and dignity. Back home with his People, he was recognized as a shaman—a spirit-talker—and the magic flowed from his fingertips as he fashioned his art, invoking his spirit guides. Where the power came from, he never questioned, knowing as far back as he could remember, that all things came from the Great Spirit. He was a man of peace, not of strife, though was not known to back down from a just fight. He'd rather give than receive and didn't ask *why* he was in the world. He understood that he was simply a conduit, channelling something greater than himself, and he accepted that for what it was.

For Skye Ravencloud there was much work to be done, much wisdom to gain and *the calling* provided insight into that which was, and that which was to come. He had traveled to old Colorado because his spirit guide, the Raven, had landed on a tree branch outside his shop one day, and spoke plainly to him that it was time to take a wife—and so he went forth and found her. She was the one for him, for sure, his spirit bearing witness when she chose the cedar box, the one with the special markings foretelling of his mate. Now they were heading back to his village on the coast, to his People, and the road was before them—each day an adventure, each night like heaven in the arms of his golden-haired goddess, Anna, his sun-sister, who carried their offspring in her fertile womb.

She had talked him into a detour on the way back—to pass by the Wind River Range up in Wyoming to visit her sister, Elise, and Elise's partner, Hunter, whom Anna hadn't seen since they'd last visited New Eden two summers before. Skye arranged for friends from the caravan to escort his mules and wagon back by the overland road where he would pick them up on the coast road near the Gathering in three month's time. Anna provided their mounts and pack animals from the community herd, and with her family's blessing, they headed north towards South Pass.

She recounted her previous journey along this way, and Skye was surprised and encouraged that his Anna was such a fearless and able woman. He learned her history a little at a time, and was impressed when she shared the battle of New Eden and the heroics of Elise's man, Hunter. He looked forward to meeting such a mighty warrior, who could do whatever he decided was necessary to honor an oath once given.

The weather was mild this time of year, and the days passed pleasantly with temperatures in the seventies—dropping into the fifties at night—under wide open skies alive with brilliant stars and planets. Occasional rain showers were rare here with most of the precipitation taking the form of snowfall during the long, cold winter months. The landscape was breathtakingly beautiful in its vastness, rich and varied in red and yellow sandstone canyons with towering granite mesas and stone monoliths refusing to succumb to the weathering of time. Big skies stretched the limits of one's eyesight, and there was always something interesting to see among the myriad native plant and animal species.

Around the campfire in the evenings, they would sit together and share stories of their lives, and speak about how they felt and what they believed. He told her the ancient tales of his People, and how they first came to be The People in the mists before the reckoning of time. She spoke of her family and community, and their struggles and triumphs, of the End War and the Siege. In this way, they came to know each others' histories, and hopes and dreams, and they made plans for their own new chapter in this unfolding human saga of generation-following-generation since time immemorial into whatever distant future lay in store for their descendants.

After South Pass, they skirted the foothills of the Wind and rode north toward the Tetons and Yellowstone Valley—and beyond that, Skye's old Canada. The snow-covered peaks of the Continental Divide towered to the east as they drew ever closer to their interim destination, with Mt. Gannet, the tallest of them, rising 13,800 feet into the blue. At the Green River they turned east and followed it up to the headwaters, crossing over the ridge into Hunter's valley.

From the crest, Anna looked down and spotted the two-story stone and timber cabin that Elise had told her they were building. She was excited to see what they'd accomplished in their five years together here. It looked like a respectable ranch—with a barn, sheds, corrals, a garden and orchard, and goats and sheep, wearing tinkling bells, wandering about the hillsides.

Someone exited the house and Anna immediately raised her mouth to the heavens, calling out a long coyote greeting. Skye looked on surprised, and even more so when, far off, Elise returned the spirited howl, beckoning the travelers, who nudged their curious horses forward down the faint trail towards the bottom.

2
THE OFFERING

HUNTER CROUCHED IN the shade of a massive rock overhang, senses poised, crossbow ready, waiting for a clear shot. The wounded cougar was out there hiding in the scrub, camouflaged in the jumbled rocks and sagebrush of the rugged mountain pass. It was lying very still, very close, watching, wound up tight as a spring and ready to explode in a bursting flash of fury; as dangerous and unpredictable a threat as only an eight foot, two hundred pound wounded mountain lion armed with six-inch fangs and two and a half inch retractable claws could be.

Hunter knew it was badly injured, saw his bolt pass right through its body before it jumped sideways off the kill and vanished into the bush. He'd checked over Elise's badly-mauled foal for any sign of life, but the three-month-old filly was already gone, its spine crushed by the big feline's vise-like jaws. Hunter immediately gave chase, tracking its blood sign into the rocks. He glanced at the height of the sun in the stark azure sky as the July heat caused droplets of perspiration to bead up on his tanned, wind-blown brow.

In the blink of an eye, the enraged lion sprang across the rocks and Hunter shot it straight through its heart as it flew through the air above him. In the nick of time he rolled left and the beast fell dead where he'd been kneeling a moment before. Removing its hide, he opened the skull and took out the brain, wrapping it in the skin to be used in the tanning process to make the pelt feel baby soft. Heading home, he pondered the best way to present Elise with the bad news about her precious filly and decided that there was no easy way to go about it. She so loved that little thing—but that was just her way.

* * *

AN EXCITED ELISE cantered out to meet Anna and Skye on her newly saddle-broke mustang mare. Walking the pretty paint beside her sister's chestnut gelding on the way back, the two sisters chattered a mile a minute. When introduced to Skye, Elise could tell at once that he was the perfect match for Anna, who had become quite the grown up young woman since seeing her last. When she heard the news about the baby, Elise was thrilled for her sister, but inwardly wounded by the reminder of her own disappointment at still being childless after five years with Hunter. She'd always wanted to have children, but not way out here alone, away from community—so perhaps it was a blessing in disguise. Children needed others their age to grow up and play with, and to come of age with in this world, but her longing for tribe was a pain she bore quietly alone.

When Hunter arrived home a few hours later, he was surprised and happy to see Anna and glad to meet her man. They were welcome to stay as long as they liked, and he could see the joy it brought Elise, who he knew suffered greatly, though stoically, from the lack of female companionship. It was a touchy subject between them and avoided most of the time, but there was nothing to be done about it. He had never been comfortable around a lot of people, especially since the End War. Not much of a herd animal, Hunter was more the solitary predator type, preferring the quiet solace of the wilderness to the constant busy comings and goings associated with towns.

Well aware of his self-imposed social isolation and its effect on Elise, Hunter tried to accommodate her in other ways. Like moving from cave to house, for example, or in his embrace of a more agrarian lifestyle than he would have personally preferred. When he received the happy news about the baby, he smiled and nodded his head, remaining silent. He and Elise had hoped to have children, but there was something not working right—he wasn't sure what. Maybe they couldn't. It was a fairly common scenario since the End War that some couples weren't blessed in that way.

After supper, they sat around the table and Anna and Skye shared their vision of the future out on the Pacific Northwest coast. Elise listened with rapt attention and Hunter read between the lines. He was interested and curious to know what was happening out there and was rather surprised by some of what Skye related. Civilization, it seemed, had returned. Towns and villages were vibrant, and all manner of arts and crafts had experienced a tremendous renaissance. There were blacksmiths and brewers, carpenters and masons, jewelers and potters, glassblowers, basket makers, weavers and tailors. Shepherds tended flocks and herds, and wineries and orchards prospered in the mild micro climates of the Willamette and Yakima valleys. Northern old California still grew plenty of pot and a powerful cannabis guild coordinated with its northern sister guild in old B.C. to set prices and keep the quality of the bud at a premium level—to the enjoyment of all.

Amidst this period of cultural renewal and human industry, there was, of course, the usual chaos. Bandits plagued the coast road, hijacking wayfarers and kidnapping women and girls to sell or keep for themselves. Slavers were an even worse scourge of the new world, indiscriminately taking the young and strong of either gender to sell to work farms and plantations down south and back east. Walled towns and communes were well armed with organized defenses against depredation. From their base on Vancouver Island, brash pirates plied the seas in swift vessels, raiding up and down the coast by night, and plundering and pillaging whoever and wherever they could.

Overall, the Northwest Pacific Coast was reasonably hospitable and navigable as long as you kept your wits about you and knew how to take care of yourself. Traveling alone was not recommended so folks banded together in caravans, if their journeys were protracted. A common defense force of sorts had evolved along the road, with local volunteers manning stockades with guardhouses positioned along the highway where wayfarers could stay the night, safe from the ubiquitous creepers and leeches who sniffed out an existence on the fringe, conscienceless predators, stalking the edges of the safe zones for unwitting prey.

And then there was *The Sisterhood.* A controversial calvary of warrior-women, avenging crimes against the weak and helpless—women and children in particular—and dedicated to "making the world a safer place for the fairer race." Many admired their courage and supported their cause while others felt threatened by their methods and maligned them unjustly.

Men without malice towards those less physically powerful than themselves need not fear them. It was the misogynistic who quaked at the knock on the door in the black of night, when they'd come for you, hundreds strong, and there was no place to hide from their vengeance. Their flag was an all-seeing eye, red on white fabric, with rays emanating from it in every direction, and an inverted cross at the bottom.

They trained in the martial arts and were silent weapons experts, specializing in the bow and throwing knife. They especially abhorred slavers, pirates and pimps, and had been known to coordinate ferocious large-scale attacks on their strongholds and bordellos to free their sisters from bondage. Their numbers grew larger, and their army more powerful, each season, as rescued women and children found love and acceptance within their ranks. Some towns and communes refused to allow them inside their walls for fear they would lose wives and daughters to what the less enlightened inaccurately referred to as *that man-hating cult.*

New forms of self-government had randomly sprung up across the region, decentralized and responsive to those they immediately served. Ruthless warlords, too—as in the Middle Ages—ruled certain districts with an iron fist, coveting the resources of others and subjugating whole populations by use of force. Their brutal private armies were another scourge upon the land, and as they squeezed their people for some sort of tribute or tax, woe unto those who refused to meet their demands.

Without a national anything or mass communications capability, news traveled slowly and conversations took place face to face. Books were treasured, even revered. Libraries had become irreplaceable repositories of knowledge—cherished by all those with a view towards a brighter future. Within the various enclaves, tremendous ongoing creativity and invention took place, and the ingenuity born of necessity resulted in the unusual—and unexpected—use and reuse of components from the old world. Some locales had even restored some form of electric power, either through the repair of a dam or salvaging bits and pieces of wind and solar systems.

The most famous and infamous of all of the new cultural creations in the region was *The Gathering*, something new and unique in the world: a sprawling walled city that was declared neutral territory—the vortex for a constant stream of bustling humanity. Anything needed or wanted could be found there. A town had grown up around it—the place where deals were made and news passed along. A communications hub where merchants brought their goods and received credits which they, in turn, could trade for desired goods from others. It was a vast living entity, breathing in goods and services and breathing out the dreams and desires of the neo-culture.

* * *

SKYE AND ANNA stayed for three days, and Elise was overjoyed to have someone to share her secret thoughts with. On their final evening together, they all sat at dinner, enjoying some tender lamb chops and fresh salad from the abundant garden. In the midst of the meal Skye stood up and walked over to stand behind Elise's chair. Hunter half stood, unsure of what was happening, but Elise gestured to him that it was okay. Skye closed his eyes and spread out opened palms toward her lower back, speaking words unknown to the others in a sing-song voice. After a minute or so, he ended and returned to his seat. Afterwards, Elise experienced a warm tingling within her belly and a realization that some kind of quickening had occurred inside her body. For some inexplicable reason, she had the definite sense that her barrier to conceiving a child was now somehow removed!

She turned to tell Anna and they embraced while Hunter sat back observing, curious but skeptical, not knowing exactly what had happened. Later that evening, when they were alone, Elise shared what she believed had occurred within her, and he was intrigued, though not yet convinced, trying to work out with logic how Skye could have made a difference in her longstanding barrenness. Hunter was familiar with how babies were made, and his understanding of the process didn't include faith healing or magic. It wasn't until a month later, when Elise was late and the morning sickness began, that he really got it.

* * *

WITH THE COMING of their child, Elise understood that her life with Hunter was about to undergo a significant transformation. He, too, felt a restlessness, a stirring desire to go someplace new. Not that he wanted to suddenly embrace community, but he had been living in the wilderness for seventeen years in this same territory, and the familiarity—though comforting in many ways—was also limiting to his innate curiosity and yearning for discovery.

The intriguing conversation during Skye and Anna's visit had altered his perception of the world beyond his mountains. The biowarfare viruses seemed to have played themselves out, with those having lived through them, developing an apparent immunity. The social landscape, as well, was evolving rapidly and transforming itself in many positive directions and ways. The *Great Purging* had done a remarkable job in selective adaptation, bringing out the best in the human DNA and psyche. There was a brand new world out there to be discovered and Hunter had the growing realization that perhaps he had been in exile long enough.

When he informed Elise that he was ready to travel to the coast to see this new land of milder winters, abundant water, and game-filled forests for himself, she almost fell out of her rocking chair! She had wrestled with the thought of joining Anna and Skye and his People up in old B.C., and had even considered going there alone, just until the baby was born and old enough to return. She was completely taken by surprise at Hunter's decision to move on and was pleased beyond words!

What to do with their livestock and belongings that would remain behind was another challenge that solved itself rather nicely when Hunter suggested that they offer the livestock they wouldn't be taking with them to a young couple who had arrived in the territory about three years earlier and had a modest place two valleys west. When Hunter and Elise traveled the twenty miles to their homestead, they were overwhelmed by the generous offer, and returned to see what they would be inheriting. Two weeks later, Hunter and Elise said their goodbyes to home and valley, heading northwest with a string of mounts and pack animals to rendezvous with Anna and Skye in old B.C.

3
WINDSONG

THE SLENDER WOODEN vessel skimmed buoyantly across Beggar's Bay under full sail, heeled slightly to starboard, slicing the whitecaps with her sharp, gracefully curved dragon prow—like a Norse warship of memory past. Her mainmast was spruce, tall and solid, her ivory sails stretched, lines taut as she chased the wind down the coastal waters south of Vancouver Island. Lars was her captain, strong and steady, with curly, red-blond hair and beard, and eyes like the sea that he loved. Sometimes bluer than the deep water, at other times gray like the storms that pounded the rugged coastline in winter, but mostly they were a misty sea-green, like the foaming breakers churning up the kelp beds where harbor seals chased fish near the shore.

He stood amidships at the helm, hair blowing wildly in the brisk onshore breeze of morning, eyes concentrating, counting the rock formations jutting from the water on both sides of his ship. He steered her through the passage with precision as he had a hundred times before, each voyage, risky, each journey flirting with disaster. His course was strewn with shoals and shallows, and half submerged rocks and shipwrecks, all just waiting to rip the keel out of his darling—his mistress. She had taken two painstaking years to build. Piece by piece, board by board, a labor of love for a man who was only at peace on the ocean, riding the swells, surrounded by endless horizons.

He'd discovered his prize while scavenging a wrecked marina north on the coast road. She was hidden beneath a rotting tarp in the back of a custom shipyard, in a large warehouse near the wharf, where someone had commissioned a wooden sailboat fitted with the upswept dragon prow of a Viking ship. The frame was already in place atop a rolling gurney that would facilitate moving her to the water when complete. Her owner had left behind a detailed set of plans and all the lumber and hardware necessary to finish her! So there he lived and there he worked, the inherited genes and skilled hands of his finish-carpenter father helping the vessel take shape, day-by-day, beneath the skylights of the lofty warehouse ceiling with the huge bay doors rolled open inviting in the mist-soaked world.

When his beauty was finally complete, he moved her from the workshop to the water on the gurney, rolling her out to the end of the wharf with a series of cables and winches all the way to the launching ramp where she slid down, crashing into the cold waters of the Pacific, bobbing sweetly on the gentle swells.

He had done it alone, without any help. Lars didn't need help—didn't need people, couldn't trust them. Besides, he was alone here. Stepping the mast on his own was a bit of a challenge, but the shipyard was filled with all manner of useful tools, supplies, and equipment, and he used his wits and the laws of physics to his advantage and got the job done.

When the End War came more than two decades earlier, everyone, who didn't die right away, went south, fleeing the brutal two-year nuclear winter, but Lars had headed north, away from the desperate survivors. Here he lived much better than most on the old world's leftovers. When the thaw finally came he turned to the sea for food and lived off her bounty. With rod, net, or spear gun, he fished for cod, flounder and salmon, or donned a wet suit and scoured the bottom harvesting crabs and mussels.

* * *

SUNRISE PAINTED THE dawn sky crimson, and the onshore wind blew a steady ten knots, smelling of rain. It was mid-April and still cold enough to wear layers. Lars was very excited, for today was *the* day! Everything had been made ready. He looked his graceful ship over and was pleased. His final task was to painstakingly paint her name across the stern in dark green oil: *Windsong* and was she ever a beauty!

Thirty-three feet long at the waterline with a four-foot draft. Nimble in the wind and agile in the water, responsive to his slightest touch. She was well-provisioned and well-appointed, having spare sails and lines, spare hardware, and two extra anchors with chain, all in waterproof lockers on deck. Below decks was a forward cabin, amidships galley and bath with an aft captain's cabin hosting a king bed. Windsong was set up for a single man to sail her, which Lars found challenging at first, even harrowing at times.

After going over his mental seaworthiness checklist a dozen times, he decided to make a practice run over to an island about twelve miles off the coast, that on a clear day, he could barely make out with his telescope. From a set of laminated charts scavenged from a former harbor patrol office, he'd plotted a course and made final preparations to get under way.

Lashing the helm to starboard with bit of line using a quick release, he cast off the dock lines and ran back to tighten the slack jib sail. As Windsong came around, the wind blew the luff out of her sails and she jumped ahead, cutting nicely through the swells on a WNW heading away from the dock. Minding the rocks and shoals, he headed her out into the straits, referring constantly to chart and compass, tacking toward the distant island, wind off his starboard bow, full mainsail and jib taut and lines humming.

On the western side of the rock-guarded isle he cut back some sail and slowed, discovering a perfect little inlet, protected by a curved rock jetty, built sometime in the distant past by men and machines long since forgotten. Inside the half mile-long cove was a rocky shoreline with a sturdy dock at the far end next to a narrow darkened opening that appeared to be, yes, a cave! Back and forth, plastered to the cliff face, a steep stairway zigzagged eight hundred feet or so to the only house in sight perched precariously on the extreme edge of the precipice, and underpinned by what appeared to be the massive beams and footings used in bridge building! Putting out the bumpers he coasted in next to the cedar and redwood structure and jumped to the dock, tying Windsong off to the darkened green brass cleats that, surprisingly, still held firmly to the wood.

With his adrenaline kicking in, Lars swept the rocky beach for signs of life or recent activity, but came up negative. Just in case, he strapped his sidearm to his waist and grabbed an oil lantern, heading towards the narrow cave. Inside it was dark and he held the lantern aloft as he climbed the aluminum steps that ran along the beach side to the grotto. Beyond the tiny entrance, it opened up into a roundish, playing field sized cavern with high ceilings, and he was surprised to see another small dock hidden safely within, perfect for tying up Windsong out of the weather!

From inside the grotto a second set of stairs led up and out a metal door near the roof. He scouted these stairs which emerged from the cavern to join the same stairway that was visible from the water, scaling the cliff to the house perched on the edge of the world. He decided to go on up and take a look and was glad to discover that the stairway infrastructure was also aluminum and, thus, practically corrosion-proof. Still, he took no chances, and made his way carefully to the top, checking for loose fittings or storm and weather damage as he went along.

Cautiously ascending the last few steps to the top, he came to a large balcony decked with composite flooring—apparently some sort of acrylic or epoxy planks designed to look like wood. The house itself was amazingly intact, with huge floor to ceiling windows looking out over the water below. He looked down to see Windsong resting peacefully next to the dock. Trying the door, the handle turned freely and he stepped inside. The stale smell of disuse and dust assailed him and he covered his mouth with his shirt. Re-lighting the lantern, he scouted the place, which was larger than it looked from below. Upstairs was a bedroom loft with a second balcony boasting an expensive high-powered telescope on a tripod. Looking through it out to the sea, he felt like he had just returned home from a long, trying journey, and he dubbed it his *Crow's Nest* and claimed the house, cave and docks all for himself.

Over the next few weeks, Lars investigated the small island and found it empty but for skeletons and a mummified corpse or two, and so named it Skeleton Island. The fourteen luxury vacation homes occupying the rocky paradise were more or less intact—some faring better than others. It seemed that no one had been back here since the End. Before the War, all food supplies must have been ferried or flown in. There was a small helipad down on the far side of the island which was approximately two miles wide and five miles long with high cliffs and small rocky beaches here and there, covered in huge piles of driftwood logs and trees. There were several freshwater springs supplying drinking water and even a small waterfall. The fishing here was excellent and he was content with plenty of everything he might need. Lars enjoyed nothing more than taking Windsong out everyday, weather permitting. Sailing was an incredibly *in the moment* experience—in total concert with the natural world, gliding through the water, wind on his face and salt spray his hair.

* * *

AS SUMMER PROGRESSED, he familiarized himself with his island paradise and fixed up the Crow's Nest to better suit his needs. One bright day, with a ten knot breeze out of the west, Lars was a couple of miles offshore, hauling in an overnight net he'd set the day before when he saw something moving out of the corner of his eye. Reaching for his binoculars he scanned the horizon and spotted some type of low-riding vessel passing by—a large canoe with outriggers—about a mile away and heading toward the mainland, but coming from where? He watched it until it disappeared over the horizon.

He was puzzled and went to his maps and charts to consider the possibilities. Whoever they were, he wasn't sure they'd spotted him. His sails were down and the varnished hull was reflecting the colors of the sea and the sky. *Who could they be?* he wondered, not happy about the prospect of having other seafarers in his territory. If they navigated the ocean currents, they could find him. If they found him, they could make trouble. Maybe even ransack his place when he was out fishing, or worse. There must have been several men aboard to paddle the forty-foot sea-going canoe. He had seen such a vessel in a book once. The oceanic islanders use them on long-distance journeys from Polynesia.

Lars spent the next ten days fortifying the Crow's Nest and beefing up his defenses. He devised several alternate battle plans, customized according to how many attackers might be in the raiding party and their assault approach. Finally, he felt very well-prepared. When the End War had arrived almost two decades earlier, everyone on his island had either left never to return, or died here. One of the residents choosing to stay on was apparently a gun aficionado, who literally died with his finger on the trigger.

In addition to the stainless steel 12 gauge and .45 Glock pistol that Lars brought with him from the mainland, he selected two battle rifles from the local mummified corpse's collection: an M-21 sniper rifle in .308 with a wicked scope, and a standard AR-15 in .223 caliber with red dot. There were ten cases of vacuum-sealed ammunition for each rifle, plus a case of .45 CAP's for his pistol, and a thousand 12 gauge shells in various configurations—slugs, double-ought buckshot, and birdshot—depending on the specific application they were to be used for. The stash was worth a fortune on today's market so Lars removed all of the weapons and ammo to a hidden location in the center of the island. He made sure the weapons he took for his own use were clean, well-oiled, and functional, and had full bandoliers and loaded clips ready to go.

Down below in the cave, he prepared some oil bombs—Molotov cocktails made from wine bottles filled with spirits pilfered from a house hosting a full bar, with a piece of cloth stuffed into the top—that he could light with one of the ubiquitous butane lighters he always carried with him.

Two uneventful weeks passed and he started to relax when a three-day storm moved in, bringing torrential rainfall with lots of thunder and lightning. The morning of the fourth day dawned clear and sunny with a mild breeze and sparkling waters. Deciding it was time to get back to a normal routine, he prepared to take Windsong out for a little fishing, when he heard something unusual in the distance.

Looking out to sea, a dark ship belching smoke suddenly appeared from around the jetty guarding the little inlet's entrance, powered by some type of motor! It was a forty-five foot pilothouse motor-fisher and Lars could make out several people moving about on deck! As it headed into his inlet, he turned and started sprinting back up the steps, headed for the *Crow's Nest* where he could watch her through the telescope. He made the top breathing heavy with his heart jumping out of his chest and peered down through the scope. It was halfway across the inlet heading straight towards his dock! He could make out a crew of about eight men and it looked like they had two or three women on deck with them. His mind raced through twenty different scenarios. *They might try to assault the house—no, if they did that they would be exposed the entire way on the stairs.* He watched her approach, and as the noisy boat got closer, he counted at least ten heavily armed men and three scantily dressed women, probably slaves.

The unfamiliar smell of exhaust fumes from the internal combustion engine eventually reached him through the open window and he wondered where the hell they were from, amazed that people were still able to maintain that old technology—but why not? Motors had been invented back in the 1800's. Fuel was easy to distill. There were tons of spare parts and tools lying around if someone had the knowledge and skills as a mechanic. It made sense, but did seem bizarre, almost as if he'd been suddenly transported back to civilization before the Fall!

He heard gruff voices over the sound of the motor as she tied up alongside his dock and several of the crew jumped off heading toward his cave! He'd forgotten about *Windsong! What if they tried to take her?* The cave entrance was too narrow to drive their wide beamed boat into, but the men disappeared into the opening, reappearing a few minutes later carrying armloads of his precious supplies! He turned and picked up his long-range sniper rifle, resting the bipod on the deck railing. The crack of the shot echoed off the cliff walls and rang out across the calm inlet. Down below, the crew dropped their pilfered goods and raced back aboard their boat. He could hear the captain in the pilothouse yelling at his men to hurry as he pulled the exhaust-belching, steel-hulled workhorse away from the dock, heading back towards the entrance to the cove. Suddenly, one of the women broke free from the others and leapt off the side into the sea! He watched the crew run to the rail, yelling and gesticulating wildly. The girl swam hard for shore as the captain turned his boat around to go back for her.

Instinctively, Lars took careful aim at the roof of the pilothouse and slowly squeezed the trigger. *Boom!* He blew a large hole in the cabin roof, top dead center, and the boat swerved back toward the mouth of the inlet. Her captain increased her speed and drove in a zigzag pattern to avoid being picked off. The crew hustled the remaining females belowdecks as the boat made fast tracks towards the open sea. Down in the icy water, the young swimmer was nearly to the dock. Grabbing a towel and an extra sweater off a peg, Lars dashed out of the house and raced down the stairway to the beach...

WATCH FOR

THE GATHERING - AFTER THE FALL

12–21–2010